SHELTER FROM THE STORM

Spence hesitated, then put his arms around her, holding her close and soaking her gown, he was sure, with the water that dripped from his hair and seeped through his shirt.

The sky lit up and another crack of thunder shook the ground beneath the wagon. He felt the tremor that ran through her as she buried her head under his chin.

"I'm all right. Really," she said. "You're here, and that's all that matters." She raised her head, and even though it was dark as pitch he knew she stared at him. Then he felt her tender lips brush his, tentatively at first, then with more concentration.

"I don't think you know what you're doing," he warned.

"Maybe I do."

She brushed his lips again, pressing her body into his.

"I'd better leave," he said, mostly to give her the chance to change her mind. He would go if she wanted him to; if not....

Defiant Hearts

MELODY MORGAN

LEISURE BOOKS NEW YORK CITY

A LEISURE BOOK®

August 1996

Published by

Dorchester Publishing Co., Inc.
276 Fifth Avenue
New York, NY 10001

Printed in the United States of America.

To Betty Lewis,
Thanks so much for the ''bat'' research. <grin>
M.M.

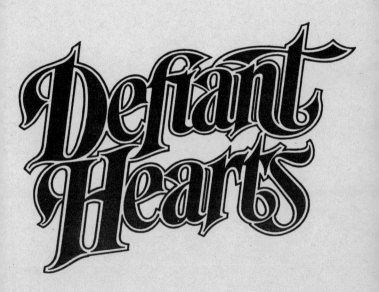

Chapter One

New York City, 1879

Spence McCord took in the sight of the tree-lined street before him where large houses crowded together and each well-kept miniature front lawn sported a carriage block and hitching post. The clopping of his horse's feet could barely be heard over the laughter and shrieks of delight from the children playing tag nearby. Added to these, though filtered by distance, were the sounds of busy New York City assaulting his ears and making him look first to his left, then to his right.

He didn't belong in such confining surroundings where there was barely enough good air to breathe and almost no clear view of the sky. Two weeks ago he'd been standing on Colorado soil with all the fresh mountain air a man could want and clear skies as far as the eye could see. If the choice had been his, he would have been the one trailing herd up to Montana instead of riding a train east to the biggest city he'd ever seen.

Melody Morgan

At last he brought his horse to a halt in front of a stately two-story house with a wide front porch. Beside the bottom step was a plain sign announcing: O'ROURKE PHOTOGRAPHY. This was where she lived. Miss Katie O'Rourke. With a resigned sigh, he dismounted from the rented horse, tied the reins to the metal ring on the hitching post, which resembled the scowling features of a bird, then followed the brick walk to the steps. Before going further, he pulled a piece of paper from his pocket and read it again.

Dear Katie,
This is Spence McCord. He's come to escort you across the country to Montana unless you've changed your mind about this ridiculous idea. I would have come myself but Rachel is expecting our third child and I can't leave her. Spence is a good and honest man.
Your brother, Tim

The letter was a little too sparse of detail to suit Spence, which meant he'd have to do a lot of explaining and he didn't relish that idea at all, especially if Miss O'Rourke had as much Irish spirit in her as her brother. Actually, none of this suited Spence, but he was under a pressing obligation. He'd had no choice in the matter whatsoever. Tim had made that very clear. A debt owed was a debt that had to be paid. And Spence owed Tim.

He folded the letter and held it in his hand as he climbed the steps. After knocking on the door, he backed up several spaces and waited. Within minutes the door opened to reveal an older woman in an apron holding a towel.

"Yes?" she asked.

"I'm looking for Miss O'Rourke," he replied, remembering belatedly to remove his hat.

"Who's calling, please?" she asked, giving him a thorough once-over until he wondered if he might have a smudge of horse dung on his face.

"Well, ma'am, even if I told you, it wouldn't matter much, because Miss O'Rourke doesn't know me. Just tell her that her brother Tim sent me." He handed her the letter of introduction.

"Tim? Is he in some kind of trouble?" A worried frown creased her brow as she accepted the paper.

"No, ma'am, nothing like that. At least, he wasn't when I left him." He couldn't keep back a small smile as he realized that Tim's reputation as a scrapper stretched from one side of the country to the other.

"Praise be for that!" exclaimed the woman as she crossed herself. "Just a moment and I'll find Katie." She turned to go, leaving the door open, then stopped. "Where's my manners," she said. "Please, come in."

Spence backed up another step, shaking his head. "I'll wait out here. Thanks just the same." He didn't want hospitality; he just wanted to get this settled so they could get started as soon as possible.

She nodded and hurried away.

Spence replaced his hat on his head and leaned against a porch post as he glanced down the row of other porches all within spitting distance of each other. No privacy at all, he thought. Hardly enough room to think, let alone live. Once again he thought about the men trailing herd up to Montana to the new ranch near Fort Keogh where you'd have to travel miles just to see another face. He missed that solitude. Normally he wasn't given to fits of anger or even irritation, but he had to admit that for the last few weeks he'd had plenty of time to mull over the unfairness of Tim's choice of repaying a debt.

He turned his head in the other direction and found a similar long line of porches stretching out endlessly. Pushing away from the post, he paced the length of the boards thoughtfully, watching the toes of his boots with each step. The quicker he got back to ranching, the better. Now if Miss O'Rourke would only be agreeable to his suggestions.

On the return trip across the porch he stopped in front of the door to wait. Within minutes Katie O'Rourke stood before him. He barely had time to take in her disheveled appearance before she rounded on him with her blue eyes snapping.

"Mr. McCord," she began slowly. "You have foolishly made this journey all for nothing."

She was taller than he'd expected, but she had the same bright red-gold curls as her brother and that familiar stubborn set of her jaw. He knew instantly that she was a determined, independent woman with more spunk and grit than her slender frame could hold onto. Every move was graceful and unpracticed; she was totally unaware of her simple beauty, and the effect she had on him. Suddenly the speech he had prepared to talk her out of her plans just plain evaporated. Instead, he felt surprisingly as though he'd been ambushed. He strained to hold onto a rush of anger toward Tim for putting him in this awkward position, and toward this woman for dreaming up such a foolhardy notion. Who ever heard of a woman wanting to drive a photography wagon across the country just to take pictures?

He ignored the fact that she had just called him foolish and focused on the problem at hand, which was how to get her safely to the new ranch in Montana as he had promised her brother.

"I take it you didn't get the telegram Tim sent last week?" he asked, realizing full well that Tim probably hadn't sent it.

"No, I did not. If I had, you wouldn't be here, because I would have wired Tim to mind his own business." A slight twist of her head was meant to add emphasis, but instead gave him a new angle to view the deep dimple in her cheek.

Independent, determined and straightforward, too. These were qualities Spence might have admired if he weren't nearly two thousand miles from home, he reminded himself.

Peeking over Katie's shoulder, the older woman smiled pleasantly at Spence. "Katie dear, let's ask the gentleman in for a cool drink. After all, he's come a long way."

"I doubt if he can stay," Katie said, steadfastly staring Spence in the eye and practically daring him to accept.

"Actually, a cool drink sounds good," Spence said, holding her stare. "Thank you, ma'am."

"I'll bring it right out," the woman said cheerfully before she bustled away.

Katie crossed her arms at her waist.

Spence hooked his thumb in his belt as he shifted his weight to one foot.

Neither spoke for several seconds, then Katie broke the silence.

"And how did Tim find out about my plans?" she asked.

"Your sister wrote to him," he replied casually.

Her arms slowly unfolded until they lay straight at the sides of her hoopless skirt. "Erin?" she said in disbelief. Then understanding seemed to dawn in her eyes, and her rigid body became fluid in its suddenly angry movements. She stepped close to him, poking her finger in his chest. A soft flowery fragrance he couldn't identify drifted toward him each time she moved.

"Mr. McCord," she said, accenting his name with a jab of her finger, "there's no need for you, my brother or my sister to concern yourselves with my plans. So you may as well turn around, get on your horse and ride back to where you came from."

If he thought her eyes were snapping before, they were positively blue fire now. Each toss of her head brought the red-gold curls across her face, and she an-

13

grily brushed at them. He would have thought this fit of temper a little uncalled for, but then he suspected it was a family trait. He'd seen Tim get set off under lesser circumstances.

"To tell you the truth, I'd like nothing better," he said honestly. "But I can't do that."

"Oh, yes, you can. It's really quite simple."

"Looks like you're wrong about that, ma'am." He didn't figure that making a hell-bent-for-leather trip clean across the country to get her was a simple matter at all. Especially if he went back empty-handed. The way he saw it, he'd still have a debt that had to be repaid, and hard telling what Tim would come up with next time. No, sir, he wanted this debt paid, once and for all. And right now it was half paid; the only thing he had to do was get her to Montana safe and sound.

With a shake of her head, she replied, "I'm afraid you're the one who's mistaken. And since the choice is mine, there is nothing that can make me decide to travel with you. Nothing. And least of all, Tim's orders."

Suddenly she was in control of herself again, cool and calm on the outside but bristling with animosity on the inside. He'd seen porcupines that were friendlier, and probably less dangerous.

"Does that mean," Spence began, "that you intend on heading west by yourself?"

"Well, not that it's any of your business, but yes."

"I can't let you do that, Miss O'Rourke."

"Let me?" Her voice was low and quiet, and carried more than a hint of what was to come if he persisted in minding her business.

"That's right, ma'am."

"There is no *letting* about it. I will make my own decisions, just as I've been doing for the past four years. And in spite of Tim's opinion, I am quite capable."

"I'm not here to dispute that, ma'am, I'm just . . ." He paused, having almost said "repaying a debt," but he didn't imagine that would help the situation any. Instead, he finished with, "helping a friend."

"I'm not your friend, Mr. McCord, and I didn't ask for your help. So you may as well head back to Montana." Then with slow, deliberate movements, she began tearing up the letter. "And tell Tim I think he's an arrogant"—she paused as she tossed the little pieces of paper into the air—"jackass."

Spence watched the fluttering pieces drift downward to land on the toes of his boots. Sometimes, he thought, getting a woman riled could be a pure and simple pleasure. Sometimes. Other times it just brought out their true nature. He could tell that cussing didn't come natural to her, but she sure did enjoy it.

"I guess you can tell him yourself when we get there," he said as firmly as he could without pushing her too far.

"Ha!" was her only reply before she turned and stalked into the house, leaving a sputtering, embarrassed Mrs. O'Shea to deal with him.

But before the older woman could get out an intelligible word, Katie whirled back through the doorway.

"And furthermore," she went on, "I can't imagine why Tim ever thought he could coerce me into making this journey, which I have dreamed about for years, with someone I didn't even hire. And I will tell you this, when I hire someone it won't be you." A smug smile suddenly lightened her features as she crossed her arms over her chest. "And that's final."

Spence leveled an honest, direct look at her. "If you try to hire someone else," he said, "I'll pay him off or run him off."

She held her position. "You wouldn't dare."

He wasn't a man to belabor a point once he'd made it, so he gave her a nod of farewell as he put his hat on his head. "We'll leave at daybreak." Then he turned, crossed the porch and descended the steps.

"Don't hold your breath, Mr. McCord! I wouldn't go with you to the corner and back. Tell that to Tim!"

Mrs. O'Shea shushed at Katie. "Keep your voice down. What will the neighbors be thinking?"

"I don't care what they think," he heard her say as he mounted his horse. But the rest of their conversation was lost to him as he headed back up the street.

Katie stood immobilized in her fury. Tim wouldn't get away with this! And he was a jackass! No, he was worse than a jackass but she wasn't exactly sure what that would be so she settled for a picture in her mind of her brother with long ears. And if she didn't have so much respect for an actual photograph, she'd find one of him and paint long ears on him.

That almost made her smile.

Well, she wouldn't let Tim, Mr. McCord or Erin make her decisions for her, and it was a great misconception on their parts if they thought they could. She would simply continue on the way she had been before Tim and Erin had meddled in her affairs. And Mr. McCord could just catch the first train back to Montana. Alone.

"Come along, Mrs. O'Shea, we've got more packing to do."

With an exaggerated, resigned sigh, Mrs. O'Shea followed her into the house, muttering, "And what is this world coming to, traveling women photographers and strange men as escorts."

Returning to the chore she'd begun before she'd been interrupted, Katie put her anger to work for her as she tugged a crate of clothing up the stairs. Thank goodness this was her last crate, she thought as she hefted and shoved it into the large walk-in attic. Out of breath, she sank down onto a chest for a moment.

How she wished that everything was going smoothly enough for her to leave tomorrow, but it wasn't. She hadn't found a suitable guide in spite of the many newspaper advertisements she'd placed, and she'd been careful not to mention even a hint of that to Spence McCord in the event it should get back to Tim. For a month now she'd advertised for an experienced man who could drive a photographer's wagon west. But the only responses had come from a few peddlers who thought they could sell their wares with hers and a drifter who smelled as though he had a penchant for strong drink.

With a swipe at the damp curls stuck to her forehead, she contemplated her next task: the studio. She knew she'd saved the most difficult for last.

Katie glanced into the four bedrooms before going back downstairs. They were neat and tidy and dust free, thanks to Mrs. O'Shea. The rooms looked just as they had when her mother had been alive. She would miss her home, of course, with its familiar patterned carpets, comforting squeaks of certain floorboards and most of all, the memories. If this journey turned into all she hoped it would be, perhaps she wouldn't return except to display her pictures in a gallery alongside those of the best.

But she couldn't let her hopes get too high. After all, a woman was hardly taken seriously where photography was concerned, certainly no more than she was in any other area, except in the kitchen. Well, she intended to do her best and see what happened. At the very least she would experience the journey of a lifetime, and at the very most. . . . No, she chided herself, she wouldn't think that far ahead. She had enough to think about as it was.

She turned at the bottom of the stairs and walked to the studio attached to the back of the house where everything was set up for one last picture. She had pulled down the screen with the forest background and removed all the other props. Once the sun rose fully, the room would brighten by means of the skylights in the slanted ceiling. Then she and her guide would stand side by side as Mrs. O'Shea exposed the plate, under Katie's direction.

That is, if she ever found a suitable guide.

Shrugging off an inescapable feeling of hopelessness, she organized a box of photographic plates, going over once again the supplies she would need for such a long trip. She had no exact destination. How could she, since she'd never been beyond the edge of New York City? But was that so important? Her only goal was to take real pictures of real people, so she would leave the traveling decisions to her guide.

She gazed around the studio lovingly. She'd spent the very best days of her childhood and adolescence here watching her father work among the chemicals, lenses and all that went with their occupation. But as the years had gone by, she began to feel stifled, confined, especially after her father's illness and death.

Seating herself in his worn leather chair, she touched the places where his hands had smoothed the leather to a brittle thinness. It was here that she felt his presence the strongest; it was here that she could still commune with him. She remembered now the dreams and hopes he'd once had and how he'd shared them with her. They were the same dreams she held close to her own heart. But he had put his dreams aside in order to care for his family, providing for them quite well. She didn't need to do that, since the only family she had left was a married sister and a married brother. So, in reality, she was her own boss and in control of her own life.

She rolled the chair so she could better see the pictures she had yet to remove from the walls. Still, lifeless portraits stared back at her, their studio facades merely a pretense of who the people really were and what they really felt. Then she gazed with admiration at the two pictures hanging in a place of honor. These were Mathew Brady's pictures in which the people were not posed and propped with humorless smiles, but had emotions behind frightened eyes, proud eyes and smiling eyes. These were real people. Only Mathew Brady could capture life and death the way it actually happened. Even her father had said so.

As much as she'd loved her father and appreciated his skills, she idolized the works of Mathew Brady. Perhaps she would never have the chance to photograph a country at war as he had, but she could at least travel west and capture the farmer and his family, the rancher and his cattle, the trapper, the Indian and his home.

It was a grand goal. And while sometimes it overwhelmed her, she'd remained dedicated to her dream. And deep within her heart, she knew it was the same dream her father had had.

But she knew that dreams could turn to dust unless acted upon. So she forced her tired body from the chair and went in search of Mrs. O'Shea.

"Here you are," Katie said as she entered the kitchen.

"Yes, here I am." Mrs. O'Shea sounded forlorn. "And probably for the last evening, too."

Katie put an arm around the woman's shoulders and squeezed. "Just think, without me to look after, you'll have a life of your own."

"Hmph. What's a life of my own without someone to look after, I ask you," she said softly as she wiped the last dish.

"Don't say that," Katie said, giving her another hug. "You make me feel so guilty. You know Erin is always going to need help with that small brood of boys she's raising. And besides, we've already talked about this. I *have* to go. It isn't a matter of just wanting to, it's a matter of having to. Can you understand?" Katie tried to put some of her feelings into her words but she knew it was useless. This dear, dear woman had taken care of Katie and her father for all those years since her mother's death. Leaving her would be as hard as leaving Erin and her family. Even so, she had to go.

"All I understand is that you're being a foolish young woman, traipsing off with a strange man into heathen country where you'll likely get yourself killed."

That wasn't the way Katie saw it at all. There was no adventure in Mrs. O'Shea's words, no freedom and no opportunity to attain her goal.

"I absolutely will not get myself killed. You certainly don't give me much credit," she said.

"That I don't," she replied emphatically. Then with a thick Irish brogue, she muttered, "Gallivanting over the land like a Gypsy. And what would your poor mother say, God rest her soul."

Katie leaned down and kissed the graying hair at Mrs. O'Shea's temple. "She'd say exactly what you said." Katie smiled at her. "Now does that make you feel better?"

"Only you changing your mind will make me feel better. It would make Tim and Erin feel better, too."

"I don't want to discuss Tim and Erin," she stated, taking a stack of dishes and packing them in a crate. They were at a stalemate once again, which meant there was little reason to continue the conversation, and they both knew it.

"This should be all of the kitchen supplies, shouldn't it?" Katie asked as she glanced around the nearly bare room. All of her mother's good dishes had been packed in the attic along with most of the everyday pots and pans right down to the utensils. They had left only the essentials in the cupboard so that most of the packing would be done in advance.

"Yes, that's the last of it."

As she quickly scanned the room once more, her eye caught the movement of a figure outside the window. A tall, broad-built man was making his way toward the rear of the house. He wore rugged clothing and put her in mind of the perfect guide. She hurried through the house to the back door in the studio room. He just had to be there in response to her ad! And bless the Lord, he was just in the nick of time. Now she would be able to leave on schedule after all.

She opened the door, breathless from anticipation as much as her rush to greet him before he even had a chance to knock.

"Hello!" she said, smiling happily.

He pulled a folded-up newspaper from inside his shirt and said, "I've come about the ad."

"I knew it!" She looked him over once more, taking in his sensible clothing and sturdy shoes, and she didn't miss his friendly smile. "Please, come in." She stepped back, opening the door wide and nearly tripping over Mrs. O'Shea.

"I'll bring some cool drinks," Mrs. O'Shea said. Then she clucked disapprovingly as she left the room, muttering, "Strange escorts, indeed."

"Sit down," Katie said, offering the chair opposite her father's desk. When he was seated she went on. "So, tell me about yourself and what experience you've had with wagons and cross-country traveling."

He adjusted himself several times as though he was uncomfortable on the small chair. "Well, I can't say I've ever been across the country before, but I've got a hankerin' to go to California and not much money to do it on, so I thought the ad might just be the answer. Is your husband traveling on business?"

"I don't have a husband. I'm the one you'll be escorting. As you can see, I'm a photographer."

"Oh." He glanced around the room, then back at her, looking more uncomfortable than before. "Just you?"

"Yes. Is that a problem?"

He cleared his throat. "No, not for me. But . . . well, it wouldn't exactly be, well, uh, proper. Would it?"

"Don't worry about that, Mr. . . . . ?"

"Lewis. David Lewis."

"Mr. Lewis, I'm an excellent shot and I always carry a weapon," she said with a smile. "I'm not afraid nor do I worry about propriety."

He nodded but looked skeptical about traveling alone with a woman. She counted that in his favor.

"I'll give you the same rate of pay that a wagon train would require and half again as much," Katie went on.

Mrs. O'Shea returned and set down two glasses with a solid thump for each.

"Well," he said, smiling broadly, "I can't hardly say no to that. And you won't have no use for that gun you'll be totin', ma'am. I'm an honest man and you can trust me. I'll do my very best to protect you and get you there safe and sound. When do you want to leave?"

"Is tomorrow too soon? I've been planning this for a long time," she said, practically unable to contain her excitement.

"I'll be here bright and early."

"Good." She rose and he followed.

"I'll be here," he repeated, with a nod.

When he'd gone, Mrs. O'Shea announced, "I don't like this at all. I didn't like it before and now I like it even less." She gathered up the still full glasses. "A woman's got no business gallivanting off with a strange man. At least Mr. McCord is someone that Tim knows and trusts."

"I don't want to discuss Tim or Mr. McCord."

"Hmph."

"It's settled. I'm leaving in the morning with Mr. Lewis. I'll start packing the wagon tonight."

"Hmph."

Chapter Two

Katie was up before the sun. She'd packed the wagon the night before with everything she knew she would need. Now she packed and repacked her valise, unsatisfied with each choice of clothing. How was a woman to travel and still look like a lady? Then her own words came back to her: She was not worried about propriety. Was she? Of course not! This was an adventure as well as a journey to fulfill her dreams. Perhaps if she dressed less like a lady, Mr. Lewis would feel less concerned about propriety himself, and she would probably be safer if she was taken for a man. She'd only told that story about being a great marksman with a gun to put Mr. Lewis at ease. She'd never so much as held a gun, let alone shot one.

Her mind suddenly made up, she quickly scoured the attic for any shirts and trousers that would fit. She filled two valises, one with men's clothes and one with her underclothing. Satisfied now, she hurried downstairs to the nearly bare parlor, where she caught a glimpse of a man headed toward her house. At first she thought it must be Mr. Lewis, but a closer look told her otherwise.

Riding his horse up the carriage drive toward the back of her house was Spence McCord, and he was leading two horses.

"Of all the nerve!" Katie tugged at the window but it wouldn't give. "What is he doing back here?" But before Mrs. O'Shea could respond, Katie was making a mad dash through the house to the studio where she pulled the door open to find Spence McCord poised to knock.

"I just wanted to let you know that I'll be working on the wagon before we leave," he said, gesturing toward the carriage house in the corner of the lot.

"You'll do no such thing." The man was a true pain in the behind.

"Tim's orders," he said, then turned and walked away.

"And just what do you intend to do to my wagon?" she asked, hurrying to catch up to him.

"Tim said it's been out there for as long as he could remember and probably needs some repairs, if it's usable at all." He stopped and turned toward her. "And if that's the case, we'll have to travel by train."

"We will not! I mean, I will not!"

He resumed his progress toward the carriage house, leaving her to follow if she wanted.

Once inside, she stood back while he made his inspection of the wagon, feeling especially glad about the work she had done on it. The two front wheels were new, all were greased, and the canvas top had recently been tailor made. After he studied its sturdiness, she knew he'd have to agree.

"Satisfied?" she asked, smiling smugly.

But before he could reply, a shadow blocked a portion of light from the doorway. Both Spence and Katie turned to look.

A man about Spence's height and build stood in silhouette. His clothing indicated that he was used to being in the outdoors most of the time. Katie immediately recognized Mr. Lewis.

"Mornin'," he said to Spence. "You plannin' on headin' west with us? A little more company would be real nice."

Spence gave Katie a surprised glance, then said to the man, "Good morning."

"This is Mr. Lewis, my guide." Katie couldn't help but feel a little self-satisfied at outmaneuvering Spence McCord and Tim.

Spence stepped away from the wagon and closer to Mr. Lewis. "Sorry," he said, his tone friendly but firm. "But I've already been hired."

Katie gasped and turned on him. "You have not!"

The man stared first at Katie, then at Spence. "Uh, well, the lady seems to have changed her mind."

"I never hired him," Katie corrected.

The man frowned in confusion.

"Her brother did. I'm hired."

"I told you, Tim's a jackass. And you're not hired, you're fired!"

"Sorry, Miss O'Rourke, you can't fire me." Then extending his hand toward Mr. Lewis, Spence said, "Better luck next time."

Bewildered, the man shook Spence's hand. "But if she doesn't want you . . ."

"She does. She doesn't know it yet."

"I do not want you!" she cried in desperation.

Irritation started to replace the other man's bewilderment, and he leaned forward, intent on settling the situation. "If the lady doesn't want you, then why don't you forget it?"

"I can't," Spence replied sincerely. "I've already been paid. It's a matter of honor."

At that the man visibly calmed down and nodded

thoughtfully. "Well, then I guess I'll be on my way." He politely tipped his hat and turned to go.

Dumbfounded, Katie stared at the retreating back of the best prospect she'd had so far.

"No! Don't go!" she cried, running after him.

He halted but shook his head when she stopped beside him. "I don't want the job after all, ma'am. A man's honor . . . well, it just wouldn't be right."

Katie watched in disbelief as the man smiled apologetically and walked away. He was the only one who had answered her ad that had all the qualifications she'd been looking for, and he was turning her down. More specifically, he'd changed his mind. No, she corrected herself, Spence McCord had changed his mind.

"I hope you're satisfied!" she said, rounding on Spence. "I've been planning this trip for months. Years! And you've just chased off the one and only man I could have hired." There probably wasn't another able and willing man in all of New York City, and if there was, how long would she have to wait before she found him? It was the beginning of May already and she had hoped to be on her way by the end of this week. But what chance did she have now?

"I'll help you load your things," Spence said. "Do you have supplies yet for cooking on the trail?"

"Cooking?" she repeated vacantly, trying to focus on his words instead of the defeat she suddenly felt. "I . . . I hadn't thought about cooking . . ." That was one of those details she'd intended to leave to her guide.

He smiled for the first time. "Well, I am partial to eating, although I can't say I care much for beans."

"I'd have to be very hungry to eat beans," Katie replied. But she was thinking that if she had to do all the cooking, beans just might be the mainstay of their meals. "So I guess we do agree on one thing."

With that said, she realized she'd just accepted him as her guide and escort. Looking him over from head to toe, she took in his broad yet lanky frame, the wide-brimmed hat that seemed to add several inches to his height, and the sturdy boots which had obviously seen better days. He was rugged, and she sensed that he was more than capable of handling the job before them. She would simply have to put aside her personal differences with him and concentrate on her journey, her goal.

"Well," she said with a resigned shake of her head, "since you're here and I do need someone, I suppose we might as well get on with it. I assume that as Tim's hired hand you've had experience with most kinds of wagons. But this," she said, indicating her wagon, "is not at all like driving for a cook on a cattle drive."

He coughed and nearly choked. "Maybe we should get something straight—"

"I only want to make it perfectly clear that transporting photographic equipment isn't the same as hauling flour."

The frown between his eyes told her that he wasn't pleased about something she'd said. "Don't worry, ma-'am. The cook never lost an egg," he replied in a long, friendly drawl.

Well, she couldn't worry about whatever it was she'd said that upset him, she had a new problem now. "I suppose I'd better send Mrs. O'Shea for the cooking supplies." Katie only hoped that she wouldn't have to make up a list, since she had no idea what or how to cook "on the trail."

"Good idea," Spence replied.

Katie went to find Mrs. O'Shea, leaving him to check the harness and other equipment for himself.

After a thorough inspection, Spence found the harness to be in as good shape as the strange contraption she called a wagon. It was no more than four wheels with a shallow box for a bed, a ribbed roof similar to that of a buggy, and four black walls of canvas neatly attached to the bottom edge. It was completely enclosed except for the flaps in front and back, and probably hotter than Hades inside when it stood in full sun. A small extension of the roof offered some protection of the exposed front seat, which could accommodate only two people.

He walked to the rear of the wagon and lifted the canvas aside. Not much room for anything, he thought, as his eyes scanned the dark interior where small cabinets lined the outside edge.

"It's all packed," he heard her say from behind him. When he turned around she raised a small valise. "Except for this."

But he hardly noticed the carpetbag in her hand when he got a look at the clothes she wore. Even in the dimly lit building it was easy to see that she had traded in her dress for men's clothing.

"What are you doing wearing that?" he asked.

With red-gold curls springing into action, she looked down at her britches and shirt and sensible walking shoes.

"I think it's the practical thing to do," she returned, unruffled.

Time was ticking away. Spence could spend all day squaring off with her. He knew he shouldn't care if she wanted to be gawked at by the ladies of New York, but if the men saw her as a tantalizing bit of baggage with her contrary hair, and those long legs of hers . . . well, that could be a problem. He decided another tack might be in order.

"It's your decision," he said, pulling off his hat and scratching a spot above his left ear. "I'm not sure, though, if you won't be turning folks away, especially women, when you ask to take their pictures."

He could tell that that idea took root when her hand dropped away from her hip.

"I think it would be better if you changed back to your regular clothes," he said.

Katie considered his words for a moment, but only a moment. She had never been one to conform to fashion. She wore what was comfortable, and that meant no bustles of any sort, and she had long ago thrown out her hoops, much to Mrs. O'Shea's horror. Katie preferred to be unfettered and unconfined, but Mrs. O'Shea disapprovingly said that "too defined" was a more appropriate description of her appearance. What better time than now to show her truly unconventional side?

"No," she stated. Then she walked around him, pulled back the canvas and crawled in on her hands and knees to stow her valise near the front.

Spence cleared his throat and immediately looked the other way when presented with the backside of her britches. Either she was ignorant of the view she'd just given him or she thought he was immune to such things. He mumbled something about hitching up the horses and went to get the harness.

Mrs. O'Shea hugged Katie tight and threatened not to turn her loose until she got some good sense in her head, but Katie pried herself free, only to return the hug.

"You've got enough supplies to last a long while if you're careful how you use them," Mrs. O'Shea admonished.

"We'll be fine," Katie replied.

"And don't be stingy with your letters."

"I promise to write often."

Katie climbed up her side of the wagon, feeling the thrill of the moment vibrate throughout her body. For years this wagon had sat idle waiting for this day, and now she was taking it and leaving behind everything that was comfortable and familiar. She looked over the house and the neat yard one last time, feeling only a momentary sadness at leaving. Although her entire life had been spent here, she was eager to get on with the rest of it. And that was why she'd already said her good-byes to Erin, James and the boys. Their tears and pleadings were things she could not deal with on the morning of her leave-taking, so she'd made it a point the evening before to hug and kiss them all good-bye. And she had done her share of crying, too.

But Mrs. O'Shea would have it no other way than to be there when Katie left.

"Don't cry," Katie called to her. "You'll make me cry."

"And you should," said the woman as she dabbed her eyes with the hem of her apron.

Katie felt the wagon dip slightly as Spence took his place on the seat beside her. Then he slapped the reins and they rolled down the drive to the street. She turned and called back, "I'll write often! I promise!"

The day was perfect for traveling as they left the city behind. The warm sunshine poured down on them as a stiff breeze blew about, occasionally puffing up the canvas sides.

Neither spoke, but that was fine with Katie. She drank in the sights and sounds of the rural area she'd never seen before. In fact, she'd seen very little of anything but New York City. Even Mr. McCord seemed to visibly relax, she noticed.

They didn't stop for a noon meal until well into the afternoon, but that was all right, too, since both were eager to be on their way as quickly as possible. When they did finally stop, it was under a tall, shady tree near a fenced pasture.

Katie jumped down from the wagon almost as soon as the horses came to a halt. Stretching and bending, she marveled once more at the freedom men took for granted in their unrestrictive clothing. Out of the corner of her eye she saw Spence first tend to the horses, then head for the woods. She would do the same after they'd eaten.

Inside the wagon she pulled open a basket filled with the food Erin and Mrs. O'Shea had insisted she take.

"Well, isn't this a feast," she said to herself as she looked over the bread, cookies, fried chicken, two kinds of cheese and an apple pie. Two glass jars of cool water were tucked along the side, wrapped in a double thickness of napkins. She had to admit that this would be the last good meal she'd be able to offer on their journey. Cooking was something she'd just never found the time to learn properly. Not that she'd ignored the problem of meals on the trail; she had intended from the beginning that her guide would do the cooking on an open fire when they weren't able to exchange a photograph for food. As far as she was concerned, nothing had changed.

When Spence returned to the wagon he found the picnic lunch spread out on the seat of the wagon with her standing alongside, biting into a piece of chicken. He helped himself and was pleased to find that she was a great cook. She handed him a jar of water, which he accepted gratefully, and drank deeply. Wiping his hand across his mouth when he'd finished, he said, "When we get to St. Louis we'll have to get a pack mule to carry more supplies. And a water barrel."

She nodded agreeably and sunk her teeth into a chunk of bread. Food had never tasted so good.

"I'll need more photographic plates, too," she said, then took another bite. After a while she asked, "How long do you think it will take to reach St. Louis?"

"Well, I figure from here to Pittsburgh will take a few weeks, more or less, at the rate we're traveling. Then from there to St. Louis we'll make better time since we'll take a boat."

31

Katie dusted her hands on the sides of pants.

"We can't do that," she said with quiet determination. "I don't think you realize the reason for this journey. I intend to photograph my way across the country. This isn't a lark, regardless of what you may think, Mr. McCord."

She had a rising feeling of helplessness when he didn't respond or even argue. What could she do if he simply chose to drive to the river and load the horses, the wagon and her equipment on a boat? Nothing.

"All right," she said, seeing that she was forced to relent. "If I agree that we take a boat to St. Louis, then will you agree that from there we do it my way?"

She held her breath while he hesitated; then he nodded.

Removing his hat, he absently scratched the spot above his left ear, and the dappled sunshine highlighted his dark hair. Then he settled his hat back on his head. She hadn't taken the opportunity to really study him until now. He had a stubborn jaw that softened somewhat when he smiled, which wasn't all that often, and warm brown eyes which he kept shaded with his hat.

A quick glance from him told her she'd been staring too long.

"Well," she began, "I'll just pack up these leftovers . . ." She gathered them up and stashed them in the box in the back of the wagon, then she made a trip to the woods. When she returned she found Spence sitting on the wagon seat with the reins in his hands, apparently anxious to get going.

The rest of the day passed as easily as the first part, with neither having much to say. He was thinking that she would want to find a town to spend the night in a hotel, and she wondered which farm to stop at for the night. She knew they would need to call it a day fairly early so she would have enough light to take some farmer's picture in trade for a meal and the use of his barn.

When at last they came upon a small farmstead where a woman was gathering in her wash and a man carried two buckets of water toward the barn, Katie reached out and touched Spence's sleeve.

"Let's stop here," she said.

Without slowing down, he asked, "Why?"

"Because I want to photograph them. And if they're willing we can stay here for the night. We'll make a trade."

Spence took in the scene. The barnyard was well kept and the barn looked solid, not likely to leak in case of rain. It would be a good place to sleep and tend the horses. The farmhouse was a frame building, which suggested that the farmer was prosperous enough to afford to trade a picture for room and board. So he turned off the road into a lane that led to the house.

"I'd better do the talking," Katie said, jumping down.

Without answering, he got off the wagon and walked alongside the horses, patting one of them in a soothing manner. Katie was several steps ahead of him as he followed her to where the woman stood staring at them, her arms full of clean clothes.

"Hello," she said to the woman. "My name's Katie O'Rourke."

The woman nodded, but was apparently leery of the two. She glanced nervously across the yard at her husband, who set down his buckets and walked toward them.

"Afternoon," he called.

Katie introduced herself again, exchanged a few pleasantries, then went on to say, "I'm a photographer and I was hoping you'd let me take your picture."

The older woman's hand immediately went to her hair, fingering the bun at the back of her neck, but Katie caught her look of interest.

The farmer frowned and looked past Katie to her wagon. "So that's what that is."

Pleased that she had at least piqued his curiosity, she answered, "Yes. Would you like to see it?"

"I never saw one of these but once, back in the war." He ambled toward it, looking it over, under and around. "Yes, sir. Reminds me of Brady's 'What's-it' wagon."

"You know Mathew Brady?" Katie asked, unable to keep the admiration she felt for the man from her voice.

"Sure did. Got my picture taken by him once or twice. Fine man." He opened the back curtain and peered inside. "Just as dark as his was, too."

"Mr. Brady was a friend of my father's," she offered in hopes of drawing more information from him. "Father was one of Mr. Brady's assistants during the war."

"Is that right?" the farmer said, looking at her more closely. "O'Rourke." He scratched his chin, thinking. "Can't say that I knew him."

"Well, there were a lot of assistants, and it was a long war," she said.

"That it was."

Spence stood by silently, just watching and letting her do all the talking, which she seemed to do so well.

"So you want to take our picture," the farmer said, suddenly straightening. "How much?"

She smiled charmingly. "I was hoping we could trade. A picture for a meal and a night in your barn."

The farmer looked at his wife and asked, "What do you think, Mattie?"

"Well, we haven't had a picture taken since we got married," she said and smiled almost bashfully. "I s'pose it would be nice to have another one. And there's plenty of room in the barn for the horses. The young couple can have the spare bedroom, because I certainly won't hear of them sleeping with the animals." Katie caught her breath at the suggestion that she and Spence share a bedroom, realizing that these people assumed she and Spence were husband and wife.

34

"Uh, Spence wouldn't mind sleeping in the barn at all. He likes animals."

The older couple looked at them with confused expressions on their faces.

"You're not married?" the man asked.

"Henry," Mattie scolded under her breath.

"Married?" Katie replied.

Spence couldn't hide a grin as he waited to see how she would talk her way out of this.

She laughed and motioned at him. "Heavens, no! He's my brother."

The older couple, relieved, laughed with her. Henry stuck out his hand to Spence and said, "Henry Jacobs. And this is my wife, Mattie."

Spence shook his hand. "Spence McCord."

Before their befuddled looks could return, Katie added, "We had different fathers."

"Of course," Mattie said. "Why don't you young folks come in and I'll fix us some coffee. I made bread today and it's still warm."

"That sounds lovely. But first I'll need to take the picture while there's still good light."

"Oh, my word," Mattie said. "But I'm such a mess." She brushed at her skirts and fingered her hair once more.

"Well, you have time to freshen up while I set up my camera and get the plates ready," Katie said, her eyes already scanning the yard for the best spot to use as a backdrop.

The air was still; not even a slight breeze stirred. She wouldn't have to worry about fluttering leaves blurring on the trees. The house was simple with a small porch in front and one on the side. A milk house stood about fifteen feet from the side door.

She decided on the cozy area between the house and the milk house. Henry brought out two kitchen chairs and set them in the grass where Katie instructed, then he, too, disappeared to freshen up a little.

From the back of her wagon, while standing in the well-step, Katie pulled the bulky camera from its place of padded security and then the tripod. Making two trips, she first set up the tripod and then the camera with its light-filtering tent over the back.

"I need a large bucket filled with water," she said to Spence. "Would you mind?"

"Anything for my sister," he answered with a grin.

"Well," she whispered, "what would you have told them?"

He shrugged. "The truth."

"You mean, that we're a couple of strangers traveling across the country together?"

"They probably wouldn't think much worse of that than they do of your trousers."

"These clothes are practical, and so was the little white lie. I don't see any reason to explain in great detail how it happens that we're traveling together. This way it's much simpler."

"Little white lies have a way of catching up with you sooner or later," he said.

"I haven't said or done anything that isn't perfectly harmless."

"Is that how you see it?" he drawled, feeling a sudden irritation that she took this journey so lightly as to believe it held no danger.

"And how do you see it?" she shot back, her eyes beginning to snap fire.

"I think traveling across the country in a small wagon is foolish and far from harmless. You have no idea what you're up against."

"So you do think I see this as a lark."

"Something like that."

"Well, I can see you're going to make this as difficult

as possible," she said with one hand propped against her waist, leaning toward him.

The pose was very enticing. Her shirt stretched tautly across one shoulder, outlining the curves clear to her hip. But he kept his eyes staring steadily into hers.

"I'm only here because of Tim." Then he grabbed up her bucket and walked away.

In the meantime the Jacobs seated themselves on their chairs to patiently wait for the photographer.

Katie climbed onto the step at the back of her wagon and entered, angrily pulling the curtain behind her and adding another one of orange calico for subdued lighting around the edges. Her mind flitted between the task at hand and her growing irritation with Spence McCord. He was going to take all the fun out of her entire journey just by refusing to take her work seriously. A lark indeed! She felt like a true pioneer. She *was* a true pioneer. How many women had ever done what she was doing? Very few, if any. Well, she didn't need his approval, just his service as an escort.

She placed the receptacles for the baths on a drop-down shelf in the order she'd memorized from her father's teachings. Within reach of her right hand was the collodion, a mixture of sulphuric ether, alcohol and salts of bromide and iodide of potassium. The smell always made her nose wrinkle, but it so strongly reminded her of her father that she never thought of it as unpleasant. In front of her was the developing bath, an iron sulphate solution including acetic acid. Ahead of that was the fixing agent of cyanide of potassium.

When everything was where she needed it, she removed a glass plate from the dust-proof box at her knees and with a pair of tongs dipped it into the sensitizing collodion. When the plate was properly coated she removed it and held it suspended until it attained the proper amount of stickiness that only experience could teach. Then she carefully lowered it into the silver nitrate and waited four minutes, humming softly "The Battle Hymn of the Republic" three times as her father had taught her. Finally she slipped the plate into the slide holder and emerged from the tent.

Spence eyed her speculatively while sniffing the air that followed her. "Smells like you're brewing up something that could blow us all to kingdom come."

Ignoring his remark, she hurried to the camera, flipped the tent over her head and inserted the glass plate. Time was important. Once the collodion had contacted the plate, she had only ten minutes to complete the process and take the picture.

To her dismay, Mattie and Henry sat unsmiling and as stiff as the backs of their chairs.

"How long have you two been married?" Katie called from under the cover, hoping to get more relaxed expressions from them.

Mattie ducked her head and said, "Forty years."

Henry had a ghost of a smile that appeared as though it might fade, so Katie exposed the plate.

Feeling pleased with her first attempt, she continued humming the same song while she removed the plate and returned to the wagon for developing.

First she put the plate through the series of developing baths, washing and fixing, then a final washing, drying and varnishing.

From outside the wagon she could hear Spence's soft whistle of "Dixie" as he leaned against the wagon wheel. Refusing to be baited or deterred from her work, she ignored him.

The next step was to transfer the picture to paper, which was the easiest part of the entire process. Quickly she placed the albumen paper in close contact with the glass negative in a printing frame and once again emerged from the wagon to place it in the sunlight.

While waiting for the picture to "take," she alternately hummed and counted to herself. Then returning to the wagon, she stabilized the print and added a toner that produced a warm brown color.

Coming out into daylight once more, she surveyed her photograph with satisfaction while Henry looked over her shoulder and Mattie studied it from beside her. The couple in the picture seemed like an older rendition of young married love, with Mattie smiling shyly while staring at her hands and Henry with an undeniable sparkle in his eye.

"I declare," Mattie said, her voice tinged with embarrassment.

Henry cleared his throat. "You do nice work."

She handed the picture to Mattie.

"Thank you, child."

"Now how about some coffee?" Henry suggested.

"Sounds good to me," Spence replied from behind Katie's other shoulder where he, too, had been surveying her work.

Surprised that he was even remotely curious, she glanced back at him. But he was already following Henry toward the house.

Chapter Three

The next morning dawned sparkling clear. Sparkling because a gentle rain had fallen during the night, and clear because every trace of gray clouds had been swept from the sky.

Henry and Mattie insisted that Spence and Katie stay for breakfast, then Spence insisted that he help with the chores.

After a round of friendly good-byes, they were finally on their way. Inside the wagon, tucked away in a box, were the extra gifts of food from the Jacobs: a loaf of Mattie's wonderful bread, a few eggs and a couple slices of ham—in other words, their lunch.

Katie watched the passing scenery with the eye of an artist. Every distant hill, every steepled church and even the animal-filled pastures called to her to set up her camera and tripod. But she had to be more selective than to give in to every whim. Her supply of glass plates was limited, at least until she reached St. Louis. At that time she would purchase new ones. Her prints she would carefully store in the back of her wagon.

When the sun was high overhead, Spence suggested they stop for the noon meal. As they pulled off the nearly deserted road near a creek with a rocky bank, Katie inhaled deeply of the fragrant pines that lined the bubbling creek. Newly leafed trees offered dappled shade where Spence, after seeing to the horses, helped her set up camp.

Faced now with the prospect of preparing a meal using Mattie's gifts, Katie remembered with mild apprehension the little white lie she'd allowed him to believe about her abilities as a cook. The truth was she had never spent much time in front of a stove, and in fact knew very little about getting a good fire going. She momentarily considered playing hooky in the wagon, checking her supplies, but she already knew exactly what she had and a recheck would only postpone the inevitable. Besides, they might as well get a few things straight right from the beginning: she was a photographer, not a cook.

Spence saw the apprehension on her face and figured she knew nothing about building a campfire, so he gathered some dead branches and a handful of pine needles. Kneeling opposite her, he assembled them tepee style, then pulled a tin of matches from his pocket and lit the kindling. He found a few good-sized rocks and placed them strategically to hold a coffeepot or skillet over the fire. Leaning back on his haunches, he pushed his hat to the back of his head, watching the fire and feeding it more wood.

Katie studied his procedure, committing it to memory. It looked simple enough. She could probably do it herself the next time. After all, this was her journey and adventure, and she planned to make the most out of it, conceding that even photographers had to eat.

She waited until the fire was white hot, then set her skillet over it. When she added the ham she couldn't hold back a smile of satisfaction at the sound of sizzling meat. After it quickly browned, she removed the ham and added some fat, then cracked two eggs into the popping puddle. With that done, she turned her attention to filling her small coffeepot at the rocky creek. Before long, the smell of burned eggs drifted toward her.

"Oh!" she cried, looking for something to wrap around the handle of the skillet. "Oh, no." Dismayed, she watched the edges of each egg curl into thin, blackened crisps.

Spence jumped to his feet, whipped his hat from his head and used it as a potholder, pulling the skillet from the fire as smoke plumed into the air. He carried the burned remains to the base of a tree, then returned to the campfire.

"Just set it down," she said, her voice sharp with embarrassment. "I'll try again."

He hesitated, then remembered the delicious chicken she'd brought along the day before. Maybe she just needed a little experience with outdoor cooking.

"Go ahead," she said, waving a hand at the fire. "Just put it down."

He was hungry enough to cook the meal himself but he sensed that the situation had become a matter of pride for her, and a challenge, so he set the skillet near the fire and waited.

Katie went through the process once more, this time keeping an eye on the cooking eggs. Even so, she managed to char the bottoms. She scooped them out onto the plates where the cold, dried-out pieces of ham waited. Her only consolation was that she hadn't tried to make biscuits.

"I have a confession to make," she said, placing the heavy iron skillet away from the fire with the potholder she'd retrieved from Erin's box of food. "I'm not very good at this."

A slow grin crept across his face. "And I'm not very

surprised." His eyes twinkled mischievously as he accepted the plate she handed him. "I just can't quite figure out how the chicken turned out so good."

"My sister Erin is a great cook," she said with a sheepish smile.

He nodded thoughtfully. "Erin. I wondered if maybe Mrs. O'Shea had sent it," he said, tearing off a bite of ham with his teeth.

"No, but she tried." Katie set the coffeepot on the fire. "I told her everything was packed away and there was no sense in dragging it all out. And besides, we'd do our own cooking as we went."

She didn't tell him that the older woman had snorted her disbelief at that notion. Right from the beginning, Mrs. O'Shea had been set against the whole idea of the journey, even more so than Erin, and Katie wondered if maybe she hadn't been part of the conspiracy that had brought Spence to her door.

When the coffeepot boiled aromatically, Spence reached out and pulled it off the fire a little.

Katie took a bite of the ham sandwich she'd made, deciding against the eggs. It was passable fare, thanks to Mattie's bread. "You don't have to eat those," she said, pointing to the eggs on his plate.

"I've eaten worse," he replied in his usual honest manner and proceeded to eat them with bread.

When the grounds had settled somewhat, Katie poured each of them a full mug of the delicious-smelling coffee.

And it was delicious, from the top of the mug to the bottom. They each savored the taste while they enjoyed their quiet surroundings.

"I've never heard so much silence," she said softly, straining her neck to see the top of the tall pines.

"It almost reminds me of home, but not quite," he replied. "I don't know how you manage to live in the city with all that noise and commotion."

"It's all I've ever known," she said with a lift of her shoulder. "But I think deep down I suspected it was like this out here. That's part of the reason I wanted to go on this journey."

"That's the only sensible reason," he said, stretching back on the ground with his hands under his head.

Something about his reply piqued her, making her feel irritated once more. The camaraderie of the moment was suddenly broken, and she felt as though he considered her a foolish woman on a foolhardy lark for a foolish reason. But how could he possibly understand her dreams and goals? He was free to travel wherever he wished, whenever he wished and for whatever reason that moved him. She wanted that freedom, too, in whatever measure she could get it.

Jumping up from the rock she sat on, she gathered up the dirty dishes, banging the skillet noisily against the coffeepot as she made her way to the creek. From the corner of her eye she saw Spence lift his head to watch her, but he said nothing, which suited her just fine since she might just use the skillet on him.

Spence raised up on an elbow, thinking she sure did get her feathers ruffled easily. It also seemed that she had a dislike for the truth, either hearing it or telling it. He figured that was a family trait as well, since Tim could tell the tallest tales without even a grin to give himself away. Even so, he'd been surprised when he heard her tell that straight-out lie about them being brother and sister. At that moment a warning bell had gone off in his head, and he planned to pay it some heed.

After breaking camp and repacking everything, they returned to the main road, where they passed a number of other travelers, some of whom gave them and their wagon curious stares, while others nodded in a friendly gesture. Katie noticed that Spence was perfunctorily polite with only a nod, as though the company of people unsettled him. He seemed more relaxed when they had the road to themselves. People or solitude, either was fine with Katie.

They spent most of the day riding in silence. She gazed with appreciation at the beauty of the wooded surroundings, where occasionally they chanced upon a deer or some other wild creature. Spring flowers were in abundance wherever the trees opened into a meadow. She felt like a child seeing these things for the first time, and also like a woman whose horizons were expanding at last.

As the afternoon sun followed a lazy line across the sky, Katie's stomach growled and she imagined Spence's must be doing the same after the light fare they'd had at noon.

Spence had hoped they would stop early. His stomach had been rolling with hunger for hours. But today she'd shaken her head at the last three homesteads when he'd suggested they stop. Then the fourth farm, surprisingly, met her approval. He glanced at the patched set of buildings, the thin cow and the stream of children running from the house when they pulled in the barnyard.

After Katie took a picture of the entire family in the bare front yard, she and Spence helped the thin woman set up a table and chairs under a side-yard tree while her husband lounged sleepily nearby.

Then a meager meal of soup containing beans and a little ham was served. Several pans of cornbread made a tasty accompaniment, but Spence couldn't bring himself to eat his fill when the family was so obviously poor. Katie graciously thanked the woman and he seconded her, pushing himself away from the table. It disgusted him to see the husband lazing around while his family barely got by, so he did what he could to help by feeding and watering the animals.

When he'd finished pumping water for the last bucket, Katie came out to lean against the sturdiest fence post.

"That was nice of you to help her out," she said.

The evening had turned to near darkness and the kitchen glowed with the light of a single lamp. The shouts and howls of children's laughter echoed across the now empty yard.

He shrugged noncommittally, not wanting to take credit for a kindness.

Changing the subject, she said, "Looks like a clear night. Not a cloud in the sky."

From his angle, she stood in silhouette against the light coming from the house. And with the darkness hiding him, he was free to study the stubborn tilt of her chin, which matched her personality so well. She had a fine straight nose and small ears that hardly showed at all through the wisps of curls surrounding her face. There was no getting around the fact that she was pretty, but that was just one more reason to keep his distance. Independent, pretty women could be the most dangerous. Add stubborn to that and you got yourself some real trouble, he thought, and looked away toward the barn.

"That's good, because I'm not sure that old barn could keep out a heavy dew."

She shook her head sadly. "No, I don't suppose it would."

"I imagine they've never had their picture taken before," he said, realizing she'd have done it as a favor for the family. Even though he thought the whole idea of picture taking was foolish, the woman had been overwhelmed.

"She didn't say so, but I suspect that's true." Then she asked softly, "Are there families out west as poor as these people?"

"Money-wise, yes. Spirit-wise, there are some worse off."

He thought about the laughing children who had earlier played in the shade of the few trees surrounding the house and compared them to those of the desolate prairie soddies. Being alone never bothered him, but he'd seen what loneliness could do to some. "I guess 'poor' can mean different things."

He had pulled off his hat while he talked and scratched that spot above his left ear. Katie doubted he even realized he'd done it. Without any light other than that coming from the distant house, it was difficult to make out his features and tell what he might be thinking. He was a serious man, far too serious, she thought. It crossed her mind how different Spence was from her brother, who was a high-jinks sort of fellow, and she wondered how the two of them had ever become friends. And she was sure they were friends or Tim would never have trusted him to escort her. The whole idea of the two men together drew up an unlikely vision of Tim slapping Spence on the back after pulling one of his pranks.

"How does it happen that you and my brother are friends?" she ventured.

Even though they'd been together for two days they hadn't shared anything more than the usual conversations, with the exception of the small altercation at the Jacobses', but she had to admit to a little curiosity about this man.

He shrugged. "We just are."

"How long have you known Tim?" she prodded further.

"A long time," he replied, backing up to the barn door and leaning against it with his arms crossed over his chest.

She didn't need to be hit over the head to realize that he wasn't going to give up any information about his past. She knew she should leave well enough alone, but her curiosity suddenly overwhelmed her.

"A long time? That could mean all the way back to the war."

A sharp glance from him told her she'd stepped beyond her bounds. "Could be," he drawled. "It's getting late. I believe I'll turn in."

"We'll leave early tomorrow," she said, her words brisk in retaliation for his almost rude refusal to say more. "Before sunrise."

"Suits me."

Searching in the dark, Katie found the single nightgown she'd brought, and punched her arms into the sleeves with enough force to tear them loose. She had only been trying to make conversation, and yes, find out a little something about the man who was to be her companion for two thousand miles. Her unwanted companion at that! Well, it still wasn't too late to send him packing. He could catch a train to Montana and go back to his precious cows and buffalo and whatever else was so important to him. She would just go on from here by herself the way she'd planned.

Lighting a candle and securing it, she settled down on her feather tick, gazing toward the back of the wagon where the canvas flap kept back the night.

She didn't need him, not really.

The unfamiliar night sounds from outside crowded into her consciousness.

And if she thought she did need someone, she'd hire a man when she reached Pittsburgh. Certainly she shouldn't have any trouble between here and there, especially since they had come across so many friendly people.

An owl hooted. She tried to ignore the lonely, eerie sound but found herself sitting rigidly, braced for the unknown. The snap of a twig nearby made her jump, and she chided herself for being a coward. Then the quiet of a woodland night settled around the wagon.

Perhaps she shouldn't be so hasty, she acknowledged truthfully. After all, what did she know about taking care of horses and harness? It rankled, but once more she was forced to admit that she needed him, at least for now. Maybe when they reached the Mississippi River she could find someone to hire. Maybe she'd even meet up with Mr. Lewis again.

With an exasperated sigh, she pulled out some writing paper along with her pen and ink. She would write to Erin and to Mrs. O'Shea as she'd promised.

Dear Erin, James and boys,

I can't tell you how beautiful the countryside is here, and I'm afraid the pictures I have taken will not be able to convey any of it. I have met the most wonderful people, all very friendly. They seem to be pleased beyond measure at the pictures I take, which pleases me more than I expected.

I am well and so is my escort, although I fail to see why Tim thought he was such a prime choice. Still, I intend to make the best of it until we part company in St. Louis.

Do not worry about forwarding letters to me, since I do not know my destination from day to day.

I love you all, Katie

She knew without a doubt there would be a mailbag full of letters waiting for her at the St. Louis post office when she arrived. If she inflicted a little worry on them, so be it. They deserved no less for meddling in her private affairs. And if she in any way stretched the truth to suit her purposes, well, it wouldn't be the first time.

Chapter Four

Katie awoke to the sound of the harness jangling and the quiet clop of horses' feet. She had slept so soundly and comfortably that she was loath to get up. Without even looking outside the canvas flap she knew it was as black as pitch, and her words "before sunrise" came back to haunt her. Tentatively she stretched her full length, arching her toes until they reached the empty space of the step-well, then quickly she recoiled into a ball, burying her nose in the soft warmth of the feather tick.

"Are you awake in there?" she heard him call to her as he passed alongside the wagon. "It'll be daybreak in another half hour."

Another day on her journey, more pictures and unknown experiences awaited her. Suddenly she was wide awake.

"Yes," she called back, her voice as hushed as his, not wanting to awaken anyone at the house.

In no time at all she was pulling on her britches and

buttoning her shirt. Then, kneeling, she tipped her head forward and brushed her long hair. She expertly rolled and pinned it, then fluffed the short mop of curls that bobbed around her face. Her shoes took the longest to fasten, and she vowed to find something simpler for traveling.

She felt the wagon dip under Spence's weight as he seated himself in front. Assured of privacy, she made a dash for the privy before climbing onto her side of the wagon seat. Without a word he clicked to the horses and they rolled slowly out of the barnyard only minutes before the sun sent rays of red and orange across the sky.

For the most part they kept to the main roads where travel was faster, which suited Spence, and slightly smoother, which suited Katie. When they stopped for meals they turned onto side roads that resembled cow paths more than roads, but these were the places that Katie loved the best.

And it was when they had stopped on one of these turnoffs that they encountered an entourage of other travelers, all driving in the same direction. At Katie's coaxing, Spence called out to one wagonload of laughing men and boys.

"Must be a gathering of some kind going on," Spence said as the heavy wagon lumbered to a near halt.

"Just a barn raising," the man called back cheerfully. "With more food than a village could put away. You from around here?"

"No. Montana." Spence figured that it was all right to call Montana his home now, since the herd had probably already arrived at the new ranch even though there wasn't much more than a shack awaiting him.

"Looks like you got a strong back. We could always use one more. You'll be well fed for your efforts. And your wife, too." The man smiled politely and lifted his hat when he spoke to Katie.

Spence glanced at Katie half expecting her to correct the man by saying they were brother and sister. Instead, she smiled and replied, "Thank you, we'd love to be a part of your barn raising."

"Just follow us!" And they drove away.

When they were out of earshot, Spence turned to her. "Do you know how long it takes to put up a barn? We'll be here for days."

"We aren't exactly in a hurry," she returned.

"Yes, we are." Not only had he missed trailing the herd, but at the rate she wanted to travel he'd probably miss getting his place built, and winter came mighty early in Montana. But more importantly, he had a business deal waiting for him in St. Louis, if he got there on time.

"Well, I'm not in a hurry. And this is *my* journey, in case you've forgotten." She headed back to the spot where they had just begun setting up camp and gathered together the coffeepot and other cooking supplies to store back in the wagon.

"If you're in such a hurry, we'll forget about eating until we get to the barn raising. It probably isn't far."

He watched while she quickly stashed everything in the back of the wagon, her backside pointed in his direction. Clearing his throat, he promptly stepped away. When she finally climbed onto the front seat, he turned back again.

"Well? Are you coming?" she asked with mild annoyance.

He was more than a little annoyed himself. As a matter of fact, he was sorely tempted to drive to the nearest train station and send her straight to Tim. All this foolishness about picture taking was driving him to distraction when he had better, more important things to do. But a promise was a promise, and he'd given his word to her brother. And there was always the boat at

Pittsburgh to make up the difference in travel time. At least, he hoped so.

He settled his hat firmly on his head until the brim edged down toward his nose, then strode to his side of the wagon and climbed aboard. The low rumble in his stomach said all would not be lost if the food was as plentiful as they'd been told. He hadn't had a decent meal since they'd left Henry and Mattie's place, and he made a silent vow that from now on he'd be in charge of the grub.

As they crested the next hill, the scene below them was a mass of confusion. Wagons moved and parked wherever there was an open space. Stacks of peeled logs and timber lay close to where the finished barn would stand. Already a skeleton of the structure had been formed, and men walked on the floor of the hay-mow as the crew of men below handed up the necessary wood.

"Would you look at that!" Katie cried. "I've never in my life seen anything like it!"

As they drew closer, the confusion was less obvious and the entire operation actually seemed to have an organization of its own. Tables, which were really rough planking on sawhorses, laden with food, stretched for several yards in a magnificent display of the best that the county had to offer. Laughter and calls of greetings spiced the air, giving Katie the feeling of welcome even though she didn't know a soul.

The men who had invited them came over to shake Spence's hand and introduce themselves.

The older one said, "My name's Ethan and this is my brother Joshua." Spence nodded and accepted their hands. "These are my sons, Eli and Matthew."

"Spence McCord," he responded.

"And I'm Katie," she said with a smile.

"It isn't my barn but I'll say it anyway. Glad to have you both. Mrs. Jefferson will appreciate another hand to help with the food, I'm sure." He turned to point in the woman's direction. "Last year we had a barn raisin' and my wife nearly wore herself out. Mary's here somewhere, too. This year it's the Jeffersons' turn, and we've come to repay their kindness. Well, can't stand around all day," Ethan said good-naturedly. "Let's grab us a handful of eatin', then head on over to the barn."

Spence followed the men while Katie hung back, desperately wanting to set up her camera. She eyed the perfect sky and scanned the nearby crowd. There was no way she could pass up an opportunity such as this, but first she must speak to Mrs. Jefferson.

Making her way slowly toward the tables, she skirted an area where children of all ages played and then dodged young boys bent on chasing each other. A cluster of tall maples provided shade for the working women as well as a few of the older ones who sat in rocking chairs offering words of advice.

"Excuse me," Katie said. "Are you Mrs. Jefferson?"

"Call me Evie. Would you pass that plate of cookies this way so I can put it back from the edge where the children can't reach it. Of course, I don't know why I'm worrying about it," she said as she rearranged pie dishes filled with every imaginable fruit. "There's more sweets here than anyone should be eating."

"Everything looks delicious," Katie said, her eyes lingering on what looked like a blackberry pie.

Evie turned toward Katie, dusting her hands on her skirts, and smiled broadly. "Didn't I just see you and your husband drive up behind Ethan?"

Katie hesitated a minute while she considered correcting Evie about her association with Spence, then decided there was no reason to go into unnecessary detail. "Yes, we did. I hope we're not intruding."

"Intruding! Not at all. We need every strong back we can get. I'll have to thank Ethan for asking you." Evie leaned over the table, picked up a plate and handed it to Katie. "Have you eaten yet? We want our workers well fed and happy. I'm going to rest my bones and join you as soon as I get a piece of Granny's apple pie."

Katie scanned the length of dishes, choosing a piece of baked chicken, a helping of stew, a biscuit and a small section of that blackberry pie. With a guilty glance in Spence's direction she took her plate to sit beneath a tree. She almost sat on the ground out of the newly formed habit she'd acquired since she'd been traveling, but on second thought, one of two vacant chairs seemed the most appropriate choice. Beside her sat a woman whose age was difficult to determine; she could have been seventy but might have been a hundred.

Evie eased gently into the chair beside the old woman. "I'm getting old, Granny," Evie said, then groaned happily with relief.

"You ain't old yet," Granny replied, her voice cracking with age. Her poke bonnet nearly hid her deeply wrinkled face, but not the bright awareness in her eyes. Katie doubted that much, if anything, got past the old woman unnoticed.

Evie laughed. "I'm not so sure about that." Then turning to Katie, she asked, "You folks aren't the ones who moved into the Atkinson place, are you?"

"No. We're just passing through," she said.

"Can I ask where you're headed?" Evie asked, then took a bite of her pie.

"West."

"That's an unusual wagon for traveling in, but now maybe I'm asking too many questions. I didn't mean to pry, especially when you and your husband have come to help us."

"I'm a photographer, a traveling photographer," Katie explained, liking the sound of her new title.

Evie sat aghast with her mouth wide open and eyes that looked as if they'd pop. "Mercy sakes! A woman photographer! Here on our farm. Granny, did you hear that?"

"My hearin's fine," Granny said. "Is that why you're wearin' those men's clothes? You look like a boy."

"Actually, Spence thought I'd be safer traveling dressed like this." Katie liked Granny's straightforward approach and smiled in appreciation.

"Safer? From what?" Evie asked.

"Bandits, Indians. I'm not really sure."

"Got any younguns?" Granny asked, her pale blue eyes searching Katie's.

Blushing, Katie replied, "Uh, no." She hadn't set out to deceive these two women but she was in too deep now to back out.

"I ain't surprised. Dressed like that. You look like a boy."

"Granny! Where's your manners? What will this young woman think of us country folk?" Evie chided.

"I say what I think."

"I know you do." But Evie didn't look approving. An embarrassed silence hung over Evie like a mantle; Granny wasn't at all embarrassed.

Hoping to break the spell, Katie said, "I've never seen a barn raising before, although I've heard of them. It's very overwhelming to be here in person and actually see everything that goes into it."

She watched the different crews of workers as they levered timbers into place and hoisted them by means of ropes and plenty of muscle. Their energy seemed limitless. Almost before her eyes the wooden skeleton began taking the shape of a real barn. She was sorry they would be unable to see it to completion.

Then she realized she was looking for one worker in particular, but there was no way to pick out one tall man wearing a hat among so many.

"There just wouldn't be any way we could put up such a big barn without the help of our neighbors," Evie said, her voice soft with gratitude. "We'll be indebted to each and every one of them for a good long time. And happily so."

They were interrupted by a crew of men who came to take their turn at the table. Katie dished up more chicken than she'd ever seen in one place before, and it just kept coming from the kitchen along with steaming biscuits, pots of coffee and jugs of milk. She chatted easily with everyone who spoke to her, enjoying the company of such friendly people.

"Ain't you gonna feed your man?" Granny asked Katie when there was finally an opportunity to sit down.

"I wouldn't want to be in the way by going over there," Katie replied, her eyes quickly searching the area near the barn where she'd last spotted Spence.

"Don't look like he intends to come over here for his meal," Granny went on. "A woman should look after her man if'n she wants to keep him from wanderin'."

Katie's charade of allowing these good people to think that the two of them were husband and wife had begun to wear on her conscience, but telling the truth now would only make matters worse. So she accepted the only natural solution and escaped from Granny's probing gaze in search of Spence, carrying a dish heaped with an assortment of food.

"Are you hungry?" she asked when she found him mopping his brow beneath a towering oak. The shade enveloped her in welcome coolness. On a bench stood several buckets of water. Spence picked up a dipper from one of them and gulped the contents.

"Starved. Thanks." He accepted the plate and motioned her toward another tree where they could sit in private. He sat on his haunches with his back to the trunk, balancing his plate on one knee, and without wasting any time he dug into the feast before him.

"Delicious, isn't it?" Katie said. "I don't know if you like blackberry pie but I put some on your plate."

He swallowed, then said, "One of my favorites."

For some strange reason his reply pleased her and she smiled.

Spence couldn't help but notice the way she sat on the ground, with her knees bent and her legs tucked up beside her. It was the most graceful movement he'd ever seen in a pair of britches.

"Did you take any photographs?" he asked, taking his thoughts in another direction.

"Not yet. It's so busy over there. I can't imagine where all that food is coming from, and who must be doing all the cooking."

"Ethan wasn't wrong when he said there was enough here to feed a village." He picked up the pie with his fingers and bit into it. It really was one of his favorites.

"I'd love to take one of the barn like it is right now," she said, looking past him at the incomplete structure. "But I could never ask everyone to stop working." She sounded a little downhearted.

"I suppose not."

"But," she said on a lighter note, "I met this wonderful old woman who would photograph very well. She has such a straightforward approach that you just can't help but like her. That is, if she'll grant permission."

A small breeze ruffled the curls that framed Katie's face, and Spence set his gaze a little farther off, just to create a little more distance between them. He didn't need to be noticing things like that, he told himself. His life was simple and he liked it that way. He also liked the way all of his bones hung together, which they wouldn't if Tim ever guessed about the direction of these latest thoughts.

"I guess I'd better get back to work," he said. "Daylight doesn't last long in these valleys, and I'm sure they aren't as far along as they intended to be."

Both of them rose. Katie took his plate, watching as he wiped his brow again and set his hat on his head.

Then each of them turned and walked away in opposite directions.

Katie hurried back to the food tables. Spence was right, daylight wouldn't last much longer, and she just had to have at least one picture of this event. After setting Spence's dish amidst the pile of dirty dishes that waited to be washed, she went in search of Evie and Granny.

"Evie," she said when she finally located her amongst a group of young mothers. "I was wondering if you would mind sitting for me while I photograph you and Granny. I'd love to get some of the background in it, too."

A look of sheer pleasure crossed Evie's face. "Would you do that? I mean, it would be beyond my wildest fancies to have a picture of this here gathering. I don't suppose you could get one of the barn, too. Could you?"

"Well, everyone would have to hold still while I exposed the plate. But as long as they all cooperate, I don't know why not."

"You go ahead and set up that camera of yours while I find Mr. Jefferson." As Evie hurried away, Katie heard her exclaim to herself, "Just imagine!"

Katie set up her camera for the most advantageous angle of sunlight and was pleased that it was also the best angle for getting the barn's details. She quickly prepared the baths and basins inside her wagon, keeping one eye on Evie and Mr. Jefferson to wait for the signal to begin. A sharp whistle brought all the crews to a halt as Mr. Jefferson called out instructions to stop working while the lady photographer took their picture.

This was the largest undertaking Katie had ever attempted. Nothing in her past prepared her for the scope of this exposure, and she found herself more than a little nervous as she checked and double checked the angle of light, the position of men and, of course, the basic structure of the barn. When she was satisfied she could do no better, she quickly processed the glass plate, inserted it for exposure, then ducked beneath the heavy cloth. Holding her breath and saying a prayer, she exposed the plate.

Everyone waited.

Inside the back of her wagon once more, she went through the familiar steps, counting and humming, washing and fixing. At last she was able to place the plate outside for developing.

And still everyone waited.

An almost reverent hush filled the air as mothers quieted the children and men shifted their weight from foot to foot, but Katie barely took notice of those things, so intent was she on her task.

Finally the print was ready. A small group of onlookers crowded around her, trying to get the first peek. Smiles and words of praise were passed along until Mr. Jefferson, having heard that the picture was successfully taken, gave another sharp whistle for work to resume.

Katie handed the picture to Evie. "It's very good, if I do say so myself."

"I'm honored to have this," Evie said, nearly overcome with emotion. "This is one of the brightest days in our lives, and now we have this picture to help us remember it always. Even our grandchildren's children will be able to see this day, and all because you stopped to help." She pulled Katie into a gentle hug. "Thank you."

Katie returned the hug, warmed clear to the center of her being by Evie's gratitude. "You're very welcome."

"If there's anything at all I can do in return . . ."

"Well, there is one thing," Katie began. "Would Granny allow me take her picture?"

"I'll see to it myself that she doesn't give you one bit of trouble," Evie replied. "You just point that camera right where you want Granny to sit and she'll be sittin' there."

Evie hurried off and returned in no time with Granny in tow.

Granny frowned, although it was difficult to tell since her brow was already well furrowed. Still, she was compliant enough and, surprisingly, she allowed Katie to reposition her chair twice.

"Can't imagine why you'd want an old woman to sit for you," Granny grumbled loudly. "Plenty of young purty things around that would do better 'n me."

"I'm sure none of them have the wisdom you do, Granny," Katie soothed.

"Hmph. You're just talkin' words, but it just so happens they're true."

Katie couldn't help smiling at the old woman's self-appraisal. Being honest and straightforward seemed to be Granny's outlook on life. Perhaps that had gained her the longevity she now enjoyed. Katie would have to ponder that later. Being straightforward came easily to her; being honest didn't.

"I'll be right back," Katie said, heading back to her wagon to once again prepare a glass plate. "Don't go anywhere," she called over her shoulder.

"Where would I go?" Granny asked.

Within minutes, Katie was back, ducking under the cloth of the camera, then exposing the plate. Then she headed to the wagon to finish it, saying, "We'll see in a little bit how it turned out."

"You're all done?"

"All done. At least with that part. I'll be right back," she said once more as she hurried to her wagon to finish the developing.

When the print was ready for viewing, another crowd surrounded Katie, who crouched down beside Granny to show it to her.

"Can you see it all right?" Katie asked.

"My eyesight's as good as my hearin'. Just let me hold it." Then after scrutinizing the brown-toned likeness, she quietly exclaimed, "Land sakes, who is that old woman?"

A reverent ripple of laughter went around the group. "It's you, Granny. Nobody but you wears a bonnet like that," said a young woman with a baby on her hip. "Even in a picture I can feel you looking right through me to see if I'm tellin' any half-truths."

Granny craned her neck to look up at the young woman, who laughed in response, then leaned down to kiss the wrinkled cheek. "I've learned my lessons, Granny. No more half-truths."

Instinctively, Katie kept her eyes from meeting Granny's as she wondered what sort of half-truth the young mother had told, and just how Granny had found out.

Granny handed the picture back to Katie.

"No," Katie said, pushing it away. "It's yours."

"What do I want with a picture of myself?"

"Perhaps one of your grandchildren would like to have it someday."

"I don't have any grandchildren."

Surprised, Katie glanced up at her wide-eyed.

"Don't have any children either."

"Oh." At a loss for words, Katie found her usual straightforwardness leaving her, too.

"Don't have a man either. But I did once. Long time ago." Then she looked deep into Katie's eyes, until Katie felt that every untruth she'd ever told was being exposed, just like one of her pictures, for all to see. "Take care of your man. If'n you don't want him to wander."

In spite of herself, Katie heard her own words. "I will."

She didn't know when it had happened, but Katie was suddenly aware that the crowd had dispersed and the two of them were alone. "And stop wearin' them britches. You look like a boy."

Katie grinned and leaned over to kiss the old woman's dry cheek. "But they're so comfortable, Granny. I can't give them up yet."

"Hmph."

But Katie knew the old woman's words had struck a strange note within her, and she would remember this day for as long as she lived.

Chapter Five

Katie stood in the pouring rain, looking out over the busy Pittsburgh wharf. Holding the orange calico fabric over her head and shoulders, she waited while Spence bought their tickets and saw to the loading of the horses and wagon.

A spear of lightning suddenly pierced the sky and she jumped involuntarily even before the rumble of thunder shook the ground. Not only did she hate thunderstorms because of their violence, but this particular one was preventing her from taking some wonderful pictures of the teeming docks on the Ohio River.

All around her, men carried one kind of cargo or another to and from the paddle-wheel boats tied at their moorings. For the most part the men seemed unmindful of the pelting rain as wagons pulled up as handily as possible for loading or unloading.

At that moment another especially vicious bolt streaked downward and Katie squeezed her eyes shut, waiting for the inevitable crack and boom to follow.

"It's just a little thunderstorm with more bark than bite," Spence shouted at her over the roar of the rain that cascaded down upon them.

She opened her eyes to find him grinning at her from under the brim of his dripping hat. His mud-colored buckskin jacket appeared to shed the rain adequately, and she almost envied him as she stood there wet to the skin.

"Could we get out of this?" she shouted back, glancing toward the sky. Another crack rent the air, making her jump again.

"You should have brought a parasol," he yelled; then his gaze moved over her soggy appearance, silently disapproving of her choice of clothes.

The cloth over her head was saturated and no longer able to keep the water from dripping into her hair. "Could we please go?"

He nodded and turned toward the steam-driven paddle wheeler. They crossed the plank bridge with Katie only two steps behind Spence, trying to use his broad shoulders as a barrier from the driving rain. He pulled open the door, allowing her to enter first.

"Oh, thank goodness," she said, heaving a sigh of relief. She squeezed the water out of the dripping calico cloth as best she could, then shook her head to rid her tight curls of droplets.

Spence made his way to a bench that had only two empty spaces left. Katie followed and sat between Spence and an older woman. The woman gave Katie's unladylike attire a sidelong glance.

"Terrible weather, isn't it?" Katie asked, trying to keep her wet shirt from sticking to her chest.

"Yes, terrible," the woman replied coolly, keeping her eyes averted.

Katie could feel Spence staring at her with an "I-told-you-so" look. Irked at his attitude, she leaned toward the woman and in a voice just barely loud enough for Spence to hear, she said, "He made me wear this."

The woman looked up in surprise, then, horror stricken, her mouth formed an "O".

"I did not." Spence replied, his eyes questioning what she was up to now.

"You told me to buy them, didn't you?" She raised an eyebrow at him.

Now he looked irritated. "No. I told you to take them off."

The woman gasped.

Muttering an oath, Spence rose from his place on the bench and strode for the door.

"Sometimes," Katie remarked to the woman, "he can say the crudest things. I don't know why I married that man. I suppose it was because of my papa's untimely passing. . . . I was so alone."

"There, there, dear," the woman responded sympathetically.

At that moment Katie had an uncomfortable feeling that Granny was clicking her tongue and craning her neck to see into Katie's eyes. She hadn't really intended to make Spence look so bad, or to be so dishonest. But he'd had that same look that Tim had always given her, making her feel like a foolish little girl, and she had simply retaliated in defense. Now, with the spirit of Granny hovering over her, she felt guilty for making Spence pay for Tim's unkind attitude.

Spence retreated through the door into the driving rain, where he sought shelter from the wind along the wall. He couldn't even guess what had gotten into her; he supposed she just had an ornery streak a mile wide. But at the moment he didn't feel much like giving her any credit, even a small amount.

She was turning into a bigger millstone around his neck than he'd first imagined. Tim was wrong. She could probably take good care of herself. All she had to do was stretch the truth when it suited her.

Huddling against the wall, he thought about all that he'd left behind: privacy, simplicity and no irritating, confusing women. Just a big sky overhead, a quiet campfire and several hundred head of cattle to keep him company. It was all a man really needed.

After a while the cold drove him back inside, where he found a seat on the opposite side of the large cabin. He wedged himself between two men, one who was burly and smelled of pigs and another who kept sipping from a bottle inside his jacket. It was going to be a long ride to St. Louis, he told himself, settling back and closing his eyes. A long ride.

From her side of the room, Katie watched Spence. He seemed oblivious to his surroundings with his head against the wall, his arms crossed on his chest and his feet stretched out before him. She tried to study him as though he were a stranger and had to acknowledge that he was handsome in a rugged sort of way. She stared at the well-worn hat that was now tipped forward. A stranger wouldn't know about the stubborn lock of dark hair that he constantly pushed back whenever he lifted the brim. But she did. And a stranger wouldn't know about the thoughtful way he had of listening whenever she talked about her growing-up years as they stood together during the quiet time before heading off to their separate sleeping quarters.

She gave herself a mental shake. She was only thinking kind thoughts about him because she still felt guilty, she told herself. The fact of the matter was, he hadn't changed his mind about her journey being foolish. Not that he'd said anything more about it, but she could tell by the way he'd hung back each night they'd stopped, either leaning on a tree or relaxing against one of her wagon's wheels, that he was completely uninterested.

As if knowing she was thinking about him, he opened his eyes and caught her staring. Refusing to back down, she continued to stare until finally he pulled his hat down over his face. With a devilish smile, she leaned back and closed her eyes.

The unsteady rocking of the boat, combined with the noise of surrounding voices, kept her wide awake, while the intensity of the storm outside unsettled her. So her mind went back over the days that had passed since they'd left New York.

They had come across so many wonderful people and a few that were less than wonderful, although friendly in their own peculiar way. Some of them, like the Jacobs, had insisted that Katie sleep in their spare room. Others could only offer their barn, which Spence always preferred.

Without fail, they'd been invited to stay for breakfast. Most folks seemed to think their hospitality would be lacking if they allowed Katie and Spence to leave on empty stomachs. And only once or twice did Katie have to cook lunch for Spence and herself, since they had generally been given a loaf of bread, a slice or two of ham or beef, varying types of sweets and even fresh garden greens.

It wasn't until they'd reached Pittsburgh that her mood had turned sour, and the downpour hadn't helped. She was not at all happy about being aboard a boat with her camera and supplies stowed so far out of reach. At first she had insisted on staying with the wagon but soon gave in to his more insistent "no's." When she'd seen the hogs and other animals being loaded, she was glad not to be below deck.

She was sorry to miss the wonderful opportunity to photograph the countryside where farmers were planting their crops, women were hanging out their wash and children were playing beneath blossoming apple trees. Surely the rain wouldn't continue for much longer. But what good would that do her since she was bound for St. Louis on a boat?

Outside, the storm whipped and lashed at the paddle wheeler, its deck awash with rain and river water. Each lightning flash seemed frightfully close, and the thunder seemed to come from the belly of the boat, so great was the noise.

Katie hated storms. When she was a little girl she'd climb into bed and pull the covers over her head and not come out until it ended. Her mother had done everything she knew to help Katie overcome her fear, but nothing worked. Not the smell of baking cookies, or even a story about princesses could bring her from under the blankets.

And this was just the kind of storm that made her wish for a big feather bed with a pile of comforters to hide in.

Gritting her teeth and squeezing her eyes shut, she waited for the crack that soon followed the brilliant bolt of lightning that lit up the darkened sky. When it came she jumped.

Maybe being on a boat wasn't so bad after all, she thought. At least they were in out of the rain, which would have been very difficult to do in her wagon.

As they traveled down the river, the storm seemed to lessen until finally it abated altogether. The sun came out in celebration, and the majority of the people seemed to want to join it. Everyone unwound their cramped bodies and headed toward the deck, and Katie gladly joined them.

She inhaled deeply of the rain-fresh air, squinting her eyes against the sparkling reflection coming off the river as she tried to see the West Virginia shoreline. Having been within the boundaries of the city all her life, she was eager to see for herself the sights that other photographers had actually photographed. She had visited the galleries of her father's friends many times and been envious of their works and their travels. At last it was her turn.

The breeze ruffled her hair and air-dried the still-damp places on her shirt and britches. The sun felt wonderful on her face, which was something new to her. Suddenly she felt as though she'd lived like a mole, always indoors or else under a parasol. Tipping her face upward, she vowed never to use a parasol again.

"I saw a girl once with hair the color of yours who spent so much time in the sun that her face sprouted freckles like mushrooms," Spence said.

Without moving she replied, "I don't care."

They stood near the railing, enjoying the improved weather and fresh air. Suddenly Spence reached in his pocket and withdrew a key.

"Oh, before I forget, this is to your cabin," he said. "It's small but at least you can wash up."

She stared first at the key, then at him.

"You were having such a good time with the passengers in there," he said, nodding his head toward the crowded room they'd just left, "that I didn't want to spoil all your fun."

Ignoring his grin, she took the proffered key he had purposely witheld in an obvious attempt to get even with her for the insinuations she'd made against his character.

She supposed she should feel properly chastised for her actions, and she also supposed she should be grateful to have the cabin, but all she could say was, "I'll pay you back." And she didn't mean with money.

"No need. You can settle up with Tim."

"Believe me, I intend to."

As he turned to go, he said, "I'm going to check on the horses."

She watched him stride across the deck, weaving

through the crowd. This river detour was his way of trying to shorten her journey, but regardless of his intentions, she would enjoy every mile of it. After all, there was a limit to the number of detours he could place in her path, and there were still many, many miles to go.

Whenever they would dock in one of the small towns along the way, Spence would appear at her cabin door or find her on the deck, bearing lunch, such as it was.

"Compliments of Tim?" she asked the first time.

He simply nodded and ate his food.

By the time they reached Cincinnati, Katie understood the term "cabin fever" all too well. She paced the confines of her tiny room, then paced the cramped and crowded space of the deck, all the while thinking she wouldn't be able to stand it much longer. At night she bemoaned her lack of stubbornness and quietly wailed to the walls that she should never have let him talk her into this. She'd never been so bored in her life.

When they reached Louisville, she watched with longing as passengers walked down the crowded gangplank and into freedom. How much longer before they would reach St. Louis? she wondered. Maybe she should just put her foot down and tell him that they were getting off whether he liked it or not. This was her journey, after all; why shouldn't she make the decisions?

Just as she'd made up her mind to do just that, the crew hauled up the walkway. Her heart plummeted as she stood gripping the handrail. Too late. At least, too late for this town.

For the next hour she dawdled along the deck, ignoring the stares she received. Her clothing had caused more heads to turn than she cared to admit, but once they were on solid ground again following the back roads, she would feel comfortable and relaxed. When she saw Spence coming toward her, she was more than a little glad.

"Get your things ready," he said. "I've heard we're having engine trouble and we'll be stopping at the next town for unloading. We could wait, but it might take a long time to get rolling again."

She felt like shouting, but only replied, "Well, I can't say I'm at all sorry to get back on the road. I'll only be a minute." She hurried back to the cabin to collect her changes of clothing and toiletries. She was also anxious about her equipment and was relieved to know that Spence had paid to have it watched. He'd scolded her for going below deck, but she'd simply turned a deaf ear on him.

Now she gathered her dirty clothes into one of her shirts and tied the arms together. Washing clothes was certainly at the top of her list, but a boat was no place for that. Excited to be back about her business, she rushed down the steps in search of Spence.

In the distance she could see a town beginning to take shape on the Indiana side of the river. Figuring that Spence must be getting the horses hitched to the wagon, she went below deck. She intended to stay as close to her wagon as possible.

She spotted him as he finished with the harnessing, and quickly joined him.

"You shouldn't have come down here," he said.

"I don't know why not."

He glanced at her and frowned, then rounded the wagon to double check everything.

It was as obvious as the hat on his head that he wasn't pleased with her; in fact he had been in a bad mood ever since they decided to leave the boat. Well, if this slowed his progress she wasn't sorry. Actually, she was quite happy, she thought, smiling to herself. He would just have to take the good with the bad, just as she had.

Katie followed along behind the wagon as they took

their turn leaving the boat. She felt exhilarated. As her feet touched solid ground, she thought, this is Indiana soil, such a long way from home! She squinted up at the afternoon sun in a cloudless sky and smiled. Now she could contemplate covering the distance by land to St. Louis with pleasure.

A feeling of being watched forced her to glance around until her eye caught the still figure of a woman on the walkway leading to the other end of the boat. People milled around the woman and occasionally bumped into her as she stood motionless, staring in Katie's direction. But the woman wasn't actually watching Katie; she wasn't even looking at the wagon. Could she be staring at Spence? Katie tried to follow the woman's gaze more directly, but the distance made it impossible.

Katie stood stock-still, glancing ahead to where Spence brought the horses and wagon to a halt. Surely, she thought, Spence couldn't know a woman this far from Montana, and if he did, why wouldn't the woman make herself known? With a shrug of her shoulders, she tried to dismiss the whole matter, but the episode was so peculiar it wouldn't leave her completely. With one last look over her shoulder, she watched as the elegant woman disappeared into the pressing crowd.

Chapter Six

Spence climbed onto the wagon seat and waited for Katie to do the same, although he was feeling far from patient. He was anxious to reach St. Louis, where he had planned to meet up with Crandall. Spence and Tim needed Crandall's backing to assure a successful start to the Circle M T Ranch. Crandall was in the business for just that purpose, but if their paths didn't cross this time, Spence wasn't sure how long their new enterprise could last. He just hoped Crandall hadn't been there and gone by the time he got to St. Louis.

Katie smiled sweetly and plopped onto the seat beside him. "I'm ready. But don't hurry on my account."

Without a word he slapped the reins, jolting the wagon into motion. Soon they rolled smoothly along the dirt road, away from the busy small town and into the quiet countryside.

All around them spring flowers grew in abundance. Tall maple trees cast their fragmented shade across the backs of the horses while the young leaves rustled gently above them in the breeze. The first sign of a farm up ahead was a fenced pasture. And while Spence knew that any true rancher held nothing but disdain for a herd of milk cows, no matter how small, he couldn't help the longing at the sight of them.

A bell clanged on the neck of one cow, and the others responded by joining that first one at the fence in a sort of welcome to the travelers.

"Oh, look! Haven't they got the most curious expressions?" Katie said, laughing at the way their heads all turned in unison. "What do you suppose they're thinking?"

"Cows don't think."

She smiled with mischief in her eyes. "What makes you so sure?"

"They'd have to have a brain to think."

"All animals have a brain," she informed him.

"Not cows."

"I thought all cowhands liked cows."

"They do. I suppose."

"Then how can you say cows don't have a brain?"

He glanced at her, thinking that this was the most ridiculous conversation he'd ever had with a woman.

"I'd like to know how you can say they do," he replied, feeling even more ridiculous for encouraging the conversation.

"Just look at those eyes! Big soft brown eyes," she said, turning to gaze at the lineup staring back at them.

"Don't let them fool you. They could run you over if they took it in their heads."

"Ah ha!" she said, quickly turning on him. "You admit it."

"That's not called thinking, it's called instinct."

"When people act instinctively, we don't discount the fact that they've been thinking."

She was splitting hairs, and undoubtedly looking for

an argument. But he sensed that arguing with her could be dangerous.

"You win," he said. "Cows can think."

The sound of her lighthearted laughter filled the air, making him smile. The more time he spent with her, the more surprises she gave him. Not only was she a determined, spunky woman who told the whole truth only when it suited her, but she could also be a carefree mischief maker, and that, he suspected, was where the danger lay.

They followed a curve in the road to a small frame house with several small outbuildings dotting the barnyard. Sheets and shirts flapped in the breeze behind the house. Not too far away stood a barn with a good-sized holding pen attached. Probably a place to keep the cows before milking time, Spence thought.

Nobody seemed to be about the place when they pulled into the yard, although a side door to the house stood wide open. A glance at the barn showed the same: open but empty.

Katie hopped down from the wagon. "I'll go to the house."

He watched her cross the short distance and step onto the porch. Sunlight haloed the riot of burnished curls that bounced as she walked, adding an energy of their own to her personality. In contrast, her tall, slim body spoke of a grace that even britches couldn't hide. He quickly turned away and jumped down from the wagon, making his way toward the barn. From behind him he could hear her calling, "Hello? Anyone home?"

"Hey there! Over here!" answered a voice.

Spence looked up to find a white-haired man wearing bright red suspenders hurrying toward them from a lane at the back of the place. The man waved a hearty greeting and soon joined Katie at the pump near the porch.

"Howdy, folks," the man said, smiling cheerily. He

extended his hand to Spence as he ambled toward him. "Don't believe I know you."

"I'm Katie O'Rourke and this is my brother, Spence. I'm a photographer," she added before Spence could speak up.

The man nodded. "Nice to meet you. Name's Silas Tanner. Mama's down the road a piece but she should be back any minute." He gave her wagon a quizzical glance, then asked, "What can I do for you folks?"

Her explanation had become a regular speech, but she punctuated it with fresh smiles that were genuine. When she'd finished, Silas removed his straw hat and scratched his head. It was plain to see that he wasn't exactly taken with the idea.

"Well, now, you're welcome to spend the night in the barn and we'd be pleased to share a meal with you . . . but picture takin' . . . I don't know."

"You wouldn't have to get fancied-up. As a matter of fact I'd prefer that you didn't." She looked toward the barn. "I'll bet you've got a prize cow you wouldn't mind showing off."

He smiled broadly and chuckled. "I do at that."

"You don't think she'd mind having her picture taken, do you?" Katie grinned, knowing she'd offered him something he couldn't refuse.

The old man laughed again, looking embarrassed. "You want to take a picture of Bossie?"

"Only if you'll stand beside her," Katie replied.

He shrugged, still smiling. "I guess she wouldn't mind. I'll call her."

As he called her name over the fence, the sound of the bell could be heard in the distance coming closer. "She's probably kinda confused about being called in so early. We don't do the milking until after supper."

At that moment a buggy pulled into the yard and "Mama" brought the horse to a halt near her husband.

Spence and Katie watched as he helped her down. They could barely hear as Silas explained the situation.

She lightly slapped Silas's arm and said, "Go on with you!"

Silas nodded his head and ushered her toward Katie and Spence before turning his attention to Bossie, who stood ready at the gate.

"Hello, Mrs. Tanner," Katie said.

"Call me Violet, please." Then she laughed, making her eyes resemble little crescents. "You want a picture of my Silas with Bossie?"

"She likes animals," Spence offered. "Especially cows."

"Oh, well, you'll fit right in around here," Violet said.

Katie wrinkled her nose at Spence in a sisterly fashion before turning away toward the wagon. She set to work immediately, going through the process of setting up her camera and preparing the plate. It had become a routine almost as much as it had been in the studio, except here there was the added element of risk. Would the cow twitch her ear and blur an otherwise perfect picture? Would a cat cross her path and ruin it? Or would she succeed in catching the embarrassed but proud look of the farmer with his prize cow, Bossie? She couldn't explain why she got such a thrill out of standing in the bright sunshine with the smell of cow stalls surrounding her, other than to say: This is life! And she felt more a part of it here than she ever had in the studio.

Pleased with the exposure, she hurried the plate back to her wagon. From the corner of her eye she saw Spence leaning against the side of one of the small outbuildings, his stance clearly suggesting that his thoughts were elsewhere.

She put the plate through the baths without a motion wasted and in no time had the prints sitting in the sun, "taking." While she waited she could see Violet talking animatedly with Spence, and he was smiling and nodding in response.

When the print was ready she gave it to Silas, who beamed at the fine job she'd done. Bossie looked great, and he didn't look so bad himself.

Then it was Violet's turn, but she flatly refused until Silas suggested her prize-winning butter. She flapped her apron but looked pleased and finally complied. That picture, too, was a winner.

Quickly, Katie tidied her wagon, then pulled out her laundry and went in search of a tub. In no time Violet had her set up in the backyard beneath a tall, large-leafed maple, her sleeves rolled high, and soapy water to her elbows.

Spence lounged in the grass nearby watching her.

"That sure is a fine-looking cow that Silas has, wouldn't you say?" Katie cast a glance in his direction.

He plucked a blade of grass and chewed on it. "If you like milk cows, I suppose. We don't really have many of them beyond St. Louis."

She wrung out the last of her shirts, leaving her camisoles at the bottom of the tub.

"Tell me what it's like in St. Louis," she said as she dipped a shirt into a tub of clear, cold rinse water.

"It's a big city, but nothing like New York. It has a different feel to it." He watched as she alternately dunked and raised the shirts, causing goosebumps to stand up that were big enough for him to see.

"Hmm," she replied almost dreamily. "I can imagine. Sort of like an air of expectancy and excitement."

"Something like that." He raised up on one elbow to see if she had nerve enough to pull out those camisoles he'd seen her dash into the washtub or if she was just going to leave them there.

"I suppose I could do a little laundry myself," he said, starting to rise. "Since you're just about finished."

Startled, she turned round eyes on him. "Uh, well, I'm not quite done."

"That's all right. I'll just wait here until you are," he replied, settling back down. "Silas told me he wouldn't need any help until after supper."

"Oh." She paused in her dunking motions. "This could take longer than you think. Maybe you could help Violet carry water or something."

"I already did."

"Oh." Then suddenly tossing the clean shirts back into the washtub, she said, "These shirts are really dirty. I'll have to wash them again. I guess I shouldn't have waited so long to catch up on all this laundry." She vigorously scrubbed each shirt until he thought she'd wear a hole in them. Her face was a mask of concentration and her red-gold curls bobbed in rhythm with her industrious movements.

"I doubt if I'll put that much energy into my washing," he commented. "If you're not careful you'll have yourself so wore out you won't be able to help with the milking."

She stopped in mid stroke, lifted her head and stared at him. "Help with the milking? I can't do that."

"Sure you can. Anybody who likes and understands cows is bound to be better at it than a cowhand who just tolerates them."

"But I just take the pictures. You're supposed to do the chores." She wiped her arms against her trousers, leaving streaks of soapy water marks as high as her armpits.

"I believe Silas is counting on you, since you took such a liking to Bossie." His voice suggested that maybe that wasn't really true.

"I *do* like Bossie. She's the kindest, gentlest creature I've ever seen. But I can't milk her! I don't even know how." By now she'd come around the tubs to stand over him.

"You won't have any trouble learning. Especially if she likes you." Spence couldn't say why he was taking such enjoyment in tormenting her, but he figured a taste of her own medicine would do her more good than harm.

"No," she said, shaking her head. "I can't. You'll have to do it."

"Tell that to Silas." Now that she was distracted, he got to his feet. "I guess if you're finished I'll just get started on my wash." He walked to a tree where he retrieved a small bundle, then headed for the tubs.

"No, wait!" she cried. "I'm not finished."

"Here, I'll help you, then," he said as he stuck one arm into the tub to fish out her shirt. But she practically dived in as she lunged past him, wadded her wet clothing into a dripping lump, then dropped it into the rinse water, barely dousing them.

"There. That should do it," she said, trying to squeeze the excess water from the large, soggy ball. "You can go ahead now. I'll just hang these on the line."

When she'd gone he searched the bottom of the tub for any missed garments. There were none. He smiled to himself as he dumped his dirty clothes into the water. It was just as well, since he didn't know what he'd do if he found her camisole anyway. It wasn't in him to embarrass her further. He'd only wanted to have a little fun at her expense.

Later, when they sat down to Violet's delicious supper, everyone participated in the conversation. Stories, laughter and experiences were shared, making the meal very enjoyable.

"If you don't mind my saying so," Silas began, "I haven't seen a woman wear such sensible clothes since my mother was young, God rest her soul. That was when we had Indians here and about and most women

81

worked like the men." He shrugged. "So she figured she'd be safer as well as more comfortable."

Katie sent Spence a look of smug satisfaction.

"Spence tells me you're partial to milk cows," Silas said to Katie, changing the subject as easily as he poured cream over his apple pie.

Katie swallowed her own bite of pie before replying just as smoothly, "But not as much as he is."

Spence choked and went into a mild spasm of coughing.

"Milking is his favorite chore at home. I've never even had the chance to get close. Isn't that right?" She raised wide blue eyes at Spence and took another bite of apple pie.

Before he could respond, Silas, who had been clapping him on the back, said, "Well, I sure could use some help tonight. The fellow who usually stops over took sick. I'm not as young as I used to be, and those four cows take a while to get milked and bedded down."

When the meal was over, Spence followed Silas out to the barn, carrying two milk pails. Katie didn't even try to hide her merriment.

Violet insisted on clearing up the dishes alone so Katie could iron her clothes while the stove was still hot. They chatted pleasantly, each enjoying the company of another woman. Katie told her about her dream to photograph "life" on her trip west to see her older brother.

"Oh, what an adventure you have before you!" exclaimed Violet as she dried the last dish and put it with the others in the tall wooden cabinet. "I imagine it's much safer than it used to be, not so many Indians and the like, but you'll still have to be very watchful. Not everyone is as honest as you are, my dear. Always keep that in mind."

Violet carried her washpan to the back door and tossed the dirty water into the yard. Katie heard the metal basin ring as it was hung on a nail alongside other basins of varying sizes. Then Violet returned, wiping her hands on her apron with a cheery smile on her face.

"There. That's done," Violet said. "How are you coming along? I can add more wood to the stove if you need it."

"No, thanks. I only have this one last shirt of Spence's to finish."

When Violet had assumed that Katie would want to iron her brother's clothes, Katie hadn't disagreed although it had been on the tip of her tongue to do so. The experience turned out to be almost too personal as she brushed the cotton material with her hand to smooth out the largest wrinkles. The breadth of the shoulders brought to mind the day they had boarded the boat in the rain and she had walked behind him, using his wide shoulders as a shield. And even though the clothes were clean, there still remained a scent that was peculiarly his.

At last she folded the shirt and neatly stacked it with the others, right alongside the pile of hers.

"I'll just take these out to the wagon," she said, heading for the door.

"Why don't you stop in at the barn when you've finished," Violet suggested, her ever-present smile reaching her eyes. "Silas always enjoys having his cows admired, as you already know."

After depositing Spence's shirts and trousers on the wagon seat and placing her own in a valise, Katie went to the barn to peek in just as Silas was carrying out two full buckets. Stepping inside the warm interior, she saw Spence sitting on a small stool hunched over and squirting milk rhythmically into a pail.

"Enjoying yourself?" she asked, grinning.

Without looking up, he replied, "If you say one word of this to Tim, I swear I'll tan your britches so you won't be able to sit for a month of Sundays."

Silas reentered the barn and bent to pick up another pail. Then he said to Spence, "Why don't you let your sister try it? She seems like the plucky kind." He winked at Katie.

Spence slowly unwound himself from his position near the ground, a broad grin spreading across his face. "She's plucky all right."

"Oh, I don't know," she said, backing away. "Spence has always done it. I don't think—"

"Now, there's nothing to be afraid of," Silas soothed. "Your brother should have taught you before this. Bossie's a good one for a beginner. You just have to know a few tricks. Spence seems to know how to handle her, so just do what he says." Then he turned and left, pleased with himself for sharing his pride and joy.

"Nothing to it," Spence said, putting his hands on her shoulders and gently pushing her down onto the stool. "Just grab hold and squeeze."

Katie would never have guessed that milking a cow could be such an embarrassing experience, but it was. She wrapped her fingers around one sticky, wet teat and squeezed.

If only Spence would turn away or, better yet, go away, she thought. But he didn't. So she kept her head down, hoping the redness of her cheeks was coming from Bossie's warm hide instead of her own.

She squeezed but nothing happened.

"You have to use two hands," he said, leaning against the post at the end of the stall. "She expects it."

Katie set her jaw and wrapped her other hand around another warm teat. She squeezed both at the same time. Nothing.

"One at a time," Spence instructed. "Do it in rhythm."

Still nothing.

"Here, let me help," he said, suddenly feeling sympathy for her. Kneeling down alongside her stool, he wrapped one of his hands around hers. "You pull down, close it off at the top and gently squeeze the milk out. It's easier when you alternate. That's why you use two hands."

With his help, a squirt of milk pinged a steady stream against the inside of the pail.

"Now do the other one yourself," he said as he kept his hand on hers.

Katie was losing her concentration and she mentally shook herself. It's only Spence, she said silently. And this is only a dumb cow, she added. But the warmth of Bossie's hide against Katie's forehead was nothing compared to the warmth along Katie's arm where Spence pressed close to her.

In spite of the distraction, she was able to make the pail ring with an almost steady stream of milk. The accomplishment made her smile.

Then, in rhythm, Spence squeezed his hand around hers and another stream rang out. Katie caught the rhythm and squeezed again.

"I've got it now, I think," she said. And Spence dropped his hand away, letting her take over, but he stayed close by.

The muted barn sounds made a backdrop for the now steady splashing of milk. The aroma of fresh hay and clean bedding mingled with the more familiar scent of Spence McCord as he leaned near her to survey the amount of milk in the pail.

"Not too bad," he complimented. "For a city girl."

She looked up, and when he smiled her concentration was quickly broken. So was her rhythm.

"Uh, oh," she said. "I think I lost it."

At that moment the barn door opened and Silas came in to stand in the lantern light.

"How's she doing?" he asked.

"Me or Bossie?" Katie returned.

Silas chuckled. "Both, I guess."

"Bossie is very patient," Katie replied. "But I don't seem to have the knack for milking."

Spence rose from his position, and Katie instantly missed his warmth.

Still chuckling, Silas said, "Here, I'll finish up for you. Both of you go on, get yourselves ready for the night. I'm sure you have a long day ahead of you tomorrow. Mama has a room for you, young miss. And Spence can bed down in the loft."

Outside, the night air was cool and damp, so opposite from the environment they'd just left. Instead of heading toward the wagon or the house, Katie and Spence stood in the shadow of the barn.

"Silas is right," Spence said.

She turned to look up at him. "About what?"

"You are the plucky kind." He grinned.

She shrugged and caught her hands on the back waistband of her trousers. "I don't think you gave me much choice in there."

He fell silent for a moment. "I didn't mean to embarrass you."

"But you just couldn't help yourself," she added for him.

Spence heard the smile in her voice even if the darkness of the night hid it from him.

"Something like that," he replied, smiling back at her. "Guess we're even, huh?"

"For the time being," she returned. Then she hurried off toward the house where a lamp burned low in the kitchen window.

Chapter Seven

They traveled without anything unusual befalling them for the next few days. The people they met were friendly and willing to share what they had in exchange for pictures. Spence ate well at the farmhouses, and not so well when it was left to Katie to provide their fare.

One day a heavily clouded sky hid the late afternoon sun, leaving a chill in the air. Katie rubbed her arms for warmth.

"We should reach St. Louis around mid week," Spence said as they plowed along the soggy road. He'd had to get out several times and pry the wheels free from the boggy mess while Katie coaxed the horses to pull harder. Now he was trying to stay to the higher ground as much as possible, but it wasn't easy.

A misty rain fell as a precursor of what was soon to follow.

"I don't suppose there's much chance of us missing that thunderstorm, is there?" Katie asked, her eye on the distant darkening sky. A light breeze caused the mist to wet her face.

"Not likely," Spence answered.

"Maybe we should stay at the first place we come to," Katie suggested. "I can't set up my camera in this weather, but we could pay them."

Spence nodded.

The trees overhead drooped their heavy wet leaves until they nearly scraped the top of the wagon and sometimes flung a spray of large drops on Katie's lap. Ahead, the narrow road lay in muddy ruts that appeared impossible to straddle or even dodge.

Pulling the wagon to a halt, Spence leaned forward, his elbows on his knees. He surveyed the situation and concluded that they could not turn around in the small area because of the bordering tall maples. They had no choice but to go on.

"What do you think?" Katie asked. It looked impassable to her, but the alternative of camping there on the road until someone came along to help them through was not even a choice. She had no desire to be out in the open during a thunderstorm no matter how mild it might be.

A roll of thunder echoed in the distance.

Spence saw her shudder. Her fear might create just the excitement the horses needed to pull them through the morass ahead.

"Take the reins, Katie, and walk them into it. And try to stay as close to the edge as you can. Talk steady and keep them moving."

She took the reins and listened carefully to his every word. He jumped down, and she moved over to better situate herself. When he walked toward the back of the wagon, she leaned over, craning her neck to see what he intended to do. "Where are you going?" she called.

"I'm going to follow and push. Just do like I told you, and keep those horses moving." His voice was quiet with patience and apprehension.

Katie squared her shoulders and grasped the reins

tightly in both hands. She flattened her lips together in concentration, took a deep breath and flapped the reins. She'd never driven a wagon before, but she didn't think now was the time to bring that up.

"Giddyup," she told them.

Lazily the horses moved forward.

"Let's go now," she said encouragingly. "We don't want to get caught in the middle of a downpour, now do we? A little faster, if you please." She flapped the reins again and was rewarded with an increased gait.

"That's good," Spence called to her. "Keep moving and don't stop."

A long roll of thunder, a bolt of lightning and another sharp clap had Katie scooting to the edge of her seat. The horses plodded into the mudhole and she guided them as best she could to the outside edge. But her lack of experience and her jittery nerves sent the wrong signals to the animals. Before she knew it, they were deeply mired in the clay.

"Oh! Oh, no!" She slapped the reins, her feet firmly entrenched against the wagon's footboard.

Spence immediately put his shoulder to the wheel when he saw they were heading for the center of the road. He braced his hands on the spokes and leaned his weight into them.

"Keep moving!" he ground out.

"I am!" she shouted back. "Can't you do something?"

Spence strained against the wheel.

Katie slapped the reins harder and called to the horses loudly. "C'mon, you fleabags! Go!" They responded with first one lurch and then another. They jerked ahead, and she heard an accompanying splash followed by an oath.

She cracked the reins once more and the horses continued to move ahead. If she could have spared a second, she would have looked around the side of the wagon to see what had happened. But her eyes were riveted on the drier land ahead and she focused intently on her destination.

"Hee-ah!" she called to them. "Don't stop now! Move! Let's keep moving!" Her words were like a chant, and she said them over and over until at last the horses stood on firmer ground. Wilted, she sank back on her seat, the thunder and falling rain all but forgotten.

Looking around the side, she said, "Spence? Are you—"

He came up alongside her, his entire body covered with mud, his hat held safely in his hand. Only his eyes showed white, and one spot on his cheek had somehow escaped becoming gritty.

Now that they'd made it through, she felt light with relief and immediately saw humor in the moment.

"Did you slip?" she asked with a half smile on her face.

"Move over," he said with deadly calm.

"Gladly." She slid away from him and the spraying globs of mud that he scattered with his every move.

But soon the storm's sudden intensity drew all her attention and she barely noticed the mud.

What had been an intermittent rain turned into a downpour as they traveled through the wooded area. The hollow thump of rain pelting the canvas roof of the wagon echoed loudly in their ears. The little shelter they received from the small overhang above them was lost in the steady runoff that fell onto Katie's lap. If there had been a dry spot on her before, there was none now.

She shivered lightly and tried to lean farther back against the wagon. Spence sat forward, his hat streaming rivulets down his muddy back.

They plodded through mudholes and rain for another hour before coming to a small, unkempt farm. Every building on the place appeared in dire need of repair, not to mention fences that needed mending and a woodshed that leaned precariously to one side.

When they pulled in the yard, both Spence and Katie jumped from the wagon and ran for the leaky front porch. The door opened to reveal a tall broad-shouldered man in overalls. He stared suspiciously at the two bedraggled people on his porch.

"We're sorry to bother you," Spence said, pulling his hat from his mud-caked hair. "But, well, we got mired in the clay down the road." He indicated their dirty clothes. "And we're not sure how far it is to the next town."

The man continued staring before he finally answered, "It's about ten miles to town."

Katie pushed her way in front of Spence. "Could we spend the night in your barn? We'd be glad to pay you. Actually, I'm a photographer and usually I take pictures in exchange for a place to stay, but"—she turned toward the rapidly darkening sky—"as you can see, the weather isn't cooperating very well. But we'd be very glad to pay." She was willing to pay twice the cost of a picture if only they didn't have to go out into the storm at night.

"I don't know," the man replied slowly. He looked past them to the wagon, a skeptical frown on his face. "A woman photographer?" Then he glance at Spence. "You the husband?"

"Yes," Katie interjected. "I'm Katie O'Rourke and this is my husband, Spence."

"I don't know," the man repeated.

"John," called a woman's voice. "Who's there?"

"A couple of folks who want to sleep in the barn," he said over his shoulder. "You think I should let 'em?"

She ambled over to stand beside John, her shoulders nearly as broad as his. "I don't know," she said, giving Katie and Spence a thorough look-over. "It is a pretty nasty night out."

The leaks in the porch roof allowed steady drips of water to fall around them. Katie tried dodging one that plunked on her head.

"Mired in the clay, huh," the woman went on as she stared at Spence.

"They say they'll pay," John put in.

"Well, then I guess it's all right. You show 'em where they can put the horses. Feed will be extra."

"Thanks. We appreciate it," Spence replied.

John grabbed a coat and led them to the barn. Through the darkness he pointed out two clean stalls, one for the horses and one for them. Then he left them alone.

"Looks like you'll be dry in here," Katie said as she listened for tell-tale drips from a leaking roof.

"Maybe," Spence replied. "If the haymow has enough hay in it to soak up the rain."

"What I want is a bath and some dry clothes," Katie said. "Do you suppose we have to pay extra for a clean bucket of water?"

"I'll get some for you as soon as I unhitch the horses and get them bedded down."

Katie would have gone after the water herself but the storm hadn't shown any signs of letting up and she couldn't bring herself to leave the shelter of the dilapidated barn longer than was necessary to fetch her nightgown.

By the time the horses were dry and fed, Katie was shivering. Usually she washed up in the privacy of her wagon, but tonight she was hoping to use the privacy of a dark, clean stall.

"Here's the water," Spence said as he stood in the barn door. "Sorry it isn't heated."

"It wouldn't matter if there were ice in it," she replied. "I'm so cold I'll never notice." She took the bucket from him and paused.

"Would you like to use the barn?" he asked.

"If you wouldn't mind. I won't take very long." Her teeth were chattering loudly now.

"Sure." He turned to go, closing the clumsy, rusty door behind him.

She carried the bucket to a rickety bench and set it down, then quickly stripped the wet clothing from her body. Her shoes had to be peeled from her feet, and she dreaded putting them back on to get to the wagon. The icy water built a second layer of goosebumps over her entire body, and she shivered uncontrollably as she ladled the water over herself with her hands. After that she quickly dried with a towel that smelled like sunshine, rubbing the rough material over her skin until she was nearly chafed, hoping to bring warmth to her body again. What she wouldn't give for a nice warm fire! Then she donned her gown, wrapping her arms around herself.

"You can come in now," she called. When there was no response, she carefully made her way, barefoot, to the barn door. She shoved it open a crack. "Spence?"

She heard his footsteps sloshing through the mud, and then he was pushing the door open far enough to slip inside.

"I just need to put my shoes on," she began, "then it's your turn."

He shook his head and drops scattered. "I cleaned up at the well," he said.

She handed him her towel. "Here. Take this and dry yourself."

He accepted it, saying, "Thanks." Then he vigorously dried his hair and bare upper body.

Nearby the soft rustle of clean straw and a low throaty "mmmoo" told them that one of the stalls held at least one cow.

"Looks like you've got company," Katie said, rubbing her still chilled arms. "Should make you feel right at home," she added with a grin.

"Nothing but bare sky overhead will make me feel right at home."

"Do you really like all that solitude?" she asked, peering through the darkness but barely able to make out his strong features.

He shrugged. "I guess I don't think of it that way. Most of the time I don't feel alone at all."

"Why not? You don't have anyone to talk to, do you?"

"Not as a rule."

"What do you do that keeps you alone so much?"

"Mending fence, looking for lost cattle or riding herd on a drive."

"Sounds like a lot of freedom."

"Yeah, I guess that's one of the things I like the most."

She heard the yearning in his voice and understood his desire for freedom, although it still sounded more like being alone than anything else. "What's Montana like?" she asked. "Lots of mountains?"

"It's too big to explain. I've been lots of places but there's no place to compare it to."

"It wouldn't matter anyway," she replied with a shrug. "Comparing it to places I've never been would be like trying to describe a sunset to a blind person."

For the first time Spence understood her need to leave the city life and travel. Freedom was important to him, and maybe it was to her, too.

"I suppose that's true," he said, but he had a strong desire to try to explain it to her anyway, to help her fill that gap in her life.

He took her by the arm and led her to the open door and pushed it wider. The sky had begun to clear, and the last of the raindrops could be heard plinking into nearby puddles. A few stars to the west bravely peeked through the waning clouds, and the crescent of a moon promised an end to the rain.

"If you look up there and block out of your mind the things around us, you get a feel of what it's like. Pretend those dark mounds are distant mountains," he said, pointing to the dark treetops. "And all around us is grazing land as far as you can see."

From inside the barn came the murmur of cattle sounds.

Katie laughed softly. "I think she's been there and you're making her homesick."

Spence grinned. "I'm making myself homesick." He turned to look at her as she stared up at the sky. A faint glow of lamplight from the farmhouse showed him that she was still smiling. Her wet curls were plastered to the edges of her face like a fancy picture frame showing off a beautiful portrait.

"When I was a girl," she said, "after Tim had left home, I used to slip away from my mother after dark and sit in the backyard. I would stare at the moon and stars, thinking that wherever Tim was he would be looking at the same moon and stars." She glanced at Spence. "It was a form of envy. I knew he was somewhere else, but I was still at home."

"Well, you're not at home now."

"No," she replied quietly. "I'm not."

He still had his hand on her arm, and the warmth of it went straight to her bone. Without realizing it, she'd stepped closer to him in an attempt to retain her balance while she looked up, but now she didn't need the steadying solidity of him so near. Even so, she didn't move, and neither did he.

Spence wasn't prepared for the feelings that ran through him at having her so close. If he'd been asked, he would have said it must have been the Montana sky overhead, although he knew quite well that they stood on Illinois soil. Whatever it was, he found himself giving in to the temptation of her parted lips as he leaned down and softly brushed them with his own. Sweeter than warmed honey and strawberries, he thought, but twice as satisfying.

A shiver went through her, and he released her arm. "You're cold," he said. "I've kept you out here too long."

"Well, maybe I am a little cold," she replied, her voice hushed.

"I left the wagon close to the barn," he said, knowing how she feared thunderstorms. "But I guess you've already found it." He lightly fingered the sleeve of her gown. The touch seemed more intimate, more forbidden, than the little kiss they'd just shared.

"Yes."

"I don't want to keep you any longer." But that wasn't exactly true.

She nodded, but said nothing as she leaned against him once more.

Spence forgot about the promises he'd made himself to keep her at a good and proper distance. He forgot about the anger Tim would likely vent on him if he found out. Between them the soft, thin cotton of her gown was hardly a barrier at all. He pulled her tight against him and simply forgot everything except kissing her deeply and thoroughly.

Katie allowed her head to tilt back as her body fit snugly against his, warming her in all the right places as well as the wrong ones. His hand slipped to the base of her neck and he slanted his mouth over hers, parting her lips with his own. Suddenly weak in the knees, she caught and held what little breath she had left in her lungs. By sheer strength alone she managed not to embarrass herself by moaning, but was unable to hold back a throaty sigh.

When at last he raised his lips from hers, he said, "I think you'd better go."

With his hands still on her shoulders, she stepped back and nodded. He couldn't see her face in the darkness so he couldn't tell what she might be thinking. She made no reply as she hurried through the doorway to her wagon. He heard the wet canvas slap as she flung it open, then soggily scrape it into place once more. For several moments he just stood there, wondering what the devil he was going to do now. They had already spent countless days and evenings together, and twice as many lay ahead of them. Once they crossed the river and headed for the prairies, they'd be alone more than ever, and he needed to get a handle on this situation before then. Truthfully, he didn't know what to make of it in the first place. Then a clear picture of Tim's face came into his mind and that ambushed feeling hit him once again, only this time he felt less resistant toward it.

Just be careful, he told himself, and keep a good and proper distance from now on.

He retrieved his bedroll from inside a canvas lashed to the side of the wagon where he stored his dry clothes as well as his sleeping blanket. Just as he was about to walk away, he heard her call to him from the back step of the wagon.

"I thought maybe you'd be hungry," she said. "This isn't much but it's better than nothing." She stood silhouetted by the dim candlelight behind her. "And here's an extra blanket."

He took the chunk of bread. "Thanks. For the blanket, too."

"Well, good night," she said, and ducked back inside.

He stood staring at the sleek wet canvas, thinking about the cozy warmth within.

"A good and proper distance," he reminded himself half out loud, then headed for the barn.

Chapter Eight

By late evening two days later, Spence and Katie stood at opposite ends of the wagon while they floated across the river by ferry to St. Louis. The uncomfortable silence that had fallen between them was practically tangible enough to be seen. Neither of them had been able to think of a single topic of conversation other than the kiss of a few nights ago, and neither was in any frame of mind to discuss it.

Katie kept a safe distance from Spence by standing at the rear of the wagon, staring across the wide water, marveling at not only its size but its speed. She'd never seen anything like it, nor had she felt such exhilaration. It was enough to take her mind off her present problem. She watched, fascinated, as they neared the shoreline of the state of Missouri, wondering how it could be that they weren't mercilessly swept downstream or even drawn under by the fast-moving current. Muddy waves lapped over the edges of the flatbed ferry, making puddles that rolled with each movement. Katie followed one such puddle which eventually pooled around Spence's boots, then her gaze moved upward and caught him staring at her. Quickly she turned her head away, but not before she saw the questioning look in his eyes.

Spence continued watching her until she must have sensed it, then she walked behind the wagon where he could no longer see her and turned his concentration back toward holding the horses, who were more docile than he could have hoped. When they finally set foot on solid ground once more, he let out a sigh of relief. There was just something about crossing this river that made a man relax, as though he sensed freedom beyond the city. And for him it was true; he'd come this way before.

Climbing onto the wagon, Katie quickly settled herself as Spence called to the horses. Without the distraction of the river, she was once more left to ponder her new situation. She hadn't anticipated feeling anything other than tolerance for her unwilling escort, and she'd expected the same in return. But tolerance was hardly the word for the feeling she was experiencing. Confusion was more appropriate. That kiss had muddled her mind. Normally she was strong willed and proud of it, focused on her goals to the point of being unable to see anything else. But that kiss had her thinking about warm embraces and tender touches, not to mention butterflies where they didn't belong.

Keeping her face averted, she resisted the urge to look at him, reminding herself that he wasn't the only man she'd ever kissed. Of course, she hadn't liked any of the others any more than she did Spence, but nevertheless, they still counted. A kiss was, after all, just a kiss.

Well, maybe.

A tentative glance toward him told her that he was all business with his attention riveted on the road before him and the big city just ahead. She would hardly call herself unattractive, and yet there he sat acting as though she had a case of the measles. Suddenly she felt like "Tim's little sister" once again, only this time the letters were all capitals.

As darkness approached, they wound their way through the streets of St. Louis, passing a lovely residential district and moving into the business section.

"You'll be staying here," Spence said as they approached a small hotel nestled between a general store and a millinery.

"Just let me off and I'll get a room," she said, wondering why he hadn't included himself in his reference to the hotel.

"Nothing doing," he declared, looking her directly in the eyes for the first time. "You're not walking around this town alone dressed like that."

"I hardly think anyone will even notice me."

"Someone will." He wasn't taking any chances of her coming up missing while he was tending to the horses. So he pulled the wagon into the nearest livery and jumped down, giving her a quick glance that said "stay put." He spoke to the man in charge, paid him a fee, then told him he'd be at Bailey's place.

When Spence returned to the wagon, Katie whispered, "What about my equipment? Do you think it's safe here?"

"I paid him extra to watch it." He helped her down, but she was reluctant to leave.

"I don't know. . . ." she began.

"There's no other choice," he said, waiting for her to give in and half expecting her to insist on staying in the livery all night. "I'll walk you back to the hotel."

Relenting at last, she retrieved her valises from the wagon, then headed for the boardwalk beside him. Without a word he took the bags from her and carried them. After passing several stores, all of which were closed, she finally got up enough nerve to ask where he'd be spending the night.

"Who is Bailey?" she asked, trying not to be too direct. "Is he a friend of yours?"

Spence gave her quick sidelong glance, then replied, "An old friend."

"I see," she said when he didn't offer more. "I suppose you haven't seen him since you came through here on your way to New York."

He nodded.

"What if I need to find you?" she prodded further. "You know, if something, just by chance, happens to my wagon."

"Nothing is going to happen. I want you to just stay put until I come back for you."

They stood facing each other before the lighted front doors to the hotel.

"Understand?" The tone in his voice said he meant business. It was the first time he'd used that tone, and she instantly balked.

Haughtily she raised her chin and said, "I'll be in my room." Then silently she added, *until I feel like going out.*

"Good."

Inside, Spence paid for the room, escorted her to her door and unlocked it. Going in first, he set her bags on the floor and lit a lamp.

The room was small, containing only a bed, a table and a chair. At least it had a window that overlooked the street out front, Katie thought. Even so, she would be bored to death after about an hour.

"I'll have them bring up a tub and water on my way out," Spence offered.

"Fine," she replied, still miffed.

"I'll see you tomorrow then."

When he'd gone she stretched out on the bed, feeling sure that it wasn't her imagination that he'd been in a hurry to leave. Nor did she miss the sly grin that the livery man had given Spence when he'd mentioned going to Bailey's. Her usual curiosity wouldn't let her rest as she wondered exactly what sort of business he had with Bailey. Or was he just trying to put more distance between the two of them?

She wriggled deeper into the thin mattress, thinking whatever he wanted to do was fine with her. She didn't need any foolish romantic notions getting in the way of her goals. She had far too many things to accomplish to even consider such a thing.

Spence walked along several side streets until he finally stood before a sedate two-story house with an ornate sign in front announcing: BAILEY & CO. Every window had lace curtains and was lit up, as was the front door.

Without hesitating, he climbed the few steps to the narrow porch and knocked.

When the door opened he was greeted by Bailey herself.

"Spence! You're back," she said, her smile warm and inviting. "That didn't take long. Where is she?" Perfectly coifed blond curls surrounded her lovely face. "You didn't bring her with you, did you?" she asked, sounding disappointed.

Spence smiled without answering.

"I don't suppose Tim would approve. I should have figured that for myself. Well, come on in and tell me how you've been." The rustle of her silk skirts was the only sound in the entrance hall as she closed the door behind him and ushered him toward the bar.

Bailey's was the only parlor house he knew of where the women were expected to act like ladies at all times. Loud, raucous laughter and tinny pianos were forbidden. The house was tastefully, though richly, decorated in the latest style, from the paintings on the walls to the carpets on the floor. For entertainment, games of chess were played on polished mahogany boards with playing pieces of ivory, and a large, well-tuned piano occupied one room for the culturally inclined. Spence had seldom visited that room on his few trips to St. Louis, being more interested in the rooms in the back where bankers, cattle growers and other businessmen met. As many deals were made at Bailey's as at any other business in town. Possibly more. She offered privacy as well as confidentiality. And when business was over, the services upstairs were incomparable.

"I'm glad to be on this side of the river, that's for sure," he said. "Heading home where I belong."

He paused a moment while the bartender behind the bar filled a mug of beer, then passed it to Spence. A long swig took some of the tension from his shoulders, tension he hadn't realized he'd been carrying.

Bailey smiled. "Long trip, huh?"

He nodded. "A long trip." He took another swallow.

"Does she remind you of Tim?"

He gave her a long, steady look and replied, "You can certainly tell they're brother and sister."

Bailey laughed, a light, melodious sound. Then she became serious and tilted her head to inspect one of the rings on her hand. "I didn't ask when you came through here the first time, but"—she paused, looking up at him—"how is Tim?"

"Fine."

"Just fine?"

"Happy, too." Spence shifted his feet uncomfortably.

"I'm glad. Really." She gave him a genuine smile. "I just wanted to know that he's doing well."

Spence nodded in acknowledgment, but still felt uncomfortable. It had been a long time since the three of them had met in St. Louis and become friends, sharing dreams of a bright future together. Their futures had turned out bright, but not together as they'd planned.

Bailey and Tim had been inseparable until Tim had gone farther west to start his herd, and that's when he'd found Rachel. Bailey had denied a broken heart, but Spence had always known better.

"Well, about that business deal you and Tim are working on," she went on as she squared her shoulders. "Mr. Crandall is in town, which is why you came by tonight, right?"

He nodded.

"I told him that you expected to be here sometime this week, if all went well, and he said he'd drop in again tomorrow. The green room is available all morning if you want it."

"I'd appreciate that," he said.

"One more thing. I think you should know that Lorena stopped here today."

There was no pretending he didn't know who she meant, though it had been years since either of them had even mentioned her name.

"She didn't say much, really, just that she wanted to renew an old friendship," Bailey said, but her expression belied that. "Old friendship, indeed. I told her I hadn't seen you and didn't expect to. And of course, none of the girls will say a thing. She ought to know that, too. The rules haven't changed since she worked here."

Being here at Bailey's, thinking about the past, made Spence feel as if time were moving backward, and at a fast pace at that. He had dealt with all of it a long time ago, had come to grips with it, and wanted to forget it.

"I wouldn't have brought it up," she explained, "but just in case you should run into her . . . well, I thought you might like to be prepared."

"Thanks, Bailey." He finished his beer in two long swallows. "Guess I'd better get on back to the hotel."

"Sure you wouldn't like a room with one of the girls?"

she asked, and he had the feeling she was watching him closely.

"No. I, uh . . . there's plenty of room at the hotel, and Katie, well, she shouldn't be by herself in a strange town and all. Not that we're sharing a room! No, nothing like that." He was stumbling over his words, feeling like a fool and even looking like one.

"Tim would have your hide." She laughed.

He winced at her words.

"Don't look so serious," she went on. "I was only joking. Besides, you're one of the most honorable men I know, and I'm sure Tim knows it, too, or else he'd never have sent you."

He didn't feel honorable. As a matter of fact, he felt pretty low, considering the direction that his thoughts had taken the last few days. Ever since that kiss.

Taking his arm in hers, Bailey walked him to the door. "It's good to see you again, Spence. Don't stay away so long next time, you hear?" Then she leaned up on tiptoe and lightly kissed his cheek. "And that goes for Tim, too. I'll see you tomorrow morning at nine o'clock."

He nodded, saying, "G'night, Bailey." And she closed the door behind him.

Spence was up early the next morning, eager to get on with the business of the Circle M T. Downstairs in the hotel dining room he ordered a hearty breakfast and drank two cups of coffee. Then before leaving for Bailey's, he ordered a similar breakfast to be sent up to Katie's room.

The night before, his intentions had been to spend the night at Bailey's just as she'd suggested, but when it had come right down to it, he couldn't. Somehow, leaving Katie alone in a strange place seemed wrong, even if she wouldn't know that he was close by. At least staying near her in the hotel had made him feel better.

And when Bailey had mentioned Lorena's name, that had just clinched his decision. He had no desire to meet up with her again. The past was over. He had a future to look forward to, and that future lay in Montana.

When he arrived at Bailey's at nine o'clock sharp, Mr. Crandall was already waiting, and Spence wished he'd forgotten that second cup of coffee. It wasn't a good idea to keep a business deal simmering even if the other fellow had arrived early.

Stepping inside the green room, Spence shook hands and said, "Morning, sir."

"Mr. McCord."

Each man sat in a large leather wingback chair. Cigars sat in a silver container on a nearby table for their pleasure, and fresh cups of coffee were poured by one of Bailey's girls who then quickly left the room.

When they were alone, Mr. Crandall spoke first.

"I haven't got much time since I've been in town waiting on you longer than I anticipated. I don't know about you, but I don't like being away from the ranch so long."

"My partner is taking care of things just fine. I have nothing to worry about," Spence said. He had no intention of begging forgiveness or accounting for his time. It was difficult enough to ask for a loan. But Crandall wasn't ready to get right down to the order of business Spence had in mind.

"Have you heard about the new breed of cattle being brought over by the English? Well," he said, not giving Spence a chance to answer, "I've got a few contacts that I'm hoping will be able to get me five hundred head to sell. Are you interested?"

Crandall lit one of the cigars, trying to give the impression that he had plenty of time, even though he'd just said he was in a hurry.

"What's the price?" Spence asked, although he had not come to buy cattle.

Suddenly the man settled back into his chair, blew a

few circles of smoke and looked as if he now had all the time in the world.

"As I said, these are prime cattle. A whole new breed, as a matter of fact." Then he launched into the merits of the stock. Spence wasn't sure if the man was simply taken with owning this breed or if he was hedging in hopes of getting a higher price. But the more Crandall talked about the things Spence hadn't come to hear, the more Spence's mind wandered.

He thought about Katie and the clothes she wore, and that this was no town in which to be dressed so revealingly. He'd have to get her a dress. And he intended to get one right after this meeting so she wouldn't be out on the street, being gawked at and possibly even followed until who knew what might happen.

"Mr. McCord." Crandall's voice was stern.

Spence looked up to find him leaning forward, elbows on knees, staring at him. "Are we having a business meeting or do you have other pressing matters to attend to?"

"I apologize," Spence said sincerely. "These cattle sound very interesting, but I'm not here to buy cattle. I'm here because the Circle M T needs a backer."

From that point on, Spence forced Katie from his mind and concentrated on Crandall, the real focus of this trip in the first place.

Katie opened the door after hearing the knock, expecting to find Spence on the other side. Instead she found the biggest breakfast she'd ever seen. Suddenly forgetting her boredom, she gratefully accepted the tray from the young man who'd brought it, then closed the door.

Setting the tray on the table, she pulled up a chair and inhaled the aroma. There were eggs and ham, steak, flapjacks, as Spence called them, some sort of pale gritty gruel, corn bread smothered in butter and two steaming cups of coffee. She tasted everything but could not possibly finish it all.

Afterwards, she felt completely rejuvenated. She'd slept especially well but far too late into the morning. Now she was ready to see St. Louis, and since Spence wasn't here, she'd go alone. The first place she headed for was the livery, where she intended to see for herself that her wagon and equipment were safe and sound. Then she planned to find some interesting subjects and photograph them even if it meant driving her wagon by herself. She'd leave word with the livery man so Spence wouldn't have to worry.

"Good morning," she said to the man she recognized from the night before.

"Morning, miss," he replied as he oiled the leather on a harness. "What can I do for you?"

The clean, pungent smell of the oil combined with fresh hay and dirty stalls was at first repellent, yet familiar. Pitchforks and shovels lined one wall haphazardly as though in constant use, while bridles and harnesses were neatly hung on pegs. If the interior had not been so dark, she would have been tempted to ask to take a picture of the liveryman, until she remembered the sly grin he'd given Spence.

"Oh, I just wanted to come by and check on the horses," she said matter-of-factly. "They're kind of special to me."

"Right out there in the corral, ma'am," he said with no more than a cursory glance.

"Hmm. So they are." She peeked through the door to see all the horses together and wondered how he could tell them apart. She surely couldn't.

"And the wagon?" she asked.

"Right out back where it's nice and safe just like the fella asked." Still, he didn't look up.

"Mind if I go take a look?"

"Suit yourself."

So she did.

Inside the wagon everything was just as she'd left it, and she breathed a thankful sigh of relief. Maybe she'd ask the man to hitch up the wagon and she'd take it for a drive around town. That way she'd save herself running back to get it if she happened to find the perfect subject. Hadn't she watched Spence handle it for several weeks now? How hard could it be? And the animals seemed docile enough, never giving one bit of trouble.

"Excuse me," she said, interrupting him again. "Would you be so kind as to hitch the horses to the wagon and bring it around front? And just point it in the direction of Bailey's." She smiled pleasantly and added, "Please."

Now the man gave her his full attention, although she wasn't exactly sure why he stared at her so strangely. She'd probably given herself away when she'd asked him to point the horses toward Bailey's, and now he suspected she knew nothing about driving. She'd only mentioned Bailey's as a sort of reference, but now she decided to ask him for specific directions just to distract him so he wouldn't question her about her abilities.

"Could you give me directions to Bailey's? My husband forgot to tell me which house number to look for. Imagine that," she said, laughing. "How will I ever find him?"

The man stared at her. "He wants you to find him?"

"Well, of course. All three of us are getting together," she said, smiling cheerily.

"All three of you?"

"That's right."

"You and your husband and Bailey," he said slowly, astonishment plainly etched in his raised eyebrows.

"That's right," she repeated, but she was beginning to feel uneasy under his penetrating gaze. Then he gave her clothing a once-over.

"Sure thing, lady," he said with a shrug.

By now she was anxious to get away from there, and driving the wagon seemed like the lesser of the two evils every time he looked her way as he harnessed and hitched the team.

At last she was in the driver's seat, pointed toward Bailey's, and listening to directions.

"Two streets over, then turn south—"

"Is that a right turn or a left?" she interrupted.

"That's a right." He paused. "You sure your husband wants you to find him there?" he asked again.

"Yes. I'm sure. Turn right, then what?" she said, beginning to feel irritated.

"Go south three blocks, then east, I mean left. You can't miss it 'cause there's a sign out front." He stepped back, giving her a skeptical eye.

"Thank you," she said perfunctorily. He had certainly taken the cheer out of her morning. With a slap of the reins, which she held tightly in sweaty palms, the wagon moved off down the street.

With her concentration so intent on the backs of the horses and the twitching of their ears, she couldn't remember if she'd gone two blocks or three or even four. Pressing her lips together, she decided to go right . . . or was that left? Yes, it was left and then right.

After a good hour and a half of wandering up one street and down another, all the while gaining more confidence in her driving skills, she finally called to a lady passerby and asked directions to Bailey's.

The woman's face colored to the roots of her gray hair; then she began sputtering as though she would die of apoplexy. Katie apologized profusely for bothering her and quickly moved the horses down the street.

Well, she told herself, it didn't take a team of horses to run over her before she recognized the writing on the wall. Bailey's was a house of ill repute, as Mrs. O'Shea would have said.

She slowed the horses to a walk as the realization swept over her that Spence had spent the night in such a house. And only days after kissing her so tenderly. A lump of self-pity formed in her throat, but she swallowed it. Salty tears burned the backs of her eyelids, but she rejected them by blinking hard.

"Foolish girl," she mumbled out loud. He'd never made her any promises or even said anything endearing. As a matter of fact, he'd practically ignored her after she'd let him kiss her. The tips of her ears burned with embarrassment. If Erin were there, Katie knew she'd be on the receiving end of a talking-to she wouldn't soon forget, and Mrs. O'Shea would give her more than that.

She pulled the horses to a halt with a gentle "Whoa!" Then she called to another woman who passed close by.

"Excuse me, ma'am, but I'm looking for that no-'count man of mine. Would you be so kind as to tell me which way I need to head to find Bailey's house?" she asked, mimicking one of the travelers they'd come across weeks ago.

"Certainly, dear," the woman said with sympathy clearly visible in the set of her frown. "But you're headed the wrong direction. It's back that way three blocks, turn left for one block, then right for three more blocks. And you give him a good swift kick for me, too."

"I shorely will, ma'am. Thank you kindly."

At the next alley she made a turn so she'd come out on the next street headed in the right direction, then, keeping track of the blocks and the correct turns, she finally found herself in front of BAILEY & CO.

A good swift kick wasn't at all what she had in mind for Spence McCord. She intended to get even. It was her turn to embarrass him.

After securing the reins, she jumped down from the

wagon and marched to the front door, where she knocked loud enough to be heard a block away.

When the door opened, a beautiful blond woman greeted her wearing a bright blue silk dress that matched her eyes perfectly. A mischievous grin created a sparkle in those eyes when she saw Katie.

"Hello, my name's Katie O'Rourke. Is Spence Mc-Cord here?"

Chapter Nine

"No, he isn't. But please, won't you come in?"

Katie stepped resolutely over the threshold, telling herself she intended to make the most of this visit since she might never get the opportunity again. Besides that, she could still embarrass him whether he was there or not.

"Tess and I were just having tea. Would you like to join us?"

"Tea?" she replied, a little taken aback. She would have thought they served stronger drink in a place like this. Then, collecting herself, she answered politely, "Yes, thank you, that would be nice."

Katie followed her hostess to a beautiful parlor with draperies the color of an evening sunset. Oil paintings that appeared to be of real value graced each wall tastefully. A large fireplace embellished with gold detailing was far from being the focal point of the room, but the furnishings were. Satin settees edged in polished rosewood sat comfortably around a center table where a silver tea set awaited them.

"Sit down, please. Tess just went to the kitchen to bring us some cups." When both women were seated on opposite settees she said, "Before I forget, my name is Bailey."

Katie wasn't surprised.

"I'm glad you stopped by," Bailey went on. "Actually, I was hoping you would."

"You know who I am?" Katie asked.

"You're a traveling photographer going west to see your brother. And that's your wagon out front." Bailey smiled pleasantly as she rested her weight against the arm of her seat.

Suddenly feeling underdressed and out of place in this gracious woman's presence, Katie brushed at the plain cotton trousers she wore and tried to hide her mud-stained shoes beneath the table.

"Yes, it is," she replied. "I've really had quite an adventure so far and met so many interesting people, too." This whole idea was backfiring in her face. Instead of embarrassing Spence, she was embarrassing herself.

"And you take pictures of everyone you meet? I mean the interesting ones?" Bailey asked.

Tess entered just then with three cups and saucers.

"I heard we had company," she said. "So I brought another cup."

"Tess, this is Katie. She's a photographer."

"Pleased to meet you, Katie," Tess said as she seated herself on the same settee where Katie perched on the edge. "I've never met a woman photographer before." Tess poured tea for each of them.

"Actually, neither have I," Bailey said. Then a new expression crossed her face. "Perhaps we could get you to take a picture of the girls and myself. Would you?"

"I'd love to!"

"Good," Bailey said, raising her cup and saucer. "But first tell us about yourself and how you came up with this adventurous idea of yours."

So for the next thirty minutes Katie shared her dream along with many of the experiences of her journey, and even talked about her family, whom she missed more than she had expected.

"Ah," sighed Tess. "What a lovely, romantic thing to do."

Katie stared at her in surprise. "Romantic? I guess I hadn't thought of it that way at all." And she still didn't. "There wasn't anything romantic about getting soaked in a thunderstorm and splattered with the mud that dripped off Spence. And then try begging for a place to spend the night looking like that. We truly did look like something the cat dragged in."

All three women laughed at the mental picture Katie drew.

"I can't imagine Spence McCord ever looking like something the cat dragged in," said Tess with an appreciative rise of her brow.

"Well, he did that night, believe me." Katie felt Bailey's eyes watching her closely and she began to feel self-conscious again. With a concentrated effort she willed herself not to think about the events following that thunderstorm, since she couldn't be sure that her feelings wouldn't be mirrored on her face.

"I suppose we'd better get started so I can make the most of the bright sunlight. I'll just get my camera," Katie said, rising.

Tess rose with her and clutched her arm in excitement, asking, "Could you take one of me in my room by myself? I'd certainly pay you well." Then Tess turned to Bailey. "Would it be all right?"

"It's up to Katie," Bailey responded.

"Well, I haven't sold a single photograph. I've been making trades."

"All right then, we'll trade. It'll be your choice of anything in my room," Tess said. "I'll go get the others and bring them down here."

In no time at all, Katie set up her camera in the parlor while a dozen or so women looked on. The myriad of colors represented in their silk dresses almost made Katie wish she were an artist and could paint them in color.

"Should some of us sit on the settee and some of us stand behind it?" Bailey asked.

"No," Katie responded, wanting to avoid the usual props. But she could hardly expect to show them in the midst of their "vocation." So she chose second best by deciding to do just the opposite and have them stand near the fireplace in as "homey" a pose as possible.

When she was satisfied with positioning them in a semicircle on each side of the fireplace, some seated on stools and Bailey taking a central position, she warned them not to move and she'd be right back.

Inside the wagon she tried not to hurry through the process. She didn't want this opportunity to get muddled, since she was sure she'd never get the chance again. Especially when Spence and her brother found out what she'd done.

She regretted the distance she had to go from the wagon to the house, but there was no help for that; her only choice was to move quickly.

She slipped the plate into place, said a prayer and exposed it. When she came out from under the cloth, she said, "Done!" Then she hurried back to the wagon, hummed and counted her way through the finishing and finally set the picture in the light to "take." After toning the print and waiting for it to dry, she hurried back to the house once more with the picture.

"I'm very pleased with this one," she said to Bailey, handing it to her while the women crowded close to see it.

The picture was sharp and clear; even the few timorous smiles hadn't blurred.

"That's the best picture I've ever had taken of me," said one young woman.

"And just how many have you had taken?" asked another in jest.

"Mercy sakes," added a third woman. "Don't Bailey's eyes just seem to sparkle even in a picture!"

The comments and admiration mixed naturally with laughter and teasing until Katie completely forgot she was in a house of pleasure.

"I'll put it in a silver frame and set it on the mantel," Bailey said. "But I insist on paying for it."

"No, this one isn't for sale or trade," Katie replied sincerely. "This is a gift to you from me."

Bailey stared at her intently, a lingering smile on her features. "You really do favor Tim," she said, and gave her a warm hug.

Before Katie could respond, Tess was tugging at her arm, whispering, "It's my turn. Follow me."

Katie folded up her camera and carefully hauled it along, trying not to gawk at her surroundings.

Upstairs, they passed a number of doors before Tess opened the one to her room. Whatever Katie had expected, this wasn't it. A beautiful wardrobe stood in one corner with the doors open, and sunshine from the nearby window poured in, showing off the brilliance of the dresses within. A bed, looking as though it had a feather tick thick enough to get lost in, occupied one wall along with side tables which were graced with lace, and on top of those were crystal lamps. A small, lady's writing desk sat in a sunny alcove.

But the one thing that really caught Katie's eye was the shiny copper tub.

"First," said Tess, "what would you like in trade?"

Katie stared at the huge tub and without a second thought, she said, "A bath full of bubbles in that tub."

Tess laughed with delight. "That's all?"

"That's more than enough," Katie replied, already

feeling the warm water clear to her neck. The night before, the hotel had sent up a tub barely big enough to bathe a child, and the water had been cool. She'd managed to get a full bath, but it had been more work than luxury.

Shaking her head in disbelief, Tess said, "Deal." Then she walked to the alcove where the little desk sat at an angle to the window and said, "Could we take a picture of me writing a letter? I have a gentleman I would like to give it to."

Katie surveyed the angle of sunshine, determining it was an excellent location, and nodded. Then she quickly set up her camera, all the while thinking about what it would be like to take a bath in a parlor house. Erin would be speechless when she heard.

"I'll order the water now," Tess said.

Each went their separate ways, Tess to the kitchen and Katie to her wagon. When Katie returned, she found Tess seated at the writing desk, a feathered quill pen in one hand and her chin in the other. And, to Katie's amazement, she was wearing nothing more than a thin silk wrapper which left little to the imagination.

Reminding herself that she wasn't taken with propriety, or she wouldn't be in this house in the first place, Katie tried to ignore the lack of dress and concentrated on getting the best picture. But her mind wouldn't let her forget that Tess had said this picture was for a gentleman friend. Katie didn't think it was likely she would share any of this episode with Erin, and especially not Mrs. O'Shea.

After exposing the plate, she made another trip back to her wagon and went through the familiar steps. When she'd finished and had the print ready to hand over to Tess, she put her chemicals and baths away, and tidied up her wagon. The only thing left to do was to put the camera in its secure box, but she would wait until she'd finished with her bath.

Upstairs once more, she gave the picture to Tess, who was now dressed as lovely as before.

"Thank you," Tess said, apparently pleased with what she saw. "And now I'll leave you to your bath."

When the other woman had gone, Katie didn't strip her clothes off immediately. A strange sense of wrong-doing flowed over her as Granny's frowning features flitted through her mind. But she shook the feeling, telling herself she'd done nothing wrong. So, before the water cooled any further, she slipped out of her clothes and into the water and bubbles.

Spence left Bailey's and the meeting with Crandall two hours later than he'd anticipated, and the deal hadn't been settled. He'd thanked Bailey, paid his share of the fee for the use of the green meeting room, and headed back to the hotel. But before going inside, he decided to follow through on the idea of appropriate new clothes for Katie. So he entered the ladies shop next door.

"Good afternoon, sir," said the clerk. "What can I do for you?"

"I'd like to purchase a dress that would be suitable for traveling." He scanned the room in search of one already made.

"And will the lady be traveling by train or coach?" she asked.

"By wagon," he answered, his gaze coming to rest on a blue cotton dress over the back of a chair. "Is this for sale?"

"Well, I suppose it could be. I could make another for the young lady who purchased it."

Spence held it up to judge the size and length. The top of the shoulders came to the middle of his chest when he held it next to him and the waist appeared to be small enough. But the bodice . . . well, that he didn't know for sure. He'd just have to take a chance.

"I'll take it," he said, fishing out the cash to pay for it.

"And will the lady need any . . . uh, undergarments?" the woman asked.

"Undergarments? Why, does anything special go with it?" he asked, ignorant of those things.

"No, not with this dress. It's just a simple day dress. Perfect for wagon traveling."

"Good."

"And what about a bonnet?" she asked. "Something to shield her from the sun, you know."

But he remembered how much she'd enjoyed the sun on her face that day on the Ohio River, and he replied, "No. I'll leave that to her." And besides, he would miss seeing her bouncing red-gold curls.

He accepted the dress wrapped in brown paper and thanked her, then headed once more for the hotel.

When he knocked on Katie's door for the fourth time without getting any response, he figured she was either sulking or gone. And most likely gone, he told himself as he took to the stairs. At the desk, the clerk couldn't help at all. He hadn't seen her after he'd delivered the tray.

With the package still under one arm, Spence headed for the livery, deciding she'd probably gone to check on her precious equipment.

Ignoring the familiar scents that usually made him feel right at home, Spence strode through the barn to the back where the wagon was supposed to be.

"Damn!" he muttered. He should have known she'd try something like this. From now on he'd either have to keep her at his side where he could watch her every minute or else find someone who would.

"'Lo!" called the man who had promised to keep the wagon safe. "Back so soon?"

"Where's the wagon?"

"Your woman took it on over to Bailey's to meet you there. Like you told her," he said grinning.

"I didn't tell her any such thing! And how the hell did she know enough to ask about Bailey?"

"Damned if I know," he replied with a shrug. "But I gave her directions just like you wanted."

"I told you that I didn't tell her to go to Bailey's!" Spence almost never lost his temper; until now he'd never had a good reason.

"Whatever you say."

"Get me a horse. Now." Spence leveled a threatening look at the man, but it wasn't just a threat, there was a lot of promise behind it, too.

In short order Spence was riding at a good clip toward Bailey's, a lecture forming on his lips that would make those curls on her head as tight as coiled springs. Almost forgotten was the brown paper parcel with a dress tucked securely against his side.

He saw her wagon before he reached Bailey's. Pulling his horse to a stop that made it dance sideways, he dismounted and tied it to the tailgate. In five steps he was on the porch, knocking at the door.

When Bailey answered, he gave her a quick nod of greeting, then marched past her.

"Where is she?" he asked.

"Well, she went upstairs to take Tess's picture and—"

"Which room?" he asked, already on the stairs.

A door above him closed and Tess stepped into view. He had his answer.

"I'm not sure . . ." Tess began as he strode by her, barely giving her his attention. His mind was set on one thing and one thing only. She had no business in this house, and when Tim found out, if he did, there'd be hell to pay.

Clutching the doorknob, he pushed the door wide. But there he stopped.

Melody Morgan

Sitting in one of the usual large copper tubs that graced each of Bailey's rooms was Katie. A lather of bubbles floated across the top of the water, hiding all but the mounds of her breasts and shoulders. Their eyes met simultaneously, and she instantly slid deeper beneath the bubbles, letting out an ear-piercing shriek.

He didn't know whether to step back out and close the door or go on in. He chose the later.

"Get out of here!" she yelled. "I mean it. Get out!" She plucked a sponge from her bath and threw it at him.

He dodged it and heard the soggy weapon slide down the door behind him.

"I want you out of that tub and out of this house. Now," he said, his voice low.

"Me! You've got your nerve telling me to leave when you're the one who spent the night here."

It wasn't true, but he let it pass. He didn't want the real issue here tangled up with anything else.

"I said get out," she repeated, but less vehemently this time. "If Tim finds out you watched me take a bath—"

"If Tim finds out you were in this house—"

"Are you going to tell him?"

"Are you?"

She shrugged, exposing one shiny wet shoulder. "I might."

"You won't if you know what's good for you," he said.

"Does that mean we're coconspirators?" she asked. Fading bubbles made her sink to her chin.

"Not exactly."

"In that case, I'm not getting out."

"Fine. I'll wait." He crossed the room and sat on the bed.

Her curly-topped head turned as her gaze followed his progress. "You can't do that!"

When he didn't respond, she said, "You're ruining a perfectly wonderful bath, you know."

"Since I can't trust you out of my sight, I have no other choice."

With an exaggerated sigh she said, "All right, I'll get out. Bring me that screen."

He set up the screen between them and returned to the bed, only this time he stood with his back toward her. Glancing down, his eye caught a photograph propped against a book on a writing desk.

"Did you take this picture?" he asked.

"Don't look at that. It isn't decent."

"It was decent enough for you to take it."

"That's different. I'm a woman." She peeked over the screen.

He set the picture back in its place and said, "I brought you a dress." Then he proceeded to pull it from the brown wrapping he still carried under his arm.

"I don't want it."

"You're going to have to wear it. This isn't a place to be running around dressed in britches. You draw too much attention." He thought about the man at the livery and his knowing grin. "And I don't want to hear any complaints. We're going to be in town longer than I expected."

"We are?" she replied, and he didn't miss the note of cheer in her voice.

"Yes. But you're not coming back here, or anywhere, without me." He held out the dress behind his back. "Here. Put it on."

"I told you I don't want it."

He turned slightly and his eyes met hers. "I'm responsible for your safe arrival at Tim's. I intend to see to it that you do arrive safe. Now, put it on."

She hesitated a moment longer, testing his patience, then she snatched the dress from his hand over the top of the screen. He could hear her pulling and tugging at the material, while she muttered the whole time.

"There," she replied, stepping out so he could see her.

"Satisfied?" Her eyes snapped with the familiar blue fire and her mouth was set in an angry straight line, but that did nothing to detract from her natural beauty. And the dress fit fine. Real fine.

"Almost," he said. He had decided that he would deposit her at the boardinghouse he'd passed on his way to Bailey's. It looked respectable, like a nice proper place for a lady. After he left her there, he'd make sure she had no way to get around town; she could have her wagon, but there wouldn't be any horses hitched to it.

Katie gathered up her shirt and britches, wrapped them in the brown paper and shoved them at Spence. Then she folded up her camera, prepared to carry it. Without a word, Spence took the camera from her and handed her the brown paper. Standing aside, he waited for her to go through the door first, the look in his eyes telling her that he would tolerate no more shenanigans.

Downstairs Katie said good-bye to Bailey and Tess, who stood unabashedly watching them. She thanked them for their hospitality and the lovely bath; she wanted to promise to come back, but didn't dare with Spence so close behind her. So she made the promise silently, knowing somehow she'd keep it.

Spence said very little to Bailey as they left the house, she noticed, but then it wasn't likely that he'd make pleasant conversation while Katie stood there, which was part of the reason she planned to visit Bailey's again. The other part had to do with Bailey's comment about Katie favoring Tim. Not only was the comment a curious one, but the tone of her voice hinted at something more. She wondered what that might be.

Katie struggled with her skirts as she climbed onto the wagon and finally seated herself.

"I prefer britches," she said.

Spence kept his opinion to himself and turned the wagon back toward the boardinghouse.

After driving two blocks in silence, Katie gave him a

sidelong glance and said, "The rooms are very nice at Bailey's."

"I didn't spend the night, if that's what you're asking."

Relieved, she nearly released the pent-up breath she hadn't realized she'd been holding. She shouldn't care whether he'd stayed the night or not, but she did care, more than she liked to admit.

"Since you didn't spend the night there, can I ask why you were at Bailey's?" Katie asked.

"I had a meeting." He looked over at her. "I could ask you the same thing."

Turning away, she gave a small shrug. "I was looking for you."

He didn't know how she'd figured out he'd gone there, but he guessed it didn't matter. In the time they'd spent together, he'd found out she was very resourceful. He reminded himself that his only concern was to see to it she stayed out of trouble, and since leaving her alone was one sure-fire way of asking for trouble, he'd either have to stay with her himself or find someone else to watch over her. He hoped the boardinghouse would provide that service, even if it was unintentional.

He slowed the horses as they approached the tidy little sign announcing, "MISS HETTY'S BOARDING HOUSE, inquire within."

"Why are we stopping here?" Katie asked as she looked over the interesting little house with its cupola and side porch. The house was painted stark white, relieved only by the purple flowering vine on a trellis near the side entrance. Four straight-backed chairs neatly lined the wall of the porch, two on each side of the door.

"You'll be staying here instead of the hotel." He almost added that she'd be more comfortable, but he knew she probably wouldn't be. "The food will be better."

"I don't have any complaints about the food at the

hotel other than they serve too much." But she was already climbing down from her seat, considering the character of the house and wondering what sort of person Miss Hetty might be.

Spence secured the reins and followed her to the side door where a small hand-lettered sign insisted they wipe their feet. Katie knocked and they waited.

Moments later, a diminutive woman of indeterminable age pushed open the windowless door. She looked as though a small wind could blow her away, but it would take more than that to unwind the partially graying hair from its bun at her nape.

"May I help you?" she asked in a tiny and quavery voice.

"Do you have a room available?" Katie smiled in an attempt to alleviate the stern features of the older woman, for all the good it did.

"Yes." Miss Hetty looked Katie over from the top of her hatless head to the toe of her mud-stained shoes. Then she looked at Spence. "But this house is for ladies only."

"Oh, that's all right," Katie said airily. "My brother is staying down the street at Bai—"

Spence poked her in the back where Miss Hetty couldn't see, stopping her in mid sentence.

"At a hotel," he finished for her.

"I see," Miss Hetty said, eying both of them skeptically. "As I said, I do have a room available. Meals are included in the cost, and all gentlemen callers, that means brothers, too, are restricted to sitting on the porch. This is a respectable house and I have a reputation to uphold."

"Of course," Katie replied, and she wondered if she dared to ask to take pictures or if she'd even be allowed to leave her wagon in the back.

"I didn't get your name," Miss Hetty said.

"Katie. And this is Spence McCord."

Spence nodded, but the older woman barely acknowledged him.

"How long will you be staying, Miss McCord?" Miss Hetty opened the door wider as though considering to allow her admittance.

Katie looked to Spence for an answer.

"As long as a week, but hopefully I'll finish with business before that," he said. "And by then Katie should be rested enough that the doctor will let her travel again."

"Doctor!" Katie exclaimed.

"Too much sun," Spence went on, "from traveling. And she refuses to wear a bonnet."

Katie moved around him in order to land a well-placed kick, but settled for a sharp jab in his ribs. He pretended not to notice.

"Oh, I see," said Miss Hetty. "Of course, we'll keep her indoors. Bring your things right in." She glanced toward the wagon, her interest obviously piqued.

Before the woman could ask, Katie jumped at the opportunity to tell her what was in the wagon.

"I hope you'll allow me to photograph you and your house, but I'll need to keep my equipment nearby, if you don't mind."

Miss Hetty's composure seemed to leave her suddenly and she stuttered a reply. "I . . . I . . . well, I . . . think that would be . . . nice. Very nice."

Within a short time, Spence set up the wagon close to the back of the house, unhitched the horses and headed back to the livery. But not before he'd promised to check on her daily, and he emphasized the word *daily*.

Katie was more than a little disgruntled that he'd taken the horses from the wagon, but she barely had time to dwell on it. Miss Hetty all but pulled her into the house, taking her from room to room, proudly showing off her prized possessions.

"This lovely table was a gift from my dear father to my mother just before the war. He was killed, you know. Well, no. I don't suppose you would know that. Here," she said, tugging Katie's arm. "This is his picture. That's my mother. And that's me."

The likeness between mother and daughter was unbelievable, and Katie had to admire the photographer's work.

"I never had any brothers or sisters," Miss Hetty mused, apparently enjoying having a captive audience. "And all I have left is this house. Do you think you could take a picture of it? Perhaps I could stand on the porch. Or would there be enough light indoors? I wouldn't want you to have a relapse."

Katie considered the placement of the windows in the small parlor, but the exposure was to the north and she knew it would never do. The dining room was the only room with a good southern exposure and two good-sized windows. Even with the excellent lighting, the room was small and she'd have difficulty maneuvering her camera into place.

"We might be able to use this room," Katie said. And that suggestion sent Miss Hetty into another bout of reminiscing. Each teacup and doily brought on an entirely different story from her past. Just talking about the teacups made Miss Hetty decide to stir up the fire in the stove and put on a kettle of water to boil for tea. When it was ready, they sat at the table. Katie sipped her tea, listening to Miss Hetty talk as the afternoon sun inched across the sky.

Occasionally Katie would have to bring her wandering thoughts back to Miss Hetty. But a small scratching noise that she couldn't define drew her attention until she no longer heard the older woman.

"Do you have a cat?" Katie finally asked.

"A cat?" Miss Hetty said, looking rather nervous. "No. No, there are no cats here." She poured more tea, which had now become cool. "Did I mention that this teapot came from Boston?"

More scratching noises and a small, seemingly distant, screeching sound made Katie turn in her seat.

"Did you hear that?" she asked.

"Hear what?" Miss Hetty held her teacup still.

All was silent.

"I don't hear anything at all." Miss Hetty gripped the delicate handle on her cup.

"It sounds like. . . . I'm not sure what it sounds like," Katie said. But for some reason it sent shivers up her spine.

"You musn't let it bother you," Miss Hetty said. "It's probably just a branch scraping a window. Now, where was I?"

It did very much sound like a branch scraping a window, but a quick glance outside verified that no breeze fluttered even a leaf, let alone a whole branch.

"Oh, yes," Miss Hetty went on, "I enjoy using my teapot from Boston especially when the Ladies Aid Society comes for a meeting. And tomorrow afternoon they'll be meeting here." Her eyes grew large in her tiny face. "Do you suppose you could take a picture of our meeting? We always hold our meetings right here in this room."

"I'd be happy to," Katie said as she strained her ears to hear the noise again.

"Well, then let's get you settled upstairs in your room. Supper will be ready in about an hour. Perhaps you'd like to lie down until it's ready."

"Thank you," Katie replied, "that would be nice." She followed the straight-backed woman up the stairs, trying to ignore the strange scratching noises that seemed to come from the walls. Instead, she willed herself to listen to Miss Hetty's explanations and introductions to the faded pictures of her ancestors which hung on both sides of the stairwell.

Chapter Ten

Early the next morning Katie put on the blue dress that Spence had given her, more to pacify him if he should catch her on the street than for any other reason. Then she went down to breakfast, where she found Miss Hetty in a crisp apron, pouring hot water into a teapot.

"I heard you stirring around up there so I thought you'd be down shortly," Miss Hetty said. "I only cook healthy breakfasts for my guests." She set a bowl of oatmeal topped with fresh strawberries before Katie. "Although I don't have many guests these days."

Katie tasted the oatmeal, which had never been a favorite with her, and was pleasantly surprised at the sweet, nutty flavor.

"This is delicious," she told her.

Miss Hetty smiled, her hands folded in a pose of careful composure at her thin waist.

"It's my mother's secret recipe," she replied. "Lavinia Boardman has been trying to get it from me for years, but I won't tell her."

Miss Hetty peeked inside her Boston teapot. Apparently pleased, she replaced the lid and went on speaking.

"Yes, Lavinia would dearly love to have it. But I won't give it to her. And why should I?" she asked suddenly.

"I don't know," Katie answered dutifully. She poked a strawberry in her mouth, savoring the tangy sweetness.

"Well, because she makes the best cherry tarts in the whole city and she won't share *her* recipe with *me!*" Miss Hetty set a flowered cup and saucer with gilt edges before Katie. "I dare say that she'll even bring some with her for this afternoon's meeting." She peeked into the teapot once more, then poured each of them half a cup.

"And what will you be serving?" Katie asked, certain that Miss Hetty would never allow Miss Lavinia to overshadow her.

"The other recipe that Lavinia has tried desperately to pry out of me. Taste this," Miss Hetty said, indicating the tea she'd just poured. "My own special blend of herbs that I grow myself."

Katie carefully sipped her tea, enjoying the warm, soothing brew. Not only did it please her taste buds but it seemed to affect her head.

"Mmm! This is wonderful, Miss Hetty."

"I knew you'd like it. Everyone does."

"I can understand why Miss Lavinia would want the recipe."

"Hmmph. That's not why Lavinia Boardman wants it." Miss Hetty sipped her own tea.

"What other reason could there be?"

"It's a love potion. Or so I've been told."

Katie smiled behind her cup. She couldn't help it. The idea of two elderly women vying over the possibilities of making a love match all because of a cup of tea was nothing less than charming, if a little eccentric.

"Of course, I don't believe it," Miss Hetty said, with a no-nonsense straight face. "But Lavinia does."

"Who else will be at the meeting?" Katie asked with a new interest in the Ladies Aid Society.

"Esther Stilts, a widow-woman who's been the cornerstone of the Society since she lost her husband in the war. She comes from one of the best families in all of St. Louis."

Miss Hetty polished a spot on the wooden table with the hem of her apron, then rose from her seat and polished the back of her chair.

"And," she went on, "Gladys Pepper, who actually had the opportunity to meet President Ulysses S. Grant. Of course, Lavinia always reminds her that he wasn't president when she met him. That always puts a stop to her stories." Miss Hetty moved on to the china cupboard, where she alternately apron-polished the shining wood and pushed the china around.

"And Mary Alice Brown, who still believes her man will come home from the war." Miss Hetty tapped one finger to her head and clicked her tongue. "Poor dear, if you know what I mean."

Katie understood perfectly.

Miss Hetty cleared the dirty dishes from Katie's side of the table, giving the table another apron-polish as she went.

"Is there anything you'd like me to help you with?" Katie asked.

"No, no. You just make yourself comfortable. We'll have a small bite to eat at noon, then the ladies will begin arriving around four o'clock."

Katie had plans for the morning and was anxious to be on her way. She hadn't been able to stop thinking about Bailey's words: "You really do favor Tim." She had intended to ask her how she knew her brother, but one thing had led to another and she'd lost the opportunity.

Now she had made up her mind to find out as much as she possibly could. One never knew when that sort of information might come in handy.

"Well, I'm going to meet a friend, but I'll be back in plenty of time to set up my camera."

"But, my dear, your brother said you shouldn't be out in the sun," Miss Hetty replied.

"My brother worries too much about me. He's over-protective. Actually, the doctor said being outside was good for me but I should stay in the shade as much as possible, and with all the tall trees up and down the street that shouldn't be a problem."

"Well, if you're sure. . . ."

"I'm very sure, but if you're worried about what Spence will say, then we'll just make it our little secret."

Miss Hetty smiled broadly. "I love secrets and I'm very good at keeping them."

"It's settled then." Katie said good-bye, promising to be back before the Society meeting. She made her way around the table, past the delicate heirlooms that perched everywhere, stepped out onto the side porch and crossed the yard. The walk to Bailey's was rather a long one, but there was no alternative since Spence had taken the horses. Fortunately, he had once again underestimated Katie. Her natural curiosity wasn't about to leave this stone unturned. She had to know just how well Bailey knew Tim, and she freely admitted to herself that she wanted to know the same about Spence.

Keeping always alert for a sign of him, she finally reached Bailey's front door. When it opened and Bailey stood before her smiling, Katie breathed a sigh of relief.

"Katie! What a surprise. I didn't expect to see you again after Spence practically hauled you away."

"Well, he only thinks he's my chaperon, but he isn't really. I am an independent woman in spite of those two."

"Those two?" Bailey asked, looking puzzled.

"Spence and Tim."

"Ah, I see." Then she stepped aside. "Please, come in."

"He isn't here, is he?" Katie asked, glancing around.

"No. His business meeting is this afternoon."

"Good, because I'd like to talk with you, and I don't want him interrupting me. Again," Katie said.

Leading the way into the parlor, Bailey replied, "You needn't worry about interruptions. The girls have the morning off and they're all sleeping, and no business meetings have been set up." She sat on one of the lovely settees and patted the space near her. "We've got all morning for girl talk."

The silver tea set still occupied a place of honor on the table before them and the room was as elegant as she remembered, yet this lovely woman made Katie feel as comfortable as the britches she usually wore. Until that thought passed through her mind, she hadn't realized Bailey was wearing a plain cotton wrapper tied at the waist instead of a lovely silk dress.

Bailey laughed, a light, airy sound, when she saw Katie glance over her apparel.

"It's my morning to enjoy myself, too," she said. Then leaning back she comfortably crossed one leg over the other. "So what would you like to know?"

Her easy manner put Katie so much at ease that she barely restrained herself from blurting out all her questions at once. But choosing her words carefully, she decided to begin with Tim and leave the questions about Spence until last, if she could bring herself to ask them at all.

"How is it that you know my brother?"

Bailey nodded her head slowly, a small, winsome smile creeping to the corners of her mouth. "I suspected you might ask that." She paused and leaned forward. "I'm not sure Tim would want me to tell you."

"I'm very sure he wouldn't. But tell me anyway. I'm grown up now."

Bailey studied her, then nodded.

"It was a hundred years ago, or so it seems." She paused again in reflection. "The three of us met in a small bordello where I worked here in St. Louis. It was after the war. Tim and Spence were headed west to get into ranching, although Tim admitted he knew nothing about cattle. Spence had the background for that, not Tim. But I guess you know that."

Katie didn't interrupt to say she knew nothing about Spence, but simply nodded in agreement.

"I liked Tim from the start. More than I should have. And at that time he . . . liked me." Bailey took a deep breath. "I knew that Tim was interested in ranching, and so I thought if Tim could meet the right man he'd be all set. I also knew of a man who needed some help working a ranch in Colorado and I gave his name to Tim." A small shrug of her shoulder said she didn't intend to take any credit for what followed. "They met in Denver, and the next thing you know, Tim's in business. Of course it didn't happen that fast." She laughed softly. "I told you it was a hundred years ago."

Katie smiled at her, liking her more as the moments passed.

"Anyway, it seems that was the beginning of the idea of the meeting rooms that I have here now. I made arrangements when I could, helping to set up meetings whether it was here in St. Louis or Chicago or Denver. When the business deals worked out, most of the men brought me a share of it. That's how I bought this place."

"You mean this isn't a . . ." Katie asked in surprise.

"Oh, yes. We cater to all the needs of men, including that."

"I see." Katie blushed in spite of herself, and hated the thought that Spence had probably spent as much time here as Tim apparently had.

"How long has it been since you've seen Tim?" Katie asked.

"About six years. Our only contact is through business. Nothing personal." She held Katie's gaze. "How is Tim?"

"The same, I suppose. Ornery, demanding, and bossy. I could go on," Katie said, making a face.

"So he isn't exactly on your good side, I take it."

"And never has been."

"Maybe his actions were his way of showing brotherly love. He always spoke well of you."

"He did? Well, imagine that," Katie replied, scoffing at the idea. If telling her what to do was his idea of brotherly love, he could keep it.

"Now it's my turn to ask a few questions," Bailey said, leveling a straightforward look at Katie. "How is it that you're heading west with Spence McCord? I know a few women who would envy you if they knew."

"Tim," she answered simply.

Bailey looked puzzled, so Katie told her every detail of the events leading up to Spence's arrival and their departure. Katie added a few more of the interesting stories that she hadn't already told to Bailey and Tess, leaving out that one intimate moment she'd shared with Spence.

Talking to Bailey was almost like talking to Erin, although she'd certainly never say so to Erin. Katie found herself confessing to the white lies she'd told that put Spence in a bad light, laughing about it a little but feeling more guilty than she had when she'd done it.

Bailey patted Katie's shoulder. "I'm sure he doesn't hold it against you."

"He did at the time." She shrugged as she studied the toes of her dirty shoes. "We get along, for the most part. At least it's better now than when we left New York."

Bailey started to add a comment but was cut off by the sudden entrance of a woman at the front door.

"Well, good morning, Bailey," the woman said as she breezed into the parlor and seated herself without being asked. "I hope you don't mind that I let myself in. Old habits, you know."

Katie felt as well as saw Bailey bristle immediately. The woman had a commanding presence about her, dressed in the latest fashion, besides being very beautiful.

"Good morning, Lorena," Bailey replied, still looking composed.

"And who do we have here? A new girl perhaps? My dear, you will simply love working for Bailey. Not only does she treat her girls well, but you'll have such opportunities." Lorena raised a knowing eyebrow at Katie.

"This is not a new girl," Bailey said sternly. "This is Tim O'Rourke's sister, Katie."

Lorena's mouth fell open in a beautifully shaped "O". "Tim's little sister? Well, now that you mention it, yes, I can certainly see the resemblance."

Katie felt like a piece of discarded muslin, handled and observed but not wanted.

"How is Tim these days? And Spence?" Lorena fastened her eyes on Katie, waiting.

"Fine," Katie replied, deciding she'd tell this woman nothing. Then the faint familiarity she'd felt when Lorena first entered the house turned into full-blown recognition. This was the same woman she'd seen staring at Spence on the paddle wheel boat when they were disembarking. Immediately, Katie's hackles raised as she wondered exactly what the connection was between the two. Instinctively, she knew without a doubt that Lorena was a woman without principles of any kind.

Lorena turned her insistent gaze upon Bailey. "Is Spence in St. Louis?"

Bailey hesitated, then said, "Yes."

"Business or pleasure?" Lorena said, practically purring.

"Strictly business," Bailey answered.

"Isn't that fortunate. I haven't seen Spence in far too many years. We really do have a lot to catch up on. There's some unfinished business we need to talk over. Well, business may not be the exact word for it."

"Lorena, I don't think—" Bailey began, but Lorena cut her off.

"Bailey, dear. Spence is a grown man. I'm quite sure he can take care of himself." Then she turned to Katie and said, "Please forgive me for making such a ridiculous assumption. I should have known better than to think you worked here." With a half smile of distaste, Lorena glanced at Katie's simple dress, beginning at the hem and moving to the top of her bright curls. "You certainly do look like Tim."

The woman was probably no more than four or five years older than Katie herself, but she had the airs of an exceptionally mature woman, which made Katie feel all of fifteen.

"Are you an old friend of Tim's?" Katie asked, emphasizing the word "old" ever so slightly. Her ire was up and she knew her cheeks were bright with repressed anger.

Without flinching, Lorena replied, "I hardly think the word 'old' is appropriate. Let's just say I've known Tim and Spence for quite some time. The four of us were inseparable, weren't we, Bailey?"

Bailey paused, then asked, "What brings you here today, Lorena?"

"Well, I'm in no hurry to get to that. I'm much more interested in what Katie's doing here. Tell me, dear," she said to Katie. "Are you and Spence traveling together?"

"Actually, yes." Katie flirted with the idea of telling the biggest lie she'd ever told, but besides the fact that nothing big enough came to mind, she was reluctant to do so in front of Bailey.

"And how far have you come already?"

"From New York City."

"All that way! Just the two of you?" Lorena's green eyes turned a shade darker, and Katie was certain she hadn't imagined it.

"And this is only the halfway point. We're heading for Montana."

"By train?"

"No. I have a small wagon. I'm a photographer. And the trip is taking much longer than either of us ever imagined." Katie forced a bashful smile for Lorena's benefit.

"I suppose it would if you were traveling by wagon. A small wagon, you say?" Lorena's lovely smile appeared frozen in place.

"Yes," Katie said, warming to her subject. "We try to make the best of the close quarters, but it isn't always easy. Spence is so tall, you know."

"As I do recall . . ." Lorena left the sentence unfinished.

"And when it pours rain, well, we have no alternative but to take shelter inside since the wagon seat doesn't really have much protection over it. Of course, in the past few weeks there haven't been all that many thunderstorms."

The picture Katie painted was absolutely absurd and couldn't be further from the truth, but nobody knew that for certain except her. And Spence.

By now Lorena was livid, her pale face a lightly mottled red. Words seemed to escape her, and that was when Bailey stepped back into the conversation.

"Well, ladies, I hate to interrupt, but the morning is fast slipping into the afternoon." Bailey rose from her seat.

"My goodness, you're right. Miss Hetty will be wondering where I've been." Katie rose, too, and both women waited for Lorena to do the same.

But Lorena didn't budge.

"I have some private business to discuss with you, Bailey, so I'll just wait while you show Katie out."

Being dismissed with such blatant rudeness made Katie want to jump on the perfect Miss Lorena and pull her hair out by the roots. But before she could make a move, Bailey had her by the arm, gently steering her toward the front door.

"Come back and see me again, Katie," she said, her voice hushed, "before you leave. I have more to tell you. Don't let Lorena upset you. She isn't worth it."

Unable to talk, Katie nodded. Then Bailey surprised her by giving her a warm hug.

As Katie walked down the steps she heard the door close behind her. A strange emptiness filled her that she could neither explain nor understand, and it wasn't just Lorena's presence or her words that had brought it on. She was certain that somehow her relationship with Spence fit into the picture just as strongly. Perhaps she was as young and naive as Lorena suggested, especially when she'd put so much thought and feeling into that one moment when Spence had wrapped her in his arms and kissed her. How many times had he done the same with Lorena? And would he do it again? If Lorena had anything to say about the matter, he would do more than that. Her intentions were quite clear.

With a shake of her head to dispel the unwanted picture, Katie increased the length of her steps, wishing she'd left the dress on her bed and worn the britches instead. Tangled skirts forced her to slow down, but her thoughts raced ahead.

Foolish, foolish young woman, she told herself. Add inexperienced to that, she chided silently, and that's Katie O'Rourke to be sure! She needed to remember the reason for this journey, and it wasn't to be wooed by Spence McCord. No, the reason was to take pictures of real people just being themselves, like Miss Hetty and the Ladies Aid Society. She had grand goals that she would not set aside for any man, especially Spence. What was she thinking of anyway? One little old kiss had her head spinning unlikely thoughts, unwanted thoughts. There was no room in her life for such things, and she needed to remember that.

So she focused on the meeting at Miss Hetty's boardinghouse, and put behind her the unfortunate encounter of the morning. It had been unfortunate, not just for herself but for Bailey as well. It had also been embarrassing. She had looked like such a fool, and Lorena wasn't totally to blame for that. For that reason alone, she wouldn't be going back to Bailey's.

Chapter Eleven

Spence waited in the green room at Bailey's. The wall clock said Crandall was fifteen minutes late. Seated in one of the large wingback chairs, he tried to relax, hoping that Crandall's tardiness wasn't a bad sign. Tim had insisted that they would do better if they had a backer to increase their holdings. Spence hadn't been so sure, and now he wondered why he'd ever let Tim talk him into this meeting in the first place.

The door opened and Bailey entered the room, lovely as ever in a green silk dress.

"Don't worry," she said, "he'll be here. It's part of his game to make the other party wait, but don't tell him I told you."

Spence nodded, tempted to call it off anyway.

"But I didn't come in here to give away secrets," she went on. "Well, not that kind. I just wanted to tell you Lorena was here this morning. Right after Katie arrived."

That got his attention, and Crandall suddenly became a secondary problem.

"What was Katie doing here?" He couldn't hold back the irritation that surged through him. He had made it as clear as he knew how that she was not to come back to Bailey's.

"She just came to visit with me and to ask a few questions about how I knew Tim. We had a very enjoyable time. That is, until Lorena walked in and practically stampeded poor Katie."

"She had no business being here," he replied.

"Who? Lorena or Katie?"

He sent her a sharp glance. "I don't care what Lorena does. That's none of my business and hasn't been for a long time."

Bailey sat down opposite Spence and leaned toward him. "That's not the impression she wanted to give Katie," she said softly. She took a sealed envelope from her pocket and handed it to him. "Give this to Katie for me."

Before he could reply, the door opened and Crandall walked in.

Rising from her seat, Bailey whispered to Spence, "Watch out for Lorena." Then she breezed from the room with the words, "Good day, gentlemen."

"Sorry I'm late," Crandall said, his voice brusque in an attempt to control the situation.

Spence tucked Bailey's letter inside his shirt, where it lay as a painful reminder of the past and a foreshadowing of the future. Why had Lorena shown up in St. Louis at the same time that he and Katie had? He'd hoped to never cross paths with her again.

"I've thought this idea over very carefully and I believe that we can come to an agreement. From everything I've seen, it appears as though the ranch in Colorado was successful. Your records are well kept and up to date without any unusual problems. So it seems we have only to agree on the terms."

For the better part of two hours they discussed terms

and finally came to an agreement that Spence was sure Tim would approve. He felt certain it was the best they could expect to do. After shaking hands on the deal, both men departed.

Spence had to wire Tim to let him know the deal was done; he'd explain the details later. At the hotel, the clerk told him that a woman waited for him in his room. Taking the steps two at a time, he hoped it was Katie. With the weight of the business out of the way, he was anxious to be on the road and planned to leave early in the morning. But when he opened the door, he found Lorena seated on the edge of his bed.

"Where have you been?" she asked, posing and pouting as he'd seen her do a thousand times. "And close the door, please. This is a private conversation."

He closed the door.

With every graceful move planned to perfection, she rose and walked toward him. "It's been far too long, Spence." She reached one slender finger toward the button at the top of his shirt, teasing it but nothing more. "How have you been?"

"Getting by just fine," he replied, wondering how it was that she hadn't changed at all in the years since he'd last seen her and he'd changed so much.

"That's more than I can say." She slid her finger down to the next button.

With each move, he was reminded of other such evenings in her room at Bailey's when he was more agreeable to her suggestions and had a few of his own.

Times had been easier then. The war was over, he and Tim had survived, though just barely, and the future had looked bright as they headed west. Tim had the dreams and the ability to charm while Spence was more serious and interested only in good hard work. Together they knew they could make a go of anything Tim put his mind to, and Tim's mind was set on ranching. Being a Southerner by birth and a Texan by choice,

Spence knew plenty about working cattle, but neither of them had the money to begin an operation of any size. That's where Bailey and Lorena figured into the scheme of things, or at least Bailey. Lorena just sort of went along for whatever she could get for herself. And it was apparent she still had the same ideas.

"I haven't been getting by at all, Spence," she said, still pouting.

Her clothes were cut of good cloth and probably in the latest fashion, although he was no judge of that. She certainly didn't seem to be down on her luck.

"Aren't you going to ask me what's wrong?" She held his gaze with her own.

"What's wrong, Lorena?" he asked dutifully.

"Well, I'm so very lonely and I've thought about you constantly for months." She paused. "Haven't you thought about me at all?"

He had. More than he cared to admit, but that was a long time ago. Since then he'd come to see what a fool he'd been and what a schemer she really was. He might have been a fool once but never again.

"Spence? You aren't going to hold it against me, are you? I mean, that awful thing I did to you was unforgivable, but all I can say is, I was young and desperate to get out of Bailey's. I didn't want to stay in that kind of life." She let her hands fall to her sides and stepped back, putting a little distance between them.

"Can't you understand that?"

He could. Now.

"I had to get out. And Charles was such a nice man. He promised me money and a life of parties in the best circles. I'd be free!"

Things he could never have given her, he knew. Things he had wanted no part of, really.

"And life has been great. I mean, I've been accepted by people who would never have said good day to me if they knew my past. And I've never wanted for anything, not anything."

Suddenly she resembled a child to him. Not a spoiled child who threw tantrums when she couldn't get her way, although she'd done that, too, but a child who didn't understand the point of giving, only taking.

"Lorena, you shouldn't have come here," he said.

Moving toward him once more, she placed both hands on his chest. "I've had everything but you," she whispered. "Spence, I was such a fool to let you go."

"I didn't come as part of the same package as Charles. You had a choice to make and you made it."

Her face brightened. "But that's why I'm here now. I'm free again! We can be together. Just like I always wanted. I'm a widow, Spence. I'm free."

He put his hands on her shoulders to set her away from him. It was time to put a stop to her ideas and leave the past where it belonged.

With a small, strangled cry she flung her arms around his neck, gripping him tightly and pressing her lips to his. With her body molded against him, the scent of her perfume filled his nostrils, but the fire and passion that had once been there, ignited by a simple touch, no longer existed.

Spence reached around to pry her hands loose and bring them to her sides.

"Lorena, it's over."

"Don't say that!"

"I mean it."

"I won't listen! I'll make you want me. You never could resist me before, I'll make it happen again."

She yanked the pins from her hat and tossed it aside, then struggled with the buttons at the top of her dress, but he stilled her hands with his own.

"We can't go back."

"I can! And you'll want to, just give me another

chance, Spence. Please." Large tears welled in her eyes. "Please."

He felt like a heel, worse than a heel, but he couldn't give in to her pleas because he no longer felt anything for her.

"You'd better go," he said quietly.

"Go?" she replied. "Go where?" She backed up until she hit the bed. "I came here to find you. When I saw you with that girl on the boat, I asked the captain what your destination was. Then I knew. You would be going to Bailey's, so I planned to meet you there." When he didn't respond, she went on, "Do you know how difficult it was to go back there? Do you know how awful it felt to walk through that door? I degraded myself just so I could see you again!"

"Lorena, I didn't ask you to do that. I'm sorry you came back. You shouldn't have."

"Sorry!" she shouted. "Sorry? I only wanted to tell you that I love you and that I've always loved you. I thought you loved me, too."

"I did." But she'd chosen another man, actually played him against another man just to make him jealous. And the one with the broken heart had been Spence. But that was all over now.

"You will again," she pleaded. "Just give me another chance."

"Another chance to what? Set me up? Play me for a fool?" He shook his head. "Listen to me. It's over."

Lorena stood there for a long moment, taking it all in, calculating her chances. Then, with her eyes burning green fire, she snatched her hat from the bed and turned on him.

"You'll rue this day, Spence McCord. Mark my words." Her eyes flashed a warning, and a promise to carry out the threat. "And it won't be long either." On her way to the door she skirted him as though he were cow dung, then slammed the door behind her.

Her threats didn't worry Spence. She had no real power over him, not anymore. As a matter of fact, he felt as though a great weight had been lifted from him. Now there were no regrets to haul around, to sort through, or even to wonder about. Lorena had set him free, though that had been the furthest thing from her mind.

The first thing he intended to do was get a hearty meal, then he'd go to Miss Hetty's and tell Katie to get ready to leave in the morning. They'd be heading for Montana just as fast as her little wagon could carry them.

Chapter Twelve

Katie set up her camera, glad for the sunny skies that sent direct sunlight into the dining room. Miss Hetty had been set on having the parlor for the background, but when Katie pointed out that the china cabinet would make a lovely backdrop, she'd consented.

Being behind the camera once more reminded Katie of who she was and what she wanted from life. This was where she was comfortable and in control; this was where she belonged. There were no doubts to plague her, no misgivings, no regrets. And while the prospect of sitting through a boring Ladies Aid Society meeting didn't exactly send a thrill of excitement through her, she was doing what she'd set out to do: photographing real people where they lived. As far as the meeting itself was concerned, it was simply a means to occupy herself and hopefully keep her mind off the fiasco of the morning at Bailey's.

The ladies had already arrived and were either seated or standing around the table waiting for Katie. Miss

Lavinia Boardman, being much stouter than Katie had expected, was seated in the center chair with Mrs. Gladys Pepper on one side and Mrs. Esther Stilts on the other. Miss Hetty stood behind them and alongside a very tall, very thin Mary Alice Brown.

"This will certainly be a wonderful picture to show my colonel when he comes back from the war," Mary Alice said.

Through the lens Katie saw four sets of eyes roll heavenward at Mary Alice's words, and someone whispered loudly, "I declare!"

"Well, it will," Mary Alice insisted.

Katie squelched a smile as she came out from under the cloth. "I believe we're ready, ladies. Just hold perfectly still and I'll be right back with the plate."

As Katie hurried out the door, she overheard someone say, "She said don't move, Lavinia."

"I can't help it. This chair is hard as a rock."

Katie concentrated on the work at hand, not allowing her mind to worry whether Lavinia had moved or Mary Alice had talked. The baths were already set up before she'd positioned everyone, so she only had to wait until the collodion flowed properly before returning to the house.

"All right, ladies," Katie said as she ducked beneath the cloth again. "Hold tight for just a minute . . ."

Katie exposed the plate, wishing someone would have at least smiled. As it was, the picture was taken and five matronly women sat or stood stiffly, perpetually looking distressed. When the picture was finished and toned, Katie gave it to Miss Hetty, who had to sit down because the momentous occasion was simply too much for her.

After that, Katie carried her camera back to her wagon, where she carefully stowed it away, then cleaned the basins and finished tidying up. The familiar routine had a soothing effect on her, and she wished

151

she could just stay in the wagon working on sorting her plates or some other menial task for the duration of the meeting. But knowing that would be rude, she sighed and returned to the house.

Tiny sandwiches were served on china plates along with a number of other interesting delicacies that Katie had never seen or tasted before. Each lady contributed something, so there was plenty of discussion on the type of cooking as well as the ingredients. This was foreign territory to Katie, so she concentrated on the different personalities of the cooks rather than their cooking expertise.

Soon the cherry tarts were brought out by Miss Lavinia and the herb tea was brewed in the Boston teapot on the dining room table. Miss Lavinia and Miss Hetty bustled back and forth between the kitchen and the dining room, bringing silverware, teacups and saucers while the rest sat at the table to be waited upon.

"Did you know," Gladys Pepper said to Katie from across the table, "that I once had the opportunity to visit with President Ulysses S. Grant?"

"He wasn't president when you saw him, Gladys," Lavinia called from the kitchen.

"Well, he *became* president and that's what counts," Gladys called back.

"That must have been a very special moment for you," Katie said, trying to avert all-out warfare.

"Oh, it was," said Gladys. "My father knew him quite well before the war."

"That hardly counts," said Esther, who had said little up to this point. "And besides, we all know he was quite the drinker and womanizer."

"Esther is the leader of the temperance society," Miss Hetty offered. "We're very honored to have her in our group."

Esther smiled at the benediction placed upon her.

"Have one of my cherry tarts, Katie," Miss Lavinia insisted.

Katie bit into the fruit and crust, her eyes going wide with appreciation. Pleased, Lavinia placed another on her plate.

"I do not know why you won't give me that recipe, Lavinia Boardman," Miss Hetty said.

"I will just as soon as you give me the recipe for that tea."

A pleasant hum of friendly chatter surrounded the table as the women all sat and enjoyed their "meeting," which Katie could tell was nothing more than an opportunity to catch up on the latest gossip. Twilight descended but nobody seemed interested in going home. Sitting still was foreign to Katie's nature, so she joined Miss Hetty and Lavinia in the serving and cleaning-up process. Her hopes of forgetting about Lorena's remarks had quickly dwindled to nothing as the conversation around the table turned to matters she knew nothing about, leaving her once more to the feelings of regret and confusion.

A momentary lull in the conversation served as the perfect introduction to the strange scratching noises that Katie had listened to all night long.

"What was that?" Mary Alice asked, frowning and tilting her head.

"What? I didn't hear anything," Miss Hetty replied. But the stricken look on her face belied her words. Quickly rising from her seat, she picked up the teapot. "More tea, anyone? I'll heat the water to brew another pot." Within seconds she was in the kitchen, dropping sticks of wood into the stove and clattering the lids and ashpan door.

"Here, I'll help with that," Katie offered, trying to take the lid lifter from Miss Hetty. But Miss Hetty clung to the metal object, refusing to give it up, and banged the lid into place.

"I'll have some," Lavinia called to her above the din even though she'd already had four cups.

"It's apparent that you're as addicted to that tea as some men are to drink," Esther pointed out.

"Maybe there's a reason for that," Lavinia said. "But Hetty won't tell us what's in it, so how will we ever know?"

Mary Alice leaned over conspiratorially and whispered in Katie's ear as Katie reached for a cup and saucer. "She thinks it contains a love potion. If it did, Hetty would have married a long time ago." Mary Alice sat up straight and nodded wisely at Katie.

Katie smiled, thinking that Mary Alice wasn't as far gone as they all supposed.

Soon Miss Hetty returned with a quickly steeped pot of tea, exclaiming loudly, "Here we are!" Her face was flushed from all the exertion in the kitchen.

"Don't shout, for heaven's sake," Lavinia said. "We aren't deaf yet."

"I wasn't shouting," Miss Hetty replied more quietly. Another momentary lull allowed them to hear a squeak just as a dark object darted over their heads.

"Good Lord in heaven! What was that?" cried Gladys.

"I didn't see anything," Miss Hetty declared weakly.

But Katie did. And soon everyone else saw it, too.

"It's a bat!" shrieked Lavinia as she pulled her apron over her head.

Miss Hetty went white as a ghost before diving beneath the table. China cups and saucers rolled across the teetering table as the other women tried valiantly to move their chairs and escape the numerous darting bats, which had suddenly come from nowhere to join the first one.

Katie slid to the floor and found a niche to hide in between the cabinet and a door. With her arms over her head, she joined the others in robust shrieking. One brave glance told her the others were also busy scrambling for safety.

Esther alternately crawled then sprawled her way across the floor until she could push open the screen door on the porch, while Mary Alice headed for the parlor on all fours. Miss Lavinia tried unsuccessfully to fit her ample body beneath the table alongside Miss Hetty, but soon gave up the idea and crawled to the kitchen, where she wedged herself in a corner, flapping her apron and screaming at the top of her lungs.

Gladys, who had once visited with President Ulysses S. Grant, simply hiked up her skirts and ran from the house. Her shrieks could be heard for more than a block. Not long after her departure, Katie heard the front door slam and was certain that Esther and Mary Alice had followed suit.

"Open the door!" Miss Hetty cried over the still shrieking Miss Lavinia, who cowered in the kitchen. "Open the door and they'll go out!"

Frightened but desperate, Katie dashed across the floor on hands and knees, pushed the door wide, then crawled behind it where she safely held it open. Just as Miss Hetty had said, the bats zigged and zagged their way into the deepening twilight. From inside the house came the sound of Miss Lavinia wheezing and gasping with relief.

"They're gone," Miss Hetty said, her voice trembling. "For now."

Katie and the other two stayed where they were, shaking. Katie still gripped the screen door, which she couldn't seem to let loose of.

"Hetty Parker, I could kill you," Lavinia said, her voice quavery and distant.

Katie waited to hear Miss Hetty's reply, but the only sound she heard was soft crying.

"Oh, Hetty," Lavinia groaned sympathetically. "It's all right. Nobody was hurt. Don't cry."

Katie came out of her place of safety and went inside to help Lavinia struggle to her feet. Then both of them tended to Miss Hetty, who still crouched beneath the table in a tiny crumpled ball.

"They'll never forgive me," she cried. "I'll never be able to hold my head up in polite society again."

"Oh, for heaven's sake, Hetty," admonished Lavinia. "It was a frightful thing, certainly, but hardly your fault. There, there, now. Stop your crying and let us help you up."

"Oh, Lavinia," she said, sniffling. "I'll be the talk of the neighborhood. And I'll never get any boarders now."

"Talk never lasts, you know that as well as I do."

"Yes, it does. We do it all the time."

"Well," Katie said, hoping to add some humor to the situation, "I, for one, will never forget it. I only wish there were some way to capture it all on glass plates."

Lavinia righted a chair for Hetty and one for herself. After a long sigh of relief, she chuckled. "I had no idea Gladys could run like that."

"I'm surprised you could even see her the way you were flapping that apron over your head," Miss Hetty replied, wiping her nose on her own apron. "What a healthy set of lungs you have, Lavinia."

"And did you see Esther crawling across the floor?" Lavinia's chuckles erupted into full-fledged laughter.

"I did," said Miss Hetty, beginning to smile. "I believe she tore the bodice loose from her dress."

That brought a torrent of laughter from Lavinia, and Katie joined in. She was right, the entire scene had been absolutely hilarious.

"And poor Mary Alice," whooped Lavinia.

"She'll . . ." Miss Hetty wiped the tears of laughter from her eyes. "She'll never be the same!"

All three women collapsed into uncontrollable gales of laughter, holding their sides, wiping their eyes and nearly falling off their chairs.

"Oh my, oh my!" Lavinia said, finally gaining control of herself. "I can't remember when I've had such fun. How about you, Katie?"

"Oh, oh!" Katie tried to fight off the vivid picture of Gladys's skirts higher than her knees. "No, I—really—can't remember—anything like this!"

Miss Hetty sniffled unabashedly in an attempt to draw air into her lungs. "We shouldn't make such fun of them." But a siege of giggling overtook her.

"You're right," Lavinia agreed. "But they're probably doing the same."

"I suppose so."

All three sighed simultaneously.

"I'm wore to a frazzle," Lavinia said. "Is there any tea left, by chance?"

Miss Hetty gave her a sideways glance. "Honestly, Lavinia. It's nothing but herb tea from my own garden."

"I use a touch of molasses in my cherry tarts and day-old cream in the crust," Lavinia offered.

"And I use hops," Miss Hetty confessed.

"Hops!" chortled Lavinia. "Lord in heaven! Don't tell Esther!"

"Do you still want some tea?"

"A tall glass, if you please," Lavinia replied. Then turning to Katie, she asked, "How about you?"

"Most definitely." And with a contented sigh she realized that the worries of earlier had slipped away, replaced by the pleasant camaraderie of her present companions.

Later that night, when the broken bits of heirlooms had been picked up and the house had been restored to its normal order, Katie was summoned to the side porch by Lavinia.

"You have a gentleman caller, my dear," she said to Katie, then added in a whisper, "Should I make him some tea?"

Smiling, Katie replied, "No, that won't be necessary."

"Lavinia!" Miss Hetty reprimanded. "The gentleman is her brother."

"Oh! Forgive me." Both women quickly returned to the kitchen to discuss recipes.

Katie pushed open the screen door to find Spence standing in the deepening shadows.

"Spence?" For a moment she was filled with dread at the thought that he might have found out about her visit with Bailey, and Lorena, too. She didn't want him to suspect she'd been spying on him, or rather on his past, even though that's exactly what she'd done. But more than that, she didn't want to discuss any of it with him. As much as she hated to admit it, and foolish though it was, she still felt a little heartsore.

Stepping up onto the tiny porch, Spence said, "I just wanted to stop by and tell you to be ready to leave in the morning."

"You've finished your business?" Her spirits lifted, almost soared.

"Yes, and there's no need to stay here any longer. Tim's going to need help, and I have to get some work done on my place before winter. It's going to be a long trip."

Katie sat in one of the chairs. The night air was cool on her cheeks. It seemed they were back to their old conflict of hurry versus traveling slow, but somehow that conflict had lost its appeal. Not that she was any more willing than before to dash across the country, but some of her enthusiasm had dwindled and she wasn't at all sure why.

"Yes, it's going to be a long trip," she replied.

Spence propped one shoulder against a porch post as he stared down at her. "Do I hear a note of regret? Are you considering giving up the idea of wagon travel?"

With a quick lift of her head, she stared back at him. "No! Not at all. It's by wagon or nothing."

"Wagon or nothing," he repeated.

"That's right," she stated, rising to her feet. With only inches between them she could smell the clean, soapy scent that told her he'd shaved recently. Would he go back to Bailey's now that the worry of the business deal was over and he had some free time on his hands?

"Well, then I guess it's by wagon."

"Okay. Good," she replied lamely. If he went back to Bailey's for a good time, she knew she'd never be able to stand it. She also knew she had no right to tell him not to go.

"In the morning we'll get a packhorse and a water barrel," he said.

"Couldn't we do that tonight?" she asked hopefully. "I could go with you."

"It's late. I'd rather inspect the animal by daylight to be sure he's sound. And the barrel, too, for that matter."

"Of course."

"Is there anything you're going to need? We won't be in a city as large as this for quite a long time."

"Plates," she said. "I'll need more glass plates for the camera. And I should stop and see about the mail. I'm sure Erin and Mrs. O'Shea have sent a dozen or more letters."

"We can do that right after we get the barrel and the horse. What about supplies?"

"You mean for cooking?"

"Never mind," he said with a grin.

"We agreed there'd be no beans," she reminded him, smiling.

"Unless we come across Indians. We won't be able to build a fire if that's the case, and we'll have no choice."

"Indians!" But she knew he was teasing and poked a finger at his shirt. "You're in a good mood," she said.

"I guess crossing the muddy river and heading west

does that to me," he said. "There's not another feeling like it."

She thought about that for a moment. When they'd ferried across she'd felt the excitement, but since then she'd let other things cloud her sense of adventure.

"How early should we leave?" she asked, trying to pump a little enthusiasm into her words.

"I'll be here just after daybreak with the horses. That way we won't lose much time."

"I'll be ready."

They stood thoughtfully in silence for a while.

"Has everything been all right for you here?" he finally asked with a nod toward Miss Hetty's door.

"Oh, yes. Actually, it's been fun."

Silence.

"Well, I'll be going." He turned to leave, but stopped. Pulling a paper from inside his shirt, he handed it to her. "I almost forgot to give this to you. It's from Bailey."

She gasped involuntarily.

"I'll be back in the morning. Good night." And he walked into the night.

Katie dropped onto a chair. He'd known all along that she'd been at Bailey's! Had Bailey told him about her questions? About the awful meeting with Lorena? She squeezed back into the chair, embarrassed. Folding the letter, she stuffed it into the bodice of her dress. She didn't want to read it; she couldn't read it no matter what it said. She just wanted to forget the whole episode. Forever. The only thing she wanted now was for morning to come so they could leave St. Louis.

Katie crawled into bed and tried to think about the happy parts of the day, which brought to mind the bats in Miss Hetty's house. What had started as a boring meeting had turned into a riot of good fun. She would never forget Miss Lavinia and the tea, nor would she forget the sight of the proper Mrs. Gladys Pepper strutting out the door like a high-stepping chicken.

Poor Miss Hetty. How she regretted the incident with all its confusion and embarrassment. And what torture it must have been for her, living with the fear that everyone would find out about the bats in her walls. Well, her secret was out now and her friends knew the truth, and likely so would half of St. Louis before another sundown. Katie hoped for Miss Hetty's sake that they wouldn't hold it against her, that instead they would understand her fear of reproach, and somehow she was sure that they would. True friends would never forsake each other in their time of need, and Miss Hetty had found that Lavinia Boardman was a true friend indeed.

Katie thought about her own regrets over prying into Spence's past, and especially for the confusion it had awakened within her. Burrowing her face into the pillow, she wondered if she and Spence might become friends by the end of their journey, like Miss Hetty and Lavinia. Or did she want more than friendship?

Below her open window, Katie heard a knock at the side door. She hoped it might be Spence again, but the voice that answered Miss Hetty was feminine. Very feminine. Katie jumped from her bed and ran across the floor to listen to their conversation.

"I'm really sorry to bother you so late," Lorena said. "But if you have a room available I'd be ever so grateful."

"Why, yes, I have one room left."

"Oh, thank goodness. I just hate hotels."

Katie crept back to the clean, cool sheets.

A scratching, squeaking noise coming from inside the nearby walls caught her attention. With goosebumps layering the skin along her neck, Katie pulled the sheet over her head.

"Enjoy your stay, Lorena," she said softly, a wicked smile on her lips.

Before dawn the next morning, Katie dressed quietly, pulling on her britches, buttoning her shirt and carrying her shoes in her hands. Creeping down the stairs, she did her best to avoid the noisiest creaks, alternately hugging then sliding along the wall. In the kitchen she set down her valise, put some money under the teapot and helped herself to a few leftover cherry tarts and finger sandwiches. Then she slipped quietly out the door.

A layer of morning fog hovered over the dew-covered ground, dulling the landscape in the gray light. She listened for the sound of horses' hooves in hopes that Spence would not be late, but she heard nothing other than a few birds waking up in song. Sitting on the top step, she pulled on her shoes, taking her time in buttoning each hole. Then she listened again. This time she heard the clopping against the cobblestones and knew it had to be him.

Soon he rode into the yard with the two horses in tow.

Was it the excitement of getting back on the road that made her heart flutter like that?

"I didn't think you'd be out here ready to go," he said as he rode toward the back of the house where the wagon waited.

"Shh! Don't wake Miss Hetty," she whispered, but it was Lorena that she hoped not to wake. He nodded and set to work harnessing the horses, and it seemed to Katie that he was taking longer than he'd ever taken before.

"Is there something I can do to help?" she asked.

He gave her a puzzled glance, then went back to work without answering. Restless, Katie stashed her valise in the wagon, ate a finger sandwich that she'd intended to give to Spence, then stood around and waited.

At last two of the horses were hooked to the wagon and the other one was tied to the tailgate. Katie climbed up onto the seat and perched eagerly forward.

"Ready, huh?" Spence asked.

"Ready isn't the word for it," she replied as they rolled down the street. Katie's heart still fluttered in her chest, and this time she was sure it was because they were leaving.

A strong sense of freedom filled her with every step of the horses. One glance at Spence, seeing his familiar long legs slightly cramped in their confined space, his broad shoulders leaning forward, and she knew that he, too, seemed more eager than usual to be on the road.

As they passed the front of Miss Hetty's house, Katie turned around just in time to see the curtain slide back into place at Lorena's window.

But that didn't matter now, she told herself. They were leaving St. Louis and would never cross paths with Lorena again. And yet, a strange sense of foreboding sent a chill down her neck, and she quickly turned away from the neat little house where bats roosted in the walls, unseen and frightening.

Chapter Thirteen

Spence and Katie had been on the road for a week, traveling much the way they had been before reaching St. Louis. Only now the towns were farther apart and many of their nights were spent camped near a river or creek whenever possible, and always alone. During those times, Spence slept on his bedroll beneath the wagon, where both were conscious of the other's presence, so near and yet separate.

The daytime hours were long, hot and dusty. And quiet. Even though they had shared many of the same experiences over the days, weeks and now approaching the middle of the second month, neither broke the uncomfortable silence that had settled upon them in the past week.

Sitting on her side of the small wagon seat where the lowering sun glared at her, Katie once again opened the first of Erin's seven letters. Mrs. O'Shea had sent ten. Wasting no time, Erin always quickly dispensed with the state of her family's health and happiness, then moved right on to the heart and reason for the letters. By the time Katie had read the seventh one, she'd been told many times over just how careless and foolish a woman she was. Mrs. O'Shea wasn't nearly as kind or as tactful, ending with a promise, or was it a threat, to take a train west and personally fetch her home again where she belonged.

For the first time since leaving New York, Katie's heart sank as she wondered whether she might have made a mistake, and Mrs. O'Shea was right. Perhaps she should return to New York with her. Perhaps she should never have left. She admitted that life would have continued with her being dissatisfied, but at least she wouldn't have been confused. Although she had expected to encounter circumstances that might re-shape her thinking, she hadn't anticipated that her emotions would be involved. And certainly not with Spence McCord.

Added to all of this was the letter from Bailey, which lay at the bottom of her valise tucked beneath her undergarments, still unopened. Deep in her heart she knew she did not want to read it; she did not want to hear more about Lorena, which only served as a reminder that Katie was naive and inexperienced where men were concerned.

Replacing the letters from home inside the small leather pouch she'd purchased before leaving St. Louis, she stroked the smooth yet grainy surface as it lay in her lap. A long time would pass before they reached Montana, and undoubtedly more letters would be waiting. In the meantime, she would reread these whenever a wave of homesickness came over her.

Glancing across the breadth of unending landscape, Katie wished for a town or, at least, a small homestead to come into view. Any kind of a place would do as long as they might share a meal and conversation so she and Spence wouldn't have to spend another silent evening together. But there was nothing to indicate that anybody lived nearby, not even a slight plume of smoke. Only a copse of trees in the distance offered wood for a fire and the likelihood of a stream. Another long, quiet evening loomed before Katie.

By the time they reached the stream, the sun was ready to slip over the horizon and cast them into night. Katie helped gather dead wood, then Spence built a fire. A spit-roasted rabbit and biscuits made up their supper. Katie's only contribution to the meal was the coffee, since Spence had meant what he'd said about being in charge of the grub.

"How long before we reach a town?" Katie asked, needing to say something. She sat on a rock holding her cup. Unfamiliar crawling and slithering creatures had forced her to give up the habit of sitting on the ground.

"Towns are few and far between on the prairies. An occasional soddie is all we're likely to come across for a while."

"Oh."

Katie sat still, quietly listening. Night sounds out in the open weren't nearly as raucous as those in the east. A deeper silence existed this far from civilization, which wasn't exactly unpleasant, just lonely.

Katie retrieved her pen and paper from the wagon. In order to pass the time, she'd decided to keep a diary. Every evening she'd sit before the campfire and write about the events of the day, and if it was uneventful, she'd describe the scenery.

"By the time we reach a place to mail all those letters," Spence began, "you'll have a trainload."

"These aren't letters," she replied without looking up. "It's a journal."

When he didn't reply, Katie figured he was either being polite or he was uninterested, probably the later.

"I try to write about all the exciting things that have

happened since St. Louis," she went on, still not looking up.

"I can't imagine you've got much to say, then."

Now she looked at him. This was the longest conversation they'd had in a week. "I'm seeing it all through eyes that have never seen these things before, so even if nothing adventurous happens it's still interesting to me. As a photographer if nothing else." She'd added the last as a reminder to herself of who she really was. Out here with him on the lonely expanse of prairie it was easy to forget. In contrast, it was too easy to remember that kiss even though nearly two weeks had passed.

Spence listened to Katie, trying to maintain the distance he'd worked so hard to achieve for the last week. It was tempting to let the sound of her voice draw him to her. Too tempting.

He had felt so free and unburdened that day when Lorena had been in his room and he'd told her it was over. He'd been so sure he wouldn't want to get entangled with another woman ever again, so sure that he'd be careful not to get close enough to lose his heart for a second time. But after two days back on the road with Katie and her familiar smile, her bouncing walk and burnished mop of curls, he'd realized just how much danger he was really in, and just how deep those forbidden waters were. So he'd forced himself to remember that he was Tim's partner and he'd been coerced into paying an old debt, and most of all, he had to remember that she was Tim's sister. But none of it was easy, especially when her eagerness for life spilled over into her words and actions. That was when he had his most difficult times, because he now shared that eagerness. Being near Katie had done that for him.

So when Katie turned to him with her face so solemn and her eyes shielding her real thoughts, he was hard-pressed to keep that necessary distance.

"You write every night," he said simply.

"I have to. There's always something new to write about." She bent her head over her ink bottle, which she'd positioned on a nearby rock. Then she put her pen to paper, scratching her way across the sheet.

He knew she'd spend fifteen minutes or so at it before she folded everything up and headed back to the wagon. Usually he let her go without a word. Tonight he wanted to hear her voice, to keep her near and watch her face in the glow of the flickering firelight. It was a temptation he ought to resist, but he couldn't.

"I hadn't noticed you writing in a journal before St. Louis," he said.

"I guess I was too busy," she said, folding her papers and putting the stopper in her ink bottle.

"Busy?"

"Well, there were so many people to meet, so much to talk about and . . . just busy," she ended lamely.

He nodded, accepting her answer, and continued to watch her. "You haven't asked me very much about what sort of places might be ahead of us."

"Would it do me any good?" she replied honestly. "You've hardly said ten words since we left St. Louis. And frankly"—she rose from her seat—"I'm surprised you're talking to me now."

"I've had a lot on my mind."

"I'll just bet you have," she said and headed for her wagon.

"Wait," he called before she'd taken three steps. "I'd like to talk now."

"Well, I guess I'm fresh out of words. Used them up in my journal, I suppose. Good night." And she marched off into the darkness.

Spence continued to sit, staring into the campfire as it burned down to embers. He smiled to himself, wondering if she realized that she had just put the distance between them that he couldn't, and feeling grateful that she had.

Katie climbed into the wagon and drew the curtain closed. In the darkness she dressed for bed, then lit a candle so she could see to pull out the feather tick. Once she was situated, she dug into the bottom of her valise and pulled out Bailey's letter. With a thumping heart she carefully tore it open.

Dear Katie,

I want to apologize for this morning, and Lorena's behavior. I hope you'll come and visit me again before you leave St. Louis, but if you don't I want you to know that the past is always better if forgotten. And Lorena needs to forget. Spence has, I'm sure.
Bailey

Katie wondered just what sort of past Lorena needed to forget, and how Bailey could be so sure that Spence had, indeed, forgotten.

She didn't want to think about Lorena and Spence together, in the past or in the future, but the picture was firmly planted in her mind. She wasn't even sure what Lorena had said that had given her such a vivid picture, but it was there.

Katie blew out the candle and lay in the dark. She could plainly hear the sounds of Spence putting out the campfire, then unrolling his bedroll. After a few thumps and bumps, she knew he was settled directly beneath her. The cool night air pressed in through the canvas, and she pulled her blanket to her chin and snuggled deeper into the thin feather tick. The springs on the wagon creaked with her every move. At last all was quiet.

"Good night, Katie," Spence said, his voice slightly muffled by the floorboards.

Surprised, she lay speechless, her eyes wide. Then she replied softly, "Good night."

169

After that, a warm, secure feeling overtook her just like when she used to hide in the depth of a feather bed during thunderstorms. It wasn't long until she was sound asleep.

The following morning Katie rose and dressed quickly. Today would be a better day, she could feel it in her bones. A good night's rest had made all the difference. Bending forward, she brushed her hair, then pinned it up, fluffing the curls around her face with her fingers. The pungent smell of woodsmoke drifted inside the wagon, and she heard the lid of the new Dutch oven clang closed. Hot biscuits would soon be ready.

Once outside, Katie retrieved the coffeepot from the side box that held their supplies. Spence had made some changes in the way they stored their necessities, which not only made it much more handy but freed up some of her interior space. A water barrel with a spigot had been lashed to the side, but Katie went to the creek to fill the pot. She understood the importance of conserving water.

"Good morning, Ethan. Good morning, Silas," she said to the horses as she passed by them. Katie now thought of them as friends, so she'd named them after the two kind men back East. The horses nickered in response, then returned to eating the grass beneath the trees where they were tied.

Having mastered the art of boiling coffee, Katie could almost do it blindfolded, and it was always delicious. In no time the air was filled with the aroma.

Spence handed her a plate filled with beans and biscuits.

"What's this?" she asked.

"Breakfast."

"But it's beans!"

"I know."

"I thought we agreed we wouldn't eat beans."

"No. We agreed that if you did the cooking we wouldn't eat beans. My limit is rabbit, biscuits and beans. Sorry." Spence sat on a rock with his plate in his hand, and scooped up his beans with a biscuit.

Katie watched. She knew their supplies included more than beans, and they had, in fact, eaten fried bacon and flapjacks other mornings.

"Go ahead and eat," he said. "It's going to be a long time before the noon meal and you'll likely get hungry if you don't."

"I'm not sure if I wouldn't rather be hungry," she replied as she pushed the thick mess around her plate with a spoon. "Did you put anything in it to at least flavor it?"

"Like what?"

"I don't know. Mrs. O'Shea always added bits of things from her garden."

"She cooked beans?" he asked, surprised.

"No. When she made soups and meat dishes." She really didn't think she could eat beans. "Why don't you try making soup?"

"Why don't you?" His look was challenging.

"Well, maybe I will. We have potatoes, and if you skin another rabbit we'll have meat."

"That'll be pretty sparse soup."

"It would be better than this," she said, dropping a spoonful onto her plate.

"Are you saying that you want to be in charge of the next meal?"

With a quick glance at him, she knew he'd tricked her into sharing the cooking, but if he was only going to cook beans she'd gladly be in charge.

"Yes," she said, accepting the challenge. "But no complaints if I sometimes burn it."

"No complaints."

Katie set aside the beans and ate two dry biscuits, which she washed down with two cups of coffee while she concentrated on trying to remember the ingredients she'd seen Mrs. O'Shea put together. Ingredients that turned into things like dumplings, beef stew and apple pies.

No, no, she told herself with a shake of her head; keep it simple. But she'd really enjoy a pot of beef stew with dumplings, and an apple pie, too.

In spite of the fact that she'd been tricked into cooking, Katie felt uplifted just having Spence speak to her once more. But more than that, he seemed interested in the things she had to say. If he'd had something pressing on his mind, it was apparent he'd settled the problem, or at least put it aside for a while. Whatever the reason, she was glad.

They loaded the packhorse with their supplies, then harnessed Ethan and Silas. With the Missouri River a day behind them, Spence said he thought it best to fill their barrel to the top. Crossing the prairies could mean long stretches without coming to a river. He had told her the general route they would take, but since she'd never been that way before it meant little to her. Her only clue was that they would head northwest to the Platte and follow it for a good long ways. There would be no major cities along the way, just an occasional small town and, she hoped, homesteads where she could photograph families.

After five hours of travel they finally came across a sod house, but if not for the smoke coming from the chimney Katie would never have seen it. It took only a little urging from her to get Spence to turn the horses south, and she suspected that the rumble in his stomach had something to do with it.

They pulled up near the front of the house where chickens roamed at will and two pigs stretched out in the hot sun. Before Spence or Katie could climb down, a dog appeared in the open doorway, growling. Behind the dog stood a woman, a gun resting in her arms.

"What can I do for you?" she called to them without stepping into the open.

"I'm a photographer," Katie called back. "I just wondered if I could take your photograph."

"I ain't got no money. I can't pay you," said the woman, but she pushed the dog aside and stepped into the sunlight.

"That's all right," Katie replied, smiling. "I'd rather make a trade."

"Trade?"

Katie jumped down from her seat and walked toward the sod house with Spence right behind her. Closer inspection of the soddie proved to Katie that it was indeed made of large squares of thick sod, and the dying grass that was still attached gave the house a hairy appearance.

"Yes. I'd be happy to take something in trade," Katie said. She guessed the woman to be younger than Mrs. O'Shea but not by very much.

"Like the Indians?" the woman asked.

Katie glanced at Spence, since she had no idea how the Indians conducted business. When Spence nodded, Katie in turn nodded at the woman.

"Well," the woman said, glancing behind her into the dark interior of her house, "I don't have much in the way of trade. I can offer you some dinner, but that wouldn't be a fair trade for you."

"I think it would," Katie replied.

"All right then, come in and make yourselves at home, Miss . . . ?"

"My name's Katie and this is Spence."

"Name's Ella. Come on in."

When they stepped inside they were surprised to find a man seated at the table drinking a cup of coffee. The dog growled and bared his teeth only to be rewarded by a boot and an oath.

"Dog ain't got no manners at all," said the man.

"This is my son Jed," Ella said. "He come in from the field to have a late dinner." She motioned Katie and Spence toward the table. "You folks sit down now. We don't get much company, you know."

Also in the darkness of the soddie there were a wooden work bench, a cabinet without doors and scant dishes inside, a fireplace unlike any she'd ever seen before and a cot against the opposite wall. A strange burnt smell permeated the air, one that she couldn't quite place. Then she saw bundles of grass stacked in a corner and guessed they were a source of fuel in a place that had no trees to speak of.

"You're not from anywheres around here, are you?" Jed asked Spence.

"No. We're headed up to Montana," Spence replied.

"That's a long spell of travelin'," Jed said. "I don't envy you goin' that far, although I hear it's mighty nice country up there. 'Cept for the Indians."

Katie raised her head in surprise. "Indians? Could we really be attacked by Indians? I thought all of that was over."

Spence opened his mouth to respond, but Jed interjected, "So they tell us, but all it takes is one renegade to lose your hair."

Katie gasped. "Hair?"

"That's right," Jed went on. "Ma and I have heard stories. Course, we ain't never met an Indian, but I reckon someday we will. The government just wants everyone to think they've got 'em rounded up and put on reservations, but they only say that so's they can get voted into office again. Ain't that right, Ma?"

Ella entered the main room from the lean-to wearing a large-brimmed straw hat decorated with what appeared to be paper flowers. Her hair was tucked tightly inside the crown of the hat.

"Ma. What're you doin' with that hat?" Jed looked exasperated.

"We got company," she replied as she took two dishes from the cabinet.

"Take the hat off," Jed insisted.

"If I take the hat off how will they know they're company?" Ella asked before she set the dishes on the table.

"They already know they're company 'cause you invited them to stay."

"It ain't the same thing. And I won't take it off."

Jed shook his head in a hopeless gesture, then said, "You just can't tell about the government. They say one thing and do another."

"But we ain't like that," Ella put in. "No sir, we mean what we say." She placed a pot of boiled potatoes on the table and ladled some into all four dishes. "Taste it."

Katie sniffed the steam that rolled off her plate and was rewarded by a small rumble in her stomach. Besides potatoes, there were bits of onions, carrots and chunks of chicken plus dots of dumplings. She tasted the soup and was pleased to find it was even better than it smelled. One look across the table told her that Spence thought so, too.

Jed, on the other hand, was more interested in keeping his company informed about the workings of the government.

"Just like the war 'tween the states," he said without preamble. "We're told how bad it was, but how do we know? It's just their word."

Katie saw Spence hesitate slightly, then resume eating as though he considered commenting but didn't.

"Now don't go startin' on that," Ella reprimanded. "You know I don't like hearin' war talk." Then she turned to Katie. "Do you like the soup?"

"It's delicious."

"And you?" she asked Spence.

"Delicious," he replied with a pleasant smile.

Ella immediately filled their plates again. "We don't get much company out here, you know."

"You said that already, Ma."

"I did not."

"You did."

Ella looked slightly put out as she arched her neck and tilted the brim of her hat. "I can say it again if I feel like it. We don't get much company."

"No. We don't. Now let it go," Jed said.

"Ella," Katie interjected, hoping to prevent an all-out fight, "what did you put in your soup? I'd like to try your recipe. Is it something I could cook out on the trail?"

"Sure you could, honey. It's real simple. I'll even give you a few of the ingredients. That way our trade will be more fair."

"How far you folks haulin' from?" Jed asked Spence.

"New York City," he replied.

"God—"

"No cussin' in my house! I told you before!" Ella shouted at him. "You want me to get a broom to your backside?"

"—damn!" Jed finished.

In a flash, Ella was out of her seat and fetching the broom, which she thumped against his back.

"Ma! Ma! Quit!" Jed scooted his chair backward across the dirt floor in his attempt to escape. "You got company! Is that any way for a grown woman to act?"

As if suddenly aware that Katie and Spence were there, she halted with the broom poised in mid flight. She put it back against the wall and resumed her seat. Jed resumed his, also.

"New York City," Jed went on. "That's a God"—he glanced at his mother then finished—"awful ways to go."

Katie jumped in with the explanation of how she was traveling west to photograph the country and the people, wondering all the while how in the world they had ever stumbled onto such a strange household.

"Photograph!" Ella cried out. "You wanted to take our photograph, didn't you?"

"Yes," Katie replied. "Whenever you're ready."

"We're ready now," Ella announced, getting to her feet. "Come along, Jed."

Surprisingly, Jed complied and followed his mother outside. Katie set up her camera, positioning mother and son along with the ill-mannered dog near the front of the sod house. Spence lounged against the wagon, saying almost nothing and watching her every move.

After the picture was toned, she handed it to Ella.

"Now, would you look at that," Ella remarked. "I wish Sam coulda been here. He was my husband, you know. He was took with the sickness awhile back and died."

"It was your cookin' what done it," Jed accused. "And now I got all this worthless ground to farm on my own."

A pained expression crossed Ella's face, and Katie's heart went out to her in sympathy.

"Let me clean up my wagon and then you can give me the recipe for your soup," Katie said.

Ella's face brightened immediately. "I'll get the ingredients together while you're doin' that."

After Katie put away her chemicals and cleaned up the basins, she went into the soddie. Ella had assembled an assortment of roots and dried foods on the table.

"These should keep real good for you on the trail," Ella said as she gathered them into her apron. "I'll carry them out to your wagon."

Katie opened the lid on the side box and Ella dumped her load inside. It looked as though there would be enough to make two pots of soup.

"Now," Ella said, "you make the dumplin's with dough and water and a pinch of leavenin'. And salt if you have it to spare."

"Well, we won't be able to put chicken in it like you did, but I'm sure it will still be very good."

"Chicken?" Ella practically shrieked. "I'd never cut up one of my chickens, for land's sake! Oh, no! I need them eggs. The meat I put in the soup was snake. Now, them I can do without." Ella smiled pleasantly at Katie. "You shouldn't have too hard a time findin' one of them."

Katie blanched. "I . . . I suppose not."

Chapter Fourteen

Katie managed to keep from wretching until Spence had driven a good distance away from the sod house. With one hand on her mouth, she stumbled down from the wagon as soon as they came to a stop. Dropping to her knees, she emptied her stomach, but still continued to wretch. Finally, weak and shaky, she sat back on her feet.

"Here, this should help," Spence said. Crouching down beside her, he wiped a wet cloth across her face. When he'd finished, she let her head fall forward until it rested against his shoulder.

"Snake," she mumbled into his shirt, and shivered.

"I've eaten worse," he said, smiling.

"I haven't."

They sat that way for several minutes. She was glad for his support, while he simply enjoyed the feel of her soft body leaning into his, something he'd like to become accustomed to, he realized.

"Feeling better?" he asked.

179

"No."

The top of her curls tickled under his chin. Her hair smelled of soap and sunshine. He inhaled deeply and closed his eyes.

"I think I'm ready to go back to beans," she said.

That made him laugh out loud.

"I mean it," she muttered.

"We'll see if you still feel that way by tomorrow. A steady diet of beans has other side effects, you know."

"At least it won't kill you," she replied.

"Snake won't kill you. Not if you eat it." He grinned, although he knew he shouldn't add insult to injury.

"I'll bet that's what killed Sam," she said, raising her head to look at him. "Poor Sam."

Still grinning, he replied, "I doubt if that's what killed him. I'd be willing to bet it was beans."

She gave him a tentative smile. "They're that bad, huh?"

"That bad."

"Okay. Then I guess I just won't eat at all."

"You could compromise."

"You mean, no beans and no snakes. Just soup. Right?"

"Sounds good to me."

"Ugh!" She took the cloth from his hand and pressed it to her forehead. "Nothing sounds good to me."

"How about a drink of water?"

"Well, maybe that does sound good."

Spence got to his feet and helped her up. With his steadying hand at her back, they walked to the wagon. Katie sipped a half cup of water, then wet her cloth to mop her face and arms.

"Feel better?" he asked once more.

"Yes. I do. Just don't mention you-know-what."

Katie excused herself and climbed in the back to change clothes and freshen up a little. Afterwards, she felt ready to travel again. Much later, her stomach rumbled but she happily ignored it.

For the next few hours they traveled without incident. At one point, Katie insisted they stop so she could photograph her wagon in the tall prairie grass. She hauled her camera several yards away in order to include Ethan and Silas as well as the packhorse tied to the back. With a little more insistence, she coaxed Spence to stand alongside the front wheel. This was the first time she had asked him to participate, and she wasn't at all surprised by his reluctance.

"All you have to do is hold still," she called to him from under the camera's cloth. "This will only take a minute."

Spence did as he was told, but no sooner had she stepped away from the camera with the glass plate than he was walking toward her.

"I'll carry the camera back for you," he said, passing her. He carefully handled the awkward box, folding and covering it, then picked up the tripod.

She had barely put the plate through the finishing process when she heard him outside the flap of the wagon.

"I've got your camera."

"I won't be long," she replied, a little irritated with the urgency she heard in his voice. She knew he wasn't exactly happy about posing for her, but he ought to know she couldn't rush or all would be for nothing.

When she stepped outside she found him standing with his back to the wagon, staring off into the distance. She propped the photograph on the side box, waited and watched it "take."

"How much longer?" he asked, glancing over his shoulder at her.

But she ignored his question and took the photograph back inside to add the toner and finish it. Outside once more, she admired the picture, feeling a swell of excitement surge through her. She'd come so far and accomplished at least this part of her dream. How many times had she wondered if she'd ever actually go through with it, if she'd even get the chance to go through with it. And now she held in her hand the proof of that dream: her wagon standing in the tall prairie grass west of the Missouri River. The moment was overwhelming.

Rather than ask Spence's opinion about the picture, she simply set to work putting away her chemicals. She refused to be rushed, especially at a time like this.

When Katie finally climbed onto the wagon seat, Spence said, "We're losing daylight."

The tone of his voice startled her. In all the time they'd been traveling together she hadn't been truly frightened. She trusted him so completely with her safety that being afraid had just never come into her thoughts. Until now. Spence hadn't made a show of it, but she'd known that he carried a gun, and since leaving St. Louis he'd worn it holstered at his waist. She'd tried not to pay attention to it, but it wasn't something she could easily ignore.

"Is something wrong?" she asked, glancing first at him, then at the surrounding plains.

"I had hoped to be farther than we are, maybe near a creek," he said. But she sensed that he was covering up a deeper concern.

Then she saw the lone rider to the south. The distance between them was difficult for Katie to estimate, and it was impossible to tell if it was a man, woman or child. Or if it was . . .

"Is that an Indian?" she asked, her voice exposing her fear as she remembered Jed's words. Silently she prayed that it wasn't.

"No," he replied, but he pulled out his gun and laid it on the seat between them.

Once the rider realized he'd been spotted, he rode toward them at a leisurely trot. Before long, Katie was able to make out the obvious definition of a young woman. The long skirt of her plain dress flapped above her knees, revealing bare legs and bare feet. When she rode up alongside Spence's side of the wagon, she slowed her horse to a walk to keep pace with them. Katie could see that a broad straw hat hid sunny blond hair which she kept tied back with a string. Tugging the hat from her head, she smiled brightly and greeted them.

"Howdy! Where you folks headed?"

"Hello," Katie called back.

Spence nodded and touched the brim of his hat.

Not only was the girl barefoot, but she rode without a saddle, using a simple halter and reins to maneuver the horse.

"We're going to Montana," Katie replied.

The girl brushed the loose strands of hair from her face. "That's a certain long ways to go."

"So I'm finding out," Katie said.

"I ain't never . . . I mean, I never been that far in my whole life. Course, I sure do hope to travel like that. Someday." The girl paused, apparently just enjoying their company. "Where'd y'all come from?"

"New York City," Katie said.

"Dang! That far? I surely do envy you and your man. Now where's my manners! My name's Lily and I live over yonder, other side of that rise with my ma and pa. Got seven brothers and sisters, too. They'd sorely like to meet you. I just know they would."

Katie quickly surveyed the area Lily pointed out but was unable to discern a rise or a house.

Bringing her attention back to Lily, she said, "It's nice to meet you, Lily. I'm Katie and this is Spence." She overlooked the reference to Spence as "her man."

183

"Saw you taking a photograph back there. That was what you was doin', wasn't it?"

Katie recognized the interest in Lily's eyes, and she sensed a kindred spirit in other ways, too.

"Yes. I'm a photographer."

"Dang! A lady photographer! Y'all will come home with me, won't you?" Lily leaned precariously across her horse toward them. "Ma's got supper 'bout ready. We'd be proud to have you eat with us."

"I don't know . . ." Katie remembered the last meal they'd been invited to share, even though she'd done her best to forget it.

"It's God's truth that Ma would want y'all to come. And Pa will be glad for a reason to get out his fiddle." Eagerness flooded the girl's expression.

"I don't see how we could say no to an evening of fiddle playing," Spence said, smiling, and surprising Katie.

"Dang!" Lily cried. "I'll ride on ahead and tell 'em you're coming. Just follow me." Then digging her bare heels into the horse's sides, she flew off across the broad grassy plain.

Before long, Spence and Katie crested the rise and were able to see the acres of corn, which nearly came to the front door of the house. And just as at Jed and Ella's place, there were no trees.

By the time Katie and Spence arrived, Lily's entire family had assembled in front of their sod home.

"Welcome, folks," said Lily's father. He wore home-spun clothing that had patch upon patch. "Name's Horace and this is my wife, Maudie."

Lily, unable to hold back, finished the introductions as though it was an honor to present the company to her family. Katie tried to follow closely as she heard each of the children's names: James, Nathan, Clare, Annie, Ned and John, and little Grace.

"We'll let the womenfolk get on with their talkin',"

Horace said to Spence. "I'll show you where to put the horses." The two oldest boys, James and Nathan, who looked to be in their late teens, followed.

Unlike Jed's farm, this one had a sod building that served as a shelter for the numerous pigs, chickens and even a goat that roamed freely about. The house itself appeared large enough to hold all of Lily's family.

"Come along, Katie," Maudie said, ushering her inside. "Why, I can't tell you how pleased we are to have company. And a lady photographer at that! Now you just sit right there while the girls and I tend to supper."

The aroma that floated across the air was enough to make even Katie's stomach growl with hunger. She couldn't be sure what was stewing in the spider-legged pot, but she intended to ask before taking one single bite.

"Lily tells us you come all the way from New York City. I imagine you're getting pretty tuckered out. I know when we come up from Texas I was plumb wore out. That was five years ago, before little Grace was born and the twins were only two."

Little Grace climbed onto Katie's lap when her mother spoke her name. She twisted and turned until she sat sideways, then reached up to pat Katie's curls.

"She's a lovin' child," Maudie said, her eyes full of adoration. "We spoil her something awful, but it hasn't hurt her none."

"You spoiled us all," Lily said, kissing her mother's cheek. "And we love you for it."

Katie watched as each girl completed one task after another without being told what to do. The warmth and affection they had for one another was apparent. Even their teasing was done in a lighthearted manner.

Clare whipped a batter containing cornmeal, flour and an egg. Her younger sister Annie dusted flour on Clare, then, laughing, ran for the safety of her mother's

185

skirt. No admonition was forthcoming, just a quick re-taliation as Clare smudged Annie's nose with batter.

Little Grace giggled, saying, "See Annie! See Annie!"

Katie simply smiled to see such a fun-loving family.

"How's that fried pork comin' along?" Maudie asked Lily.

"Fine, Ma."

Maudie turned to Katie. "So you're going to Montana," she said. "Horace had wanted to go on up that way but when we got this far, I said to the Lord, 'This is far enough for me, Lord. See if you can persuade my man to agree.' And He did. There's land for as far as you can see, and Horace had a vision of it all planted to corn. And now five years later, with the help of the children, his dream has come true."

Katie sipped the strong coffee from the heavy mug that Lily had set on the table in front of her. Little Grace climbed down, then brought a rag doll for Katie to hold.

"Except for the fact that we don't see many folks," Maudie went on, "we have a good future ahead of us and we like it here. And besides, there's enough of us that sometimes we're company enough for each other."

In no time at all, the table was set and the men were called. Everyone crowded onto the benches that ran the length on each side of the table, while two chairs oc-cupied the ends. Maudie insisted that Spence take her chair and she took the end of one bench with Lily op-posite her mother, right next to Spence.

Horace, from the head of the table, said the blessing over the food, the land and the company, ending with, "Commence to eatin'."

Katie knew she had nothing to fear concerning the food since she had watched the entire meal cooked. She had also committed to memory most of the recipes and their ingredients. Now, if she could just count on the same results when she tried it over a campfire. Maudie had even interspersed their conversations with tips on cooking beans on the trail. Katie considered the likelihood of that to be kind of slim, but she thanked her anyway.

"Maudie," Horace began, "Spence tells me he's headin' back home to ranching in Montana. Mighty pretty country up that way, I hear tell."

"Might be," Maudie answered. "But here's where the Lord planted us and here's where we'll stay."

Katie wondered if maybe Horace had an idea to go wandering again. At least the look on Maudie's face suggested as much.

"I'm not about to leave this farm, not when the crops are so good." Then as an afterthought he added, "And not when the Lord pointed it out so plainly."

Maudie nodded, apparently pleased with his decision, and maybe a little relieved, too.

"So you're not from New York?" Lily said to Spence and Katie.

"I am," Katie replied, breaking open a cornmeal biscuit. "But Spence isn't."

"Ain't he your man?" Lily asked, her entire body at attention, waiting for an answer.

"Well . . . no." Katie faltered for the first time and couldn't seem to tell the usual white lie. She glanced at Spence, who stared back at her as he bit into a biscuit.

"He ain't?" Lily looked incredulous. "Well, I'll be." She smiled broadly at Spence. "Then you two are just travelin' together for protection."

"Something like that," Spence replied, but he was looking at Katie, who for some reason couldn't meet his gaze.

"Now, if that ain't something special," Lily commented. A new admiration shone on her smiling face as she openly appraised Spence. "A lady photographer and her hired protector. My!" she exclaimed, her chin resting on her palm.

Katie quickly glanced around the table to see if anyone else felt as uncomfortable as she did. Apparently not, since Spence was busy with his fried potatoes and pork gravy and Maudie tended to little Grace, who sat on her lap while everyone else seemed just plain oblivious to Lily's sudden infatuation.

As for Katie, her tasty dinner had become tasteless.

When everyone had eaten their fill, or more precisely, when the food was all gone, the girls cleared the table and prepared to wash dishes.

Spence went with Horace and the boys to finish chores. The decision had already been made that Katie and Spence would stay the night and in the morning the family would have their picture taken. Katie insisted on helping dry the dishes, which freed Maudie to work on her mending. Annie played with little Grace and occasionally shooed away a stray chicken that wandered inside.

Lily handed Katie a clean dish, which she dried, then gave to Clare, who put it away. The process was accompanied by Lily's endless chatter amid a series of questions, most of them concerning Spence.

"Where's he from? I mean, before Montana. And what's his ranch like?"

Katie realized that she knew very little about Spence but until lately it hadn't mattered. In the beginning she'd had the normal curiosity of an employer about a man she wanted to hire. He had long since ceased being an employee, but that was where her definition ended. Was he a friend? Perhaps more than a friend? And if he was, how did that figure in with the goals she had for herself? Maybe she wanted it both ways, but she knew that was impossible. She couldn't have it both ways. She was either a photographer with pioneering ideas or she wasn't.

"How old is he?" Lily went on. "Not that I care a fig about that. He ain't married, is he?" She halted her dish washing and waited for Katie to answer.

But Maudie interrupted their conversation. "Lily, the Bible cautions us to treat our company well. I don't believe that means asking personal questions."

"Yes, Ma."

That was as close to being chastised as Katie supposed any of the children ever came, but it was effective. Lily had no more probing questions, or if she did she kept them to herself.

Before long they had finished the dishes and left the darkening house to sit outside on the benches against the soddie. Soon the men joined them.

"I'll just fetch my fiddle," Horace said with the same eagerness beaming on his face that Katie had first seen on Lily's.

"Some Bible folks don't hold much with singin' and dancing'," Maudie told Katie. "But we believe in makin' a joyful noise to the Lord. And we just can't help dancin' when we do."

Horace came back through the open doorway tuning his fiddle, a thoughtful frown on his face until he found just the right tautness on the strings. Immediately, he burst into a fast-paced rendition of "Sweet Betsy from Pike." The boys and girls, including little Grace, formed two lines. Lily grabbed Spence by the hand and tugged at him until he stood across from her and alongside James. Maudie motioned at Katie and she faced one of the twins.

Following their lead, Katie marched forward in time to the music, locked arms with her short partner, swung around, then back-stepped. Vigorous hand-clapping and an occasional holler punctuated the twilight evening. The merriment was infectious, and Katie laughed along with the others at the antics of the boys. A surreptitious glance at Spence was all she needed to know that he, too, was having a great time.

And so was Lily.

After do-si-doing, swinging and bowing to their partners, each couple took their turn linking arms and marching down the center. Katie didn't miss the death grip Lily had on Spence while her adoring eyes lingered on his face. When the song ended, everyone dropped onto a bench or sat on the ground, laughing and exhausted. Except Horace, who kept up the pace with "Turkey in the Straw." This time no line was formed but everyone who was so inclined grabbed a partner, whether boy or girl it didn't seem to matter. More foot-stomping, twirling and just plain bouncing around in time to the music followed.

A surprising prick of jealousy stabbed Katie as she watched Lily pull Spence to his feet time after time. Spence did his best to keep up with Lily but he wasn't the best dancer, though he was a good sport about it. When Horace struck up one more song, Spence shook his head and refused to budge.

"Come on, Spence," Lily insisted, laughing. "You can't be tuckered out yet."

"Why not?"

"'Cause we're just gettin' started!"

"Not me," he replied. "I'm finished." His words were kind but firm.

"Oh, poot!" she said as she dropped down to sit beside him. "And here I was just gettin' warmed up."

Maudie carried a lantern from the house and hung it on a peg protruding from the door frame. Soft lighting fell in a broad circle, encompassing the dancers and those who rested.

"I ain't had this much fun since I can't remember when," Lily went on. "How about you?"

Spence nodded. "Your pa is a fine fiddle player."

Katie looked away, not wanting to see or hear any more. She made her way around the dancers, avoiding Spence and Lily, and went into the house where Maudie had a pot of coffee boiling.

"Want a cup?" Maudie asked. "It's almost done."

Katie nodded.

"Lord, will you listen to that man! He's been itchin' to get at that fiddle for a long spell. Pretty soon, though, he'll sit one out and John will warm up his harmonica. John lets a body rest with his music. It's just real relaxin'."

Sure enough, the fiddle stopped and the harmonica took over, playing "Beautiful Dreamer." The mood of the evening changed into a mellow one, and the effect on Katie was pure melancholy.

She tried to tell herself it had something to do with being so far from everyone she loved and that the haunting melody simply brought out those feelings. But deep in her heart she knew it had more to do with Spence and Lily. She was being foolish to think that a young girl's infatuation would have any effect on the friendship she and Spence had. Or maybe that was the true reason for the melancholy. Her feelings had gone beyond friendship even though Spence's hadn't.

Katie sipped the hot coffee and visited with Maudie. Little Grace climbed onto her mother's lap, snuggled into a ball and promptly went to sleep.

"I believe we've all had enough for today," Maudie said softly. "I'll just call the others, and Horace will have to put up his fiddle till another time."

Soon the family filed in, tired but happy. Everyone except John, who continued to play lovely ballads, and, Katie noticed, Lily and Spence. Excusing herself, Katie promised to be up early for the picture-taking. Outside she said a polite good night to the three sitting on benches and headed toward the sod barn where her wagon stood unhitched.

Since she was so familiar with the interior of her wagon, she didn't need a light in order to spread her feather tick and undress. With very little fumbling she managed to get the task done, then folded back the flap, as had become her habit since the weather had turned

191

so warm. She preferred having it open so she could see the stars in the broad expanse of sky, even though her view was limited. On clear nights she considered Spence to be the fortunate one since his view was the entire sky. Being on the prairie had given her a whole new feeling about herself: she was only one small person in the larger scope of things, but right now she couldn't take comfort in that. She felt pretty small as it was.

As the sun came up, Katie awoke to the sounds of chores being done and realized she'd slept longer than she'd intended.

"Hey, in there," Spence called before poking his head around the end of the wagon. "Are you going to sleep all day? Horace is anxious to get into the fields, or rather Maudie is anxious for Horace to get into the fields," he said, grinning.

"I'm surprised you're up so early," she said. She had heard the sound of his voice late into the night, talking with Lily. "And would you please drop the flap?"

Spence stepped into full view and Katie pulled the covers to her chin. "You sound as though the night should have been longer."

"I would think that you're the one who would've preferred a longer night," she replied testily.

A slow grin spread across his face. "You're jealous."

"Jealous? Don't be ridiculous! Lily is just a young girl." Then realizing that she'd just admitted to liking him, she added in defense, "who can stay up as late as she pleases talking to whomever she pleases. It's certainly none of my concern what either of you do." She paused. "Drop the flap. Please."

"We didn't do anything," he said, still grinning as though he'd just discovered a great secret. "We talked about other places because she has an interest in traveling. That's all."

"And if you believe that, I have some Confederate banknotes to sell you," Katie replied. "Drop the flap."

"No." His smile slowly turned into a frown. "You could have joined us. Then you'd know that you have no reason to be jealous. Lily is a nice girl."

"Yes, I know she is," Katie said, regretting her unkind remark about the girl. "And I didn't say I was jealous. You did. But I'm not. Now, will you please drop the flap so I can get up and take their photograph? After all, that's what I am. A photographer."

He gave her one last look before untying the strings that held the canvas flap open. When it dropped into place, she lay back on her bed with a sigh of relief mixed with vexation at herself. What had gotten into her that she let her feelings show like that? It was a wonder he didn't remind her that he was only her escort and could do as he pleased, which was, after all, the truth. Just as she was a photographer who had no business entertaining ideas of jealousy.

You can't have it both ways, she reminded herself once more. And as much as she wanted to indulge in self-pity, she couldn't because she hadn't realized her dreams yet; achieving her goals still drew her too strongly.

Chapter Fifteen

Katie and Spence were soon on their way after photographing the large family in front of their sod house where just the night before everyone had danced. Maudie was pleased with the picture, but not nearly as much as Lily.

After hearing Horace's shortcut directions to the Platte River, they struck out across the prairie. They would come across a few more homesteads, he'd told them, where they could fill their water barrels. Word had come to Horace that the dry conditions to their west should be avoided if possible. Then he wished them luck. Maudie sent along a loaf of bread, some salt pork and some dried fruit, which must have been a dear commodity.

Once again it was just the two of them. Only this time Katie was the one who didn't much feel like talking. She had said far too much already, and the safest way to handle that problem was to say nothing at all.

All around them was the endless waving prairie

grass, dipping and undulating like waves of water. And the wind was constant. The canvas on the wagon alternately ballooned, then flattened as the breezes surged and eddied. The flaps, front and back, were lifted in order to prevent a buildup of heat as the air flowed through.

Surprisingly, Katie saw a great deal of wildlife, mostly birds and rabbits that they startled but also other small creatures that she didn't recognize. She wondered if perhaps it was cooler in tall grass and for the animals' sakes hoped it was. Sudden gusts of wind brought dust up from the feet of Ethan and Silas, then an occasional back wind put the horses in a small tornado of their own making. Katie coughed and hid her nose inside the front of her shirt.

"My goodness!" she exclaimed. "How long has it been since it rained out here?"

"By the looks of the grass, I'd say quite a while."

"I hope we won't have trouble finding water."

"Horace was sure we'd be fine. We should reach the next homestead by nightfall. And even if we don't, we have enough water to last long enough to reach the river." He scanned the cloudless sky. "Sometimes weather like this can bring on a storm."

Katie, too, scanned the sky, thinking that a storm out here in the middle of nowhere would be a terrible thing. "But there are no clouds. Look at that blazing sun."

Spence nodded but didn't comment.

After that, Katie kept her eyes trained on the sky as they traveled northwest.

At noon they stopped at a dried-up creek bed where one lone cottonwood tree gave them sparse shade. Overhead, the thick shiny leaves clacked together in the wind, adding their brittle sound to that of the grasses surrounding them.

Spence watered the animals while Katie tried to live up to her bargain of cooking a meal. There wasn't enough wood from the single tree to cook anything that would take a lot of time, such as a pot of soup. So she cooked the salt pork and, as much as she hated to do it, added beans just the way Maudie told her. The bread and dried fruit was their dessert.

When she handed a plate to Spence he raised his brows at her and grinned.

"It's better than snake soup," she said, sitting on the ground beside him with her back to the tree trunk. The blackened pot of coffee boiled with noisy exuberance on a flat rock in the fire.

"Just as soon as that's done we'll put out the fire," Spence said. "It wouldn't take a whole lot to set off this grass."

Katie wasn't sure which she feared worse out here in the open, a fire or a thunderstorm. She got up and scattered the remainder of the coals in hopes it would burn out faster, then returned to sit under the tree mere inches from Spence.

The solitude quickly bore down on both of them, making each more aware of the other. Spence stared off into the distance after taking a bite of food, and Katie studied the toe of her well-worn shoes. The long silence became longer and more awkward, and harder to break.

After a while, Katie got up and poured two cups of coffee, handed one to Spence, then sat on the well-step of her wagon where she could only partially see him.

Still, neither of them spoke.

She thought of all the things she wanted to know about him, all the same questions that Lily had asked her and more. When had she become so tongue-tied? she wondered. Being straightforward was something on which she prided herself. Beating around the bush was always a waste of time and was generally misunderstood in the long run. So why didn't she just ask him what she wanted to know? She wouldn't have thought twice about it five or six weeks ago, but at that time she didn't care about the answers. Now she did, even though she had no right.

Spence poured the contents of the coffeepot over the fire, scattering the hissing coals as he did so. Brief puffs of steam rose until finally the fire was out.

"Ready?" he asked.

Nodding, she gathered up the dishes, then used the creek bottom sand to scour the plates. She wouldn't wash them until they reached a place where water was plentiful. In no time they were loaded and on their way again.

The illusion of floating over a sea of grass once again overtook Katie as it rippled in waves, one after the other for as far as the eye could see. In some places the grass was as tall as a man. She wondered how many people might actually have gotten lost in it.

From near the feet of the horses flew a covey of prairie chickens, startling Silas and Ethan. Spence settled them quickly with gentle pressure on the reins and a calm voice. Then a jackrabbit zigzagged its way past them in the opposite direction. Katie had never seen so much traffic on the floor of the prairie, but when she raised her head she knew why. A mammoth cloud loomed ominously in the sky ahead and the horizon darkened as though a lamp had been turned out. Her first thought was that a giant thunderstorm was heading their way out of the northwest, ready to greet them with all its intensity.

"I don't hear any thunder," she said, sliding over the seat closer to Spence.

"You won't, either. It's not a storm."

She tore her gaze from the cloud to stare at him. "It's not?" She couldn't control the fear in her voice.

"Fire." One word.

Too frightened to even gasp, Katie clutched the seat with both hands as the word bore through her consciousness. There would be no escape on the prairie, and the fuel to keep it burning surrounded them for miles. Now she watched as more rabbits and small creatures scurried away, creating an even greater problem for Spence in handling the horses.

"Easy, boy," Spence said to them. But their ears were back and they shook their harness, trying to get the bits in their teeth. "We're going to be fine," Spence said.

But Katie wondered how that could be true, and what a fine time to start telling lies!

By now a red glow lit up the darkened horizon, and Katie knew a fear she'd never before experienced. There was no way to tell how far away the fire was or how fast it was traveling toward them.

"Whoa," Spence said gently, guiding the horses to a halt.

"Why are we stopping? What are you going to do?"

"Hold the reins while I get down. When I've got the horses steadied, secure the reins. Then get a blanket. No, two blankets. Wet them down. Don't worry about the water. If we don't make it through this it won't matter anyway."

Katie nodded, barely able to take in the instructions, hoping she could follow them all.

He climbed down just as a bird flew over their heads, its frightened cry more like a shriek in Katie's ears. Ethan balked, danced and pranced, bringing Katie out of her seat in an attempt to hold him. It took every ounce of her strength to keep him from bolting, and Silas, too. Deep inside she wanted to cry out, to hide from the terror bearing down on them. She wanted to look at Spence and draw some strength from him, any little bit, but she feared to take her eyes off the horses. If only by sheer strength of will, she hoped to hold them in their tracks until Spence could calm them with his presence.

When he finally stood in front of her, between the

horses, holding them steady, she was able to see him. He nodded, and she tried to remember what it was she was supposed to do next. Instinct told her that he would not speak to her and risk startling the animals. *Think!* she berated herself. What should she do next? She looked at the reins in her hands and remembered. Secure them.

The smell of smoke filtered to them on the wind. It wasn't close enough yet to be a constant, smothering blanket.

Don't think about that, she warned herself. Blankets. Water.

She hurried around the side of the wagon to the back and climbed in on all fours, tugging at her bedding to get it out of its hiding place. With shaky hands and numb fingers she untied the strings and pulled two blankets free. Frantically, she backed out again, banging her shins on the well-step and falling to the ground. A quick glance told her the fire was gaining speed. Scrambling to her feet, she dragged the blankets behind her to the water barrels. She was shaking so badly she had to use both hands to open the spigot.

Somewhere in the back of her mind it seemed important not to waste the water because they *would* be around to need it, and that became a point of strength to her. After wetting the material as best she could, sparing no time, yet still conserving the water, she closed the spigot and hurried to Spence.

He positioned her so that she stood between the horses, anchoring her hands on each one. Then he took one of the blankets she'd dropped and threw it over the heads and backs of the horses, and hers, too. After that she saw nothing but darkness. The smell of wet wool permeated the small space along with those of leather and horse sweat. Standing still, she could feel her heart thudding until her chest nearly hurt from it. What was he doing out there? she thought frantically. What did he have in mind to save them?

She strained to listen beyond the sound of her own heart and the shallow breathing of the horses. First she heard the sound of crackling, then she smelled the smoke.

"Oh, God!" she moaned softly, but one look from under her blanket told her the smoke wasn't coming from the fire that bore down on them. It came from behind the wagon. Over the heads of Silas and Ethan she watched Spence use the other blanket to beat out a fire he had apparently started. His hat was gone, and he worked with frenzy until he had created a circle of charred grass that would hold three or four wagons.

Briefly, she thought about Maudie and Horace's family and sent up a silent prayer that the fire would not find them unaware.

Then he was standing beside her, his face smudged black and his shirt covered with dust and charred grass. His chest rose and fell rapidly in short breaths.

"We have to wait until the ground cools a bit, then we'll walk the horses onto the burned-out section. With a lot of luck, we should make it through."

Spence's heart nearly broke at the fear he saw on Katie's face. She possessed more grit than he'd ever thought possible. She hadn't wasted a moment when she carried out his orders. No questions and no balking. He didn't know many women who could have done as much, and certainly none who had grown up in the city. He gave her shoulders a quick squeeze of appreciation, then traded places with her.

"Drop the flaps," he told her, "then come back under here with me." In a flash she was gone.

He walked the horses to the burned-out grass and faced them away from the wind. His biggest concern now were the chemicals in her wagon. They had a smell of brimstone about them, and he could only hope they wouldn't really blow them to kingdom come like he'd teased her so many weeks ago.

Soon she was at his side and he pulled her under the blanket with him.

"Done," she said. The word burst forth on a whisper. "I covered the packhorse, too."

"Good girl." He wanted to wrap his arms around her, to keep her safe beside him and shield her from all harm. Fleetingly, the word "forever" passed through his mind. She buried her face in his chest while he was forced to hold onto the horses, and the soothing words he said to them had to replace the ones he wanted to say to her.

They stood in the darkness listening, waiting for the first sounds of crackling grass. The sun beat down on them until sweat trickled down their brows and their backs to soak in their waistbands. The horses took turns stomping their feet, and dust filtered up into their nostrils. Katie buried her face deeper, clutching at the folds of his moist shirt while Spence tucked her head beneath his chin.

Then they heard it.

Snapping and crackling, the fire closed in on them, bearing down with a vengeance that knew no bounds. As it neared, the heat became oppressive and stifling and relentless.

Ethan danced sideways, and Katie could feel Spence's muscles bunch in response.

"Whoa, boy," he soothed. "It's all right. Okay. Whoa, boy, whoa."

The roar beyond the blanket was like nothing Katie had ever heard. And then the smoke, great black clouds of it, poured in around them, choking them, causing their eyes to smart even under the shield of the wet blanket.

Ethan wouldn't be quieted now. He nickered nervously and pawed one front hoof. Spence kept a strong grip on both animals, fearing Silas would suddenly react to Ethan's fear.

And all the while, he waited for the chemical explosion that might come.

Then the inferno was gone, leaving only the acrid smoke of charred grass and the heat that the ground had absorbed. Pushing back the blanket, Spence saw that the fire had split and gone around them.

"Katie, it's over," he said. "Look."

She lifted her head, looking at him first, then turned to see the miles of blackened land that surrounded them.

"It's over," she repeated, staring off into the empty distance. A tear trickled down her cheek, drawing a white line in the dirt and smoke that clung there. Then she covered her face with both hands and began crying softly.

With the worst behind them, Spence was free to let loose of the horses and take Katie in his arms as he'd wanted to do in the beginning.

"Don't cry now," he said, holding her tight and feeling the shaking of her body. "You're safe."

Her arms went up to circle his neck, and she let go with terrible sobs. He stroked her back and hair, trying to calm her, but it seemed she needed the release and so he waited until she finished. At last, with only shuddering breaths left in her, she lay limp against him.

"Better?" he asked, stroking her hair again, feeling the bouncy curls, now damp, under his touch.

"I think so," she replied, sniffling. Still she clung to him. "I've never been so frightened in my whole life."

"To tell you the truth, neither have I." The fear that something might happen to her was the worst fear he'd ever known. That kind of fear was new to him and he didn't ever want to experience it again. Reflexively, he tightened his hold on her.

"I don't know what I'd have done if you hadn't been here," she said.

He couldn't bear to even think about it. Soothing her with sounds rather than words, he continued to stroke her hair. The moments turned into minutes, and a new awareness of an old feeling held them together. He'd come so close to losing what wasn't actually his, might never be his, that he trembled.

"I think I can stand on my own now," she said, sliding her arms down from his neck. She gave him a quick glance, then smiled. "If I look half as bad as you do I must be a sight."

"I'm not complaining."

"Thank you for those kind words, gallant sir."

He smiled. "Well, you do sort of look like the inside of a chimney."

She gave a short, tremulous laugh. "I'll just bet I do." Looking up at him, she added, "You kind of remind me of the bottom of the coffeepot."

"And that's the thanks I get for saving your wagon. I thought for sure that thing was going to blow sky high and us with it."

"Me too. That is, if I'd even been able to think about that." She wiped her sleeve across her face, further blackening the shirt. "What a mess."

"Looks like everything is a mess," he said as he pulled the blanket from the backs of the horses and shook the debris from it.

On closer inspection, they found that the canvas had tiny burn holes in the roof. Inside the wagon, everything was fine other than the dust that had sifted under the flaps.

Outside, Katie pulled the blanket from the pack-horse, saying, "Poor thing! Anyone who's been through that deserves a name, and I think Cinder is appropriate." She turned to Spence and asked, "Don't you?"

"Sounds fine to me." He was glad to see her sense of humor return.

"Could we all have a drink of water? I'm parched. Well, not really, thank goodness, but . . . you know what I mean."

"We'll call it a celebration," he replied.

Katie retrieved the cups and poured water in each.

After downing the entire contents, Katie said, "That's the most satisfying drink of water I've ever had."

"And every one after this will be, too."

With complete sincerity she said, "You're right." She paused. "I always thought nothing could be worse than a thunderstorm. I've had this fear since I was a child. I've never been able to rid myself of it. But now I know there is something worse."

"But we made it. That's important to remember."

"Yes," she answered, smiling. "We did make it."

Before getting on the trail again, Spence watered the animals and rolled up the flaps while Katie sat on the seat with still-shaky legs.

As they drove over the blackened grass, puffs of ashes rose with each footfall of the horses. Katie knew she should have taken out her camera and photographed the destruction, but she didn't have the heart for it. She didn't want anything to remind her of this day.

"All that beautiful prairie grass is gone," Katie said as she surveyed the damage left by the fire. "And so many little creatures probably perished with it."

Where there had been gracefully bending blades of grass only an hour before, now there was only barren, charred ground.

"Do you suppose it will ever come back?" she asked.

"I doubt if this is the first time it's happened. I'm sure it will come back."

"How did it ever get started? Certainly nobody started it."

"It's possible that a careless campfire could have done it. It's also possible that lightning did it."

Suddenly alert, she said, "I don't see any sign of a storm. Do you?"

"No." He let it go at that, but he knew that a prairie fire could rage for days and go for miles, which meant there could be a storm ahead somewhere. He hoped not.

Reaching down under the seat, he retrieved his hat and settled it on his head.

"You have holes in your hat," she remarked.

"And you have new freckles," he responded, smiling down at her.

"How can you tell under all this grime?"

"I saw them before the fire. I just didn't say so."

"I don't care. I like the sun. More than ever."

Just before evening they came to a homestead that looked totally deserted. Katie stayed put on the seat as she was told while Spence scouted the premises. It was an eerie feeling, one that gave her chills along her spine. What had happened to these people? she wondered.

Spence came into view at the doorway of the house, and she breathed a sigh of relief.

"Nobody's here," he said.

"How long have they been gone?" she called.

"Can't tell. Maybe a day. Maybe a week."

"You don't suppose they tried to outrun that fire, do you?"

He walked to the wagon and stopped beside her. "That would be mighty foolish, since a sod house is about the safest place to be. Most people bring their animals right in with them."

"I would, too," Katie said quietly. She'd never leave an animal to perish in an inferno like they'd just been through.

"Maybe they'll return soon," he said.

"Do you think we could use their well while they're gone? I'd love to clean up good and proper. And maybe wash some clothes, especially bedding."

"I don't see what harm it would do."

Spence found a washtub, then dipped water from the well for her. He said she'd have to take it cold since he couldn't find anything to use for firewood without burning their furniture. She said she'd gladly take it cold rather than use the poor family's furniture.

Katie shivered through her bath and washed her hair, enjoying every minute of it. There was none of the luxury she'd experienced at Bailey's, but even so, it turned out to be far more satisfying. Afterwards she washed clothes, hers and Spence's, then hung them on chair backs to dry. Katie swept out the wagon and hoped that eventually the odor of smoke would leave. For supper they finished off Maudie's bread and dried fruit, washing it down with plenty of water.

Evening settled around them as Katie and Spence enjoyed each other's company sitting in front of the house.

"I might not mind using someone else's tub but I'd never be able to sleep in their bed," Katie said.

"That's using good sense," he replied, "since you never know what you might find."

"Might find?"

"Critters."

"What kind of critters?" she asked, her mind wandering toward the slithery kind.

"Little tiny ones."

"You mean bedbugs?"

He nodded and replied in all seriousness, "They bite like the devil and stay with you longer."

She laughed out loud at the worried look on his face. "When did you ever get bit by a bedbug?"

"Years ago, and it hasn't happened since."

"That's reassuring, since you're sleeping under my wagon."

"And that's where I'm headed right now," he said, rising from his chair. He leaned over and kissed the top of her head. "Sleep tight."

She would have answered but her heart was flip-flopping so hard she could barely breathe.

Chapter Sixteen

With nothing more than the charred landscape to draw their attention, Katie and Spence found themselves faced with only their thoughts for company, or having to resort to conversation. Keeping company with his thoughts was not new to Spence, but Katie's lively presence and her curiosity about everything had him talking more than he had during the entire previous year, or so it seemed.

She wanted to know about the wildlife, where they lived on the prairie and what they ate. He pointed out the prairie dog towns, snake holes, bird nests and fox dens; then he told her they eat each other. He laughed at the face she made. As a matter of fact, since he'd been with her, he'd probably laughed more than he had the entire previous year, too.

Spence was glad when they reached the area beyond the burned prairie where the tall grasses grew once more, unharmed by fire and full of wildlife.

By the end of the week they reached the Platte River.

They planned to follow it west, eventually arriving at the fork in the river that would take them north. At that time they would need to cross over by ferry, if possible. He doubted if her wagon could handle the steady current without being swept away.

"Just looking at that water makes me feel better," she said.

"Makes me feel like we're practically home."

"Are we?" she asked, surprised.

"No. But we're not that far from the last leg of the trip."

"Oh." She sat quietly in thought. "I haven't really taken all that many photographs."

"Why not here?" he said. "This is a pretty important place. I'll even take your picture if you get it all set up." He pulled the wagon to a stop a short distance from the riverbank. A patch of cottonwoods created leafy shade overhead while a welcome stretch of shorter green grass padded the area beneath them.

"Why is this an important spot?" she asked. "Did something memorable happen here?"

"No," he responded.

The soft sighing of the tall grasses at the edge of the prairie whispered on the wind, but other than that all was silent. The wind eddied, ruffling her hair. Charmed by the effect, Spence watched the curls lift and dance, then fall back against her face. Unconsciously, she brushed at them.

"No," he repeated. "Not that I know of, but something might have."

"Like what?" she asked, returning his stare until he was sure she could see clear to the depth of his soul.

"I can't speak for the past, but I guess just getting this far makes it memorable. For us."

"I see," she replied, apparently at a loss for words.

"Is that a good enough reason for a photograph?" he

asked, but he was thinking that she had eyes the color of a clear sky.

"I don't really need a good reason. Actually, I seldom listen to reason. I thought you might have guessed that by now."

He smiled at her. "I have."

"So. . . . do we need a reason?"

He almost asked her what she was talking about, but decided that his thoughts had simply taken a turn and now he was misreading her suggestion, if it was a suggestion, which he was sure it wasn't.

"No," he said, securing the reins and putting an end to his thoughts. "We certainly don't. Let's just take the photograph anyway." He jumped down from the wagon and circled the horses to help her, but by the time he reached her she was already standing on the ground.

Brushing at her clothes, she said, "Well, I'm such a mess—"

"You sound like Mattie Jacobs," he said.

"I do, don't I." She stopped dusting herself. "I guess I should just take my own medicine quietly, huh?"

He grinned. "I'll help you with the camera."

Something about their near brush with death had affected Spence; he felt more protective of her, but in a way that Tim hadn't intended, he was sure. And there wasn't anything she'd done to encourage it; he simply wanted to keep her safe. Neither the notion nor its implications worried him, because it all seemed so natural. She needed protecting and he was there to do it. Nothing complicated about that, he told himself. Undoubtedly, it had more to do with the feeling that he was so close to home. Or maybe it just had to do with her being so close to him, day after day, week after week. He'd become accustomed to her presence, enjoyed it and, truthfully, didn't want to think about what it would be like when they parted company. He would go back to tending cattle and she would go back to New

York to her galleries and such. Maybe she'd even strike out again on another journey with another escort. He didn't want to think about it, but he was certain that she'd never give up her photography for the simple life of ranching.

With the camera set up and the plate ready for exposure, Katie perched on the wagon seat while Spence followed her directions.

With her knees crossed, her chin in her palm and an elbow resting on her knee, Katie smiled broadly at the camera. She not only looked pleased with herself, but she also seemed pleased with her surroundings. If she'd suffered any hardship since leaving New York, it didn't show, and he was reminded of Silas, who'd called her the "plucky" sort.

"Done!" he called.

In no time she was in the back of her wagon where the foul smell of the chemicals carried to him on a breeze. When the picture was ready, she handed it to him.

"You do nice work," she said, mimicking Henry Jacobs.

"No. You do." He wanted to ask if he could keep it, but for some reason he held back.

"Well," she said, accepting the picture back, "I'll just finish up and then we'll start supper. Is there enough firewood or do we have to hunt for 'chips'?" She wrinkled her nose and pinched her lips together in distaste.

She'd been totally amazed at the idea of burning animal dung, but hadn't balked when the time came to gather it up. Although her face had contorted more than once in the process.

"I'm sure there's enough for a good meal."

"I propose we make soup. If you'll produce the meat, that is. I can only hope Ella's vegetables haven't dried up to nothing. But if we simmer them long enough it won't really matter, or so Maudie says." Katie hurried off to clean the basins.

Spence checked his pistol, then went in search of game, following the river and turning around occasionally to keep an eye on camp. He'd gone farther than he'd intended, but the scarcity of rabbit or hen forced him to travel on. Another look back told him that Katie had a fire going and was busy setting up the cookpot. He continued on until a movement in the grass caught his attention and he halted. Raising his gun slowly, he took aim and fired. The shot echoed off the river and through the sparse population of trees around him. He knew the sound would carry out onto the prairie where the wind would swallow it up.

With the knife he kept inside his boot, he skinned and gutted the rabbit before taking it back to camp.

"What have we here?" Katie asked, smiling with pleasure at his offering.

In short order he cut up the rabbit and tossed it into the kettle where she already had the vegetables simmering. When she put in a few beans, she looked up at him.

"Maudie says beans won't kill you. They just make you suffer a little if you use too many. They also stretch a meal and make it go farther."

"I guess she'd know about that with such a big family," Spence replied, settling back and enjoying the smell of real food. The horses were tethered near the water and now enjoyed their own meal of tender grass.

After a long space of quiet with only the snapping and cracking of the firewood filling the air, Katie said, "I wonder if Lily will ever get the chance to see other places." She kept stirring the pot without looking at him.

"She seems like the willful sort who could probably do anything she puts her mind to. Like someone else I know," he said, grinning at her.

"You sound like Tim. He always told me that I wasn't very good at taking orders."

"I wasn't referring to taking orders. And in case you'd like to know, Tim never was very good at that either." Spence remembered one time in particular and was glad all over again that Tim hadn't been good at it.

"That's a consoling thought," she answered drily.

"Besides," he went on, "you take orders very well. If I ever needed someone to back me up, I wouldn't mind a bit if it were you."

She looked up at him and smiled. "Thanks. That's just about the nicest thing anybody's ever said to me."

The sun lowered in the sky as they sat thinking about the last week. Occasionally Katie stirred the soup. Then from his lounging position, Spence watched as she sat staring into the fire, a wooden spoon held carelessly in her hand. Her shoes were scuffed until the color of the leather was no longer visible and the bottoms of her britches were threadbare. A small hole appeared in her sleeve where the fire had singed it. She looked small and forlorn, and the new instinct to protect her suddenly overwhelmed him again, only stronger this time.

"You'll like Montana," he said, hoping to break her meditative spell. "It's open and wide like the prairie, but at the same time there's more to the land than grass."

"I'm glad. This is very lonely here. Beautiful but lonely." She paused. "Poor Ella."

It had been apparent to Spence that Ella had gone beyond normal reasoning ability, but that sometimes happened on the prairies, he knew. Just like for fires and thunderstorms, people were seldom as prepared as they thought they'd be for the isolation. It was one of the hazards of being a sod farmer.

"I hope everyone back there is all right," she said. "I mean, from the fire."

"Chances are they saw it coming."

"Do you suppose Horace and Maudie took the pigs in the house?" Katie asked, smiling.

"I'd bet that Maudie insisted on it."

Katie nodded.

"Are we going to eat that soup? Or are we going to just smell it all night?" he asked.

"I guess we might as well eat it." Katie dished up a bowl for each of them.

When the meal was finished and the fire had been doused, Katie said she was going to bathe at the river. Spence kept a respectable distance, but remained watchful. Just because the prairies were wide and open was no reason to believe they were alone. He'd had no cause to think otherwise; it was just the instinct to protect her that made him stay alert, he told himself.

When she'd finished and had bedded down in the wagon with the flaps open at each end, he went down to the river and washed up, too. Afterwards, he unrolled his blanket and crawled beneath the wagon.

"Good night, Spence," she whispered to him.

He smiled at the floorboards, listening to the creaks as she shifted her weight to find a comfortable spot.

" 'Night, Katie."

"Sleep tight down there," she said, and he could hear the smile in her voice.

"I will."

The sun was up and getting higher when Spence woke with a start. He hadn't meant to sleep so late. He turned his head and looked toward the campsite to see if Katie had gotten up before him but saw that everything was as they'd left it the night before. Sliding out from under the wagon, he finger combed his hair and reached for his hat. Then he peeked inside the wagon to find her still sound asleep with her blanket bunched up, baring the smooth skin of her slender legs. All he would have to do was reach out to touch her. But he didn't. He knew he shouldn't. So rather than tempt himself he walked to the circle of cold stones and hunkered down in preparation for building a fire. As he reached for his tin of matches, he realized he'd forgotten his gun, which lay on his bedroll.

"Hey there, peddler."

Spence whirled but was defenseless. Between him and the wagon stood a man about Spence's height and half again as bulky. He wore homespun clothes that carried the strong odor of liquor and sweat, and he held a gun leveled at Spence's chest.

"Saw your wagon from a ways back," said the man, holding the gun fairly steady. He spit a stream of tobacco juice on the ground in front of him. "What're ya peddlin'?"

Panic twisted through Spence's gut. Did the man know that Katie slept not fifteen feet away in the wagon?

"Cat got yer tongue?" Then he looked Spence over, head to toe. "You don't look like any peddler I ever seed. Look more like a cattleman without no gun and all. So what's in the wagon?"

Spence slowly rose to his full height. "Nothing much. Care for some coffee? I was just fixing to brew a pot."

The man spit another stream. "Naw. I ain't here to socialize. I come to take yer wagon and yer money. Yer horses, too." He grinned, showing a few rotted teeth. "Can't leave without yer horses."

"I don't have any money," Spence replied. "But I've got some liquor in my saddlebag over by the tree. I'll get—"

"Stay where ya are!" The man said, waving the gun. "This here Colt's got a hair trigger, and if ya like the way yer head sits on yer shoulders you'll stay put."

Spence stood still, but it wasn't just the man's words that held him there. Behind the drifter Spence caught a glimpse of Katie's bright head of hair peeking around the end of the wagon. He didn't dare shift his eyes to give her a warning of any kind for fear of alerting his captor. Forcing himself to breathe normally, he was able to vaguely follow her progress as she stepped down barefoot onto the ground. With her gown lifted high, she tiptoed alongside the wagon and knelt to retrieve his gun where he'd foolishly left it in his bedroll. When he lost sight of her, he nearly came apart with worry. One false move, one bump against the wagon, and she'd be caught.

"Although I wouldn't mind some of yer bottle. But I'll get that later. When I take yer horses. The saddlebags go with it, you know." He chuckled as if he'd made a joke.

"If'n ya ain't a peddler then what are ya doin' with this here wagon? Haulin' guns?" His eyes widened. "Now that would be a sight better than money and horses together. Maybe even better than yer bottle. Though I'd have to consider on that a spell."

"No. I'm not hauling guns."

"So you say. Maybe I'll just take a look-see for myself."

Spence hadn't been much of a praying man, but he prayed now that Katie would take the opportunity and hide herself somewhere, anywhere, before it was too late. The odds were against them, and if she made herself known, it would only get worse.

The next thing he heard made his heart sink lower than his toes.

"Drop the gun," Katie said, her voice steady, and he knew it was fear that kept it that way. She had reacted with the same control during the fire; it was afterwards that she fell to pieces.

Without turning, the drifter's face broke into a broad grin. "I done hit the jackpot," he said. "You got a woman. You know how long it's been since I had me a woman? Too long, I can tell you that."

"I said, drop the gun."

"Tell me she don't got a gun," he said to Spence, still grinning. " 'Cause even if she does, it won't matter none to you. Or to her."

"She's got a gun," Spence said.

"Damn!" The man began to guffaw as though something funny had happened. "How big is it?"

"Big enough that if she shoots at that range it'll probably go through you and hit me," Spence said. He hoped she heard him and knew that he meant it.

"Damn! A gun-totin' woman. I think maybe I don't need to keep you around to hold me back from the fun I'm goin' to have," he told Spence. "Yessirree. Have me some fun." He raised his gun, taking aim on Spence.

Katie stepped closer. "Drop the gun or I'll shoot. I'm not going to tell you again."

Spence knew that she had every intention of fulfilling her promise even if the drifter didn't. But he wondered if she could hit the broad side of a barn at five paces.

Before he could ponder that question, a shot rang out and Spence dove for the ground, rolling toward her. When he came to his feet he had his knife in his hand.

Katie stood holding the gun with both hands outstretched before her. She had hit her mark, but the drifter slowly turned, then staggered toward them, his gun pointed at her, taking aim. Katie screamed and shielded her face. Spence lunged, knocking the man to the ground and taking the gun from his weakening grasp. Then the man fell back limp and lifeless.

"Is he dead?" she asked, the steadiness gone from her voice.

"Yes."

She gasped, then broke into quiet crying. "Dead? I've never killed a man," she said. "I didn't really mean to kill him."

Spence came to her and pulled her into his arms.

"I've never even shot a gun before now." Her words

were muffled by his shirt, but he heard them. "I didn't mean to do it. It's just that. . . . he was going to kill you and . . . and . . . you know. . . ."

He did know, and she was right.

"It's over now. Don't think about it." He held her until the crying subsided, stroking her back and hair, wishing he could keep her safe always, but knowing she'd never let him.

"I don't usually cry this much," she said, drying her eyes on his shirt. "But then I don't usually go around killing people either." A fresh crop of tears burst forth.

He rocked her gently, wanting to comfort her by telling her that the man deserved to die, but he knew that would make little difference. Killing was one thing you didn't get over easily, and taking comfort was impossible no matter what the reason.

"I told you I wanted you to back me up if ever I needed help." He tipped her face up to his so he could look into her eyes. "You saved my life. Thanks." He leaned down and kissed her forehead. "I mean it."

"That helps." She took in a ragged breath and tried to smile. "I have to remember that it was him or us." She leaned against him once more as though to take strength from his body. He held her tight as though to give that strength to her.

"I suppose we should bury him," Katie said without moving.

"Be a good idea."

"I don't know if I can help," she said softly, and he knew she was trying not to cry.

"You don't have to." He didn't want her to. Killing was tough enough; burying didn't make it better.

He set her an arm's length away from him. "Go get dressed and I'll call you when I'm done."

She nodded and hurried off to climb into the wagon. He was sure she wasn't getting dressed, but was instead burying her face in her feather tick.

Spence took the shovel from the supplies that were usually strapped to the packhorse and went into the tall grass to begin digging. When he finally finished, his body sweaty from his efforts, he returned to drag the dead man to the grave. He found Katie standing alongside a meager campfire, making a pot of coffee, but she kept her back turned and went about her work.

After burying the man, Spence came back to camp, put away the shovel and went to the river to wash.

"You must be hungry," she said, and he was surprised to find that the plate she gave him had biscuits and gravy on it.

"I learned a few things from Maudie and Ella," she said simply.

He ate half of it before saying, "It's very good. Aren't you going to have some?"

She shook her head. "Coffee is enough this morning." She raised her full cup and swirled it until the grounds settled in the center.

He nodded, understanding how she felt. He had felt that way, too, when he first killed a man. But he'd gotten over it all these many years later; he'd grown into a man who had learned that trouble took on many forms.

After breaking camp, they followed the river. No longer would they have to be so careful with their water supply or spend time looking for chips as long as they gathered dead wood whenever they found it. And even though there wasn't an abundance of wildlife, they found as much as they needed.

Katie did her best to sharpen her skills over a campfire and for the most part was successful. Any compliments she received from Spence only spurred her on to try harder.

The most difficult part of their trip was the growing awareness each had for the other and a strong need to hold back. They spoke in polite tones, careful not to say too much, since there was no telling where it might lead, or rather, fearful of where it would likely lead. They did not touch at all if possible and kept a respectable distance that was good and proper. Katie knew Mrs. O'Shea would be pleased. Katie was quite capable of climbing up to her seat on the wagon and down again without aid, and did so.

She devoted more time to her photography, asking Spence to stop more often now so she could take a picture. Working with her chemicals was the best thing she could do to keep her mind on her goals, that and seeing the finished pictures. Occasionally she would arrange the photographs in an order of good, better and best, and try to discover what she needed to do to improve.

Spence, in the meantime, made sure she had privacy for bathing and sleeping, no longer peeking at her bare limbs while she slept or even studying her surreptitiously while they traveled. His job was to be an escort; his only requirement was to get her to her destination safely. This was something he needed to remind himself daily.

The storm brewing on the western horizon was similar to the one brewing within each of them. It was only a matter of time before the floodgates burst, and both of them knew it.

Chapter Seventeen

"Those are the most wicked looking clouds I've ever seen," Katie said, eying the low-hanging thunderclouds.

They had been watching the storm that approached from the northwest, the direction that they were headed in as they continued to follow the river. The clouds seemed not to move at all but just hung suspended over the land, and very little wind stirred around the wagon as Silas and Ethan plodded along with Cinder in tow.

The unusual stillness made Katie want to scream. At least with the prairie fire there had been some action to take, some preparations to prevent catastrophe. There had been panic, too, and fear, but at least they had been doing something instead of steadily moving along, waiting for it to turn its fury upon them.

She glanced at Spence, who sat apparently relaxed. If it hadn't been for the worry lines above the bridge of his nose, she would have thought he was totally unconcerned.

"I never patched those burn holes in the canvas," she said.

"We can do that now," he replied calmly, which only heightened her apprehension. He slowed the team to a halt and secured the reins. When he climbed down, he walked around the horses, soothing them with his hands and voice.

Katie hurried into the back and fished out her repair kit that the canvas maker had insisted she would want to take with her. She was glad now that he hadn't listened to her when she'd insisted she wouldn't need it. After all, the wagon was brand-new and she intended to take the best care of it. Well, she had, barring one fire and an upcoming thunderstorm.

Sitting on the floor of the wagon, she stared at the contents of the box. "I don't know how to do this," she admitted, wishing she had paid more attention to the instructions she'd been given back in New York.

Spence took the box from her and studied it. "I doubt if this will keep all the water out, but it's worth a try."

He climbed in her wagon for the first time, and had to stoop so low that it was easier to kneel. Applying a small patch, he instructed her to hold it while he did his best to thread the heavy needle in and out of the canvas. Katie knelt on a shallow box she'd pulled out, so they worked almost chest to chest with their faces upturned toward the roof and their arms over their heads. With only inches between them, Katie could not ignore the scent that was peculiarly Spence. How many times now had she buried her face in his shirt and inhaled the sometimes clean, sometimes earthy, sometimes smoky scent of him, and each and every time she'd been comforted. Once again that secure feeling swept over her, and she had to remind herself that she couldn't fall into his arms now; there was work to be done.

"Are you getting tired?" he asked, still working at the patch she held.

"I'm all right," she replied, but it seemed as though the weight of her hands had tripled.

"There won't be an all-out flood through these holes, but they're likely to leak, so keep that in mind. You might want to cover your box of photographs. And you may have to sleep crowded in one corner. If the storm lasts that long."

"All right." Her voice was tense. She couldn't bear to think that the storm would last all day and into the night.

They worked for thirty minutes patching three holes. The others were mere pinpricks and couldn't be patched if they tried.

"Looks like that's it," Spence said. He let his hands fall to his sides as he studied the ceiling for more holes.

Sitting back on her heels to put a little distance between them, Katie rubbed her arms and tried to restore the normal flow of circulation.

"Kind of sore, huh?" he asked her, smiling.

"Not bad," she said with pretended indifference. But she wasn't indifferent to the fact that he completely filled her small wagon, leaving little room for either of them to maneuver around in, which of course neither did.

"Sore arms are better than the alternative," he said lamely.

"Yes."

A silence fell between them, made unbearable by their closeness. Katie kept her eyes averted, but she was sure that the pounding of her heart could be heard in the still wagon. She knew that if she looked up at him she would embarrass herself by throwing her arms around him. If he said one word she would be lost.

The rumble of distant thunder saved her from that fate, but cast her into another one.

"We'd better leave the flaps up until the rain starts," Spence told her. "The wind could do a lot of damage if it grabs hold of a ballooning canvas."

She nodded. The return of panic held her mesmerized momentarily. Then she remembered to cover her equipment boxes with the extra canvas she'd purchased for that purpose. Only one other time had she needed it, when they'd reached Pittsburgh in a downpour. If only this storm would be no worse than that one, she prayed.

Black thunderclouds blotted out the afternoon sun entirely, leaving an eerie light creeping between land and sky. The air, already hot, became oppressive and stifling without the wind to cool them.

Katie surreptitiously unbuttoned two of the top buttons on her shirt and rolled her sleeves up to her elbows. She longed for a drink of water but hated to call a halt to their progress. The sooner they met the storm, the sooner they'd be through it, she told herself over and over.

By nightfall, the storm had produced lightning like Katie had never seen, but still it stayed ahead of them, continuing to build in intensity, she was sure.

They ate cold biscuits and drank water for their supper, fearful of what a gust of wind might do to a campfire. But Katie didn't mind; she had no appetite for more than their meager fare.

When they were ready to bed down for the night, the wind came up, gusting at first, then steadily gaining strength. With the approach of the storm, the air cooled noticeably. Katie shivered, but she wasn't sure if it was from the temperature or her trepidation.

"Are you going to be all right?" Spence asked when she was ready to step inside the wagon.

"I think so. It won't last too long, will it? I mean, it should move along rather quickly, don't you think?"

"I'd like to say yes, but you never can tell."

She nodded and tried to smile. "It'll be over in the morning."

"I'll help you tie down the flaps," he said.

Together they worked against the blowing wind, he on the outside and she on the inside. When at last they had it lashed tight to the wagon, she called through the canvas to him, "Thanks."

"If you need anything just holler," he said.

"I will."

Katie undressed in the dark, quickly pulled on her nightgown, then spread out her feather tick. If only it were thicker like the bed of her childhood, she thought, knowing that her fear was childish, but unable to help it.

A large crack of thunder told her that a lightning bolt had struck nearby, and even though she couldn't see the bright light of it beyond the pinpricks in her roof, she knew it must have lit up the entire sky.

She rolled to her stomach, burying her face in the blankets. Within minutes heavy droplets pelted the roof until they became a steady downpour that sounded like a waterfall. Sitting up with a start, she thought about Spence beneath the wagon. He carried a tarp for this purpose, but until now he'd been fortunate enough not to need it.

How could he stand it? Tarp or not, he would be soaked to the skin, she was sure. A sudden brightness of the tiny holes made her clamp her eyes tightly together, grit her teeth, and wait for the sharp clap that always followed. She pressed her hand to her breast over her pounding heart, but she wasn't sure if it was from her fear of the storm or what she was about to do.

Pulling back the bedding, she called through the floorboards, "Spence, can you hear me?"

"Yes," came his muffled reply.

"Are you okay?"

"Are you?"

She thought about that for a moment. Was she okay? The storm frightened her, but it didn't terrify her the way most of them did. Having him close by, knowing that she could call on him, helped her get through the worst of it. But having him closer was what she wanted, not separated by the floor of a wagon. She clutched her hands together over her heart and felt it accelerate at the thought of what she was about to do.

"No!" she called to him. "I'm not all right."

She heard the rustle of the stiff tarpaulin as he crawled out, then on hands and knees she quickly made her way to the back of her wagon, frantically untying the strings from the inside. Within moments she saw him standing there, in sharp silhouette against the lightning-bright sky. His hair was drenched, and rivulets of rain ran down his face.

"What's wrong?" he asked, staring at her with an intensity that matched her own gaze.

"Come in," she said, tugging at him. "You're getting soaked to the bone."

Ducking his head slightly, he climbed onto her stepwell inside the shelter of the canvas. "What's wrong?" he asked again. "You don't have to be afraid." She heard the note of concern in his voice, but there was something else, too.

"No," she responded, taking his hand. "I'm not afraid. Not now. Come in here."

"I can't. I'll get your bedding all wet."

She knelt in front of him, close enough to feel his breath on her face. "You can't stay out there in that rain."

"I've done it before," he replied quietly, and she knew he was hesitating, waiting on her.

The wind buffeted the wagon, rocking it slightly, making her gasp. He took her by the shoulders and said, "It's going to be all right."

She only nodded.

He released her. "I'm getting your gown wet."

"I know." But instead of moving away, she moved even closer.

"Katie, this isn't wise."

"Hold me. Please."

"I'll just get you all wet."

"Then take off your shirt."

"That won't help. I'm wet to the skin."

"I don't mind. Really."

He hesitated, then put his arms around her, holding her close and soaking her gown, he was sure, with the water that dripped from his hair and seeped through his shirt. He didn't know if she felt better, but he hadn't felt this good since the night they'd kissed back in Illinois.

The sky lit up and another crack of thunder shook the ground beneath the wagon. He felt the tremor that ran through her as she buried her head under his chin.

"I'm all right. Really," she said. "You're here, and that's all that matters." She raised her head, and even though it was dark as pitch he knew she stared at him. Then he felt her tender lips brush his, tentatively at first, then with more concentration.

"I don't think you know what you're doing," he warned.

"Maybe I do."

She brushed his lips again, pressing her body into his.

He wouldn't say she was practiced, but her movements were effective all the same.

"I'd better leave," he said, mostly to give her the chance to change her mind. He would go if she wanted him to; if not. . . .

"No. I want you to stay."

This time he initiated the kissing, drawing her tight against him until the soft curves of her body melded with his. Surprisingly, his grip on her was matched by the one she had on him. With experienced intensity, he explored and tasted her sweetness that was like none he'd ever known. Her fragrance filled his nostrils, and only the raging storm outside kept him grounded in the reality of the moment.

When he broke the kiss, he heard her rapid breathing. Or was it his?

"Take off your shirt," she insisted, working at his top button, and he complied. She helped him pull the wet material from his body and let it fall at his feet on the step-well.

"Unpin your hair," he said, and the next thing he heard was the sound of pins ringing against a metal basin. She shook her head until the long strands stroked his bare shoulders.

"Should I take off my gown?" she asked, and he heard the hesitancy in her voice.

"You don't have to. I enjoy holding you even with it on."

She flung herself unexpectedly into his arms, nearly sending him backwards. "I think I'll leave it on, then," she whispered. "At least for a while."

He smiled in the dark, caressing her back, thinking. Brave, sweet, innocent Katie. He would not hurt her, nor would he expect more than she was ready to give.

"Kiss me again," she said softly against his ear. "I've never been kissed like that before."

He sifted through the length of her hair to find her neck, kissing her once, twice and a third time, each one in a different place.

"And just how many times have you been kissed?" he asked before nosing his way inside the ruffle of her gown.

"Well," she replied a little breathlessly, "a number of times, but I'm thinking that none of them count anymore."

With one hand he worked the top button loose. She didn't object.

"I'm glad to hear that," he said before lightly kissing the tender skin where her heart beat a pulse against his lips. A small shudder went through her body, and her head dropped back slightly. With one hand behind her back, he slowly lowered her to the feather tick, allowing her time to adjust her legs to accommodate the shift. Keeping his weight to the side so as not to crush her, he stretched out full length.

"I don't suppose I should ask you the same question," she said.

"My answer would be the same as yours," he replied. Then, stroking her cheek, he followed the line of her neck to the barrier of her gown and stopped there. "A number of times, but none of them count anymore."

She circled his neck with her arms. "I think I love you, Spence McCord."

"For me, there's no thinking about it. Somewhere between New York and St. Louis I made a discovery, Katie O'Rourke."

"What kind of discovery?" she asked as a pleasant warmth spread throughout her entire body at his words.

"That I can't imagine tomorrow or the next day or next year without you by my side. I want you with me always." He moved closer, edging his leg across hers, and kissed her again, more deeply than before.

For Katie the world opened up a whole new spectrum of feelings she couldn't have identified if her soul depended on it. A surge of happiness encompassed her that she was sure could never be improved upon, until his hand cupped her breast through the cotton of her gown and she wondered if maybe she should amend that thought. An inner glow warmed her and each of his caresses seemed only to intensify that heat. She had a sudden need to be rid of her clothing, but kept the notion to herself.

Putting a little space between them, she said, "It's a little warm in here, don't you think?"

"What I think is that I need to take off these boots," he replied, rolling onto his back as far as the confines of the wagon would allow. He struggled with one foot against the other until she heard each of them in turn hit the step-well. When he was free of the weight, he turned to her in the dark, searching for the tip of her nose with his finger, then kissed the spot.

"That's about an inch too high," she said, then kissed his chin.

"And that's about an inch too low," he replied.

"Do you think we can get it right this time?" She pressed her lips against his.

His answer was to lever himself over her, bracing his weight on his arms. Katie raised to meet him, pressing hard against his body, creating a need within her own. She wiggled beneath him, then twined her bare feet with his stockinged ones, and still she felt the need grow. She clasped him to her, deepening the kiss as he'd taught her only moments ago, and still the need grew. Deep and low, it built until the gown she wore no longer offered virginal protection but became an offensive barrier to the release she craved.

Somehow she struggled free of the clumsy thing, pulling at it until the buttons flew. Her elbow banged against a box but she barely gave it any notice. Like a cool hand to a burning brow, his touch on her bare skin brought a sigh of relief, but only momentarily. She arched against him, instinctively knowing where her release lay.

"Don't," he said hoarsely. "Not yet."

Suspended against him, she waited for an eternity. Then he quickly shed the rest of his clothes and hovered over her. With the gentlest of kisses, he led her into a place she'd never been before, but knew she wanted to return to again and again. Nothing in her life had prepared her for this moment, and yet she always had known that a moment like this existed.

Vaguely she was aware of the rhythm of the rain outside, beating steadily on the roof, as they rocked together in a rhythm of their own. But soon she forgot about the rain, concentrating only on the emotions within her and the man who awakened them.

Holding on to each other, he showered her face with kisses while she gave in return with her heart and soul until the heavens opened for both of them, giving each the release they strived for.

Afterwards, Katie kept still, enjoying the weight of him, the musky scent of him, and the feel of his smooth bare skin touching hers.

"You're the sweetest thing that's ever come into my life," he said. "I almost feel like pinching you to be sure that you're real." His hand brushed across her bottom, lingering on the soft, tender skin.

"No pinching," she said, trying to wiggle away, but he held her still.

"I was only joking." He leaned down and kissed the soft skin of her breast.

"Listen," she said. "The storm is over, isn't it?"

"It's been over. Even the rain has slowed down a bit."

"I guess I was too busy to notice."

"I guess you were."

They lay quietly together. Then Katie cocked her head to one side and said, "What's that sound?"

"There's a leak right over my back, and that sound is a steady drop of water plopping in the middle of it."

She laughed. "Really? Would you like to move away from it?"

"Not exactly, unless I can take you with me."

He rolled them to their sides, still facing each other.

"Is that better?" she asked.

231

"I think so, except for the edge of a box that's jabbing me in the backside."

She laughed again. "Now I have a drop of water hitting me in the ribs."

"But is your backside getting jabbed?"

"No," she said, grinning.

"Then count yourself lucky."

"And what about your feet?" she asked him.

"My feet?"

"Yes, are they hanging off the end of the floor by the step?"

"They were, but now they're tangled with yours." He tickled the bottom of her feet with his toes, and she retaliated by doing the same.

"Hey! No fair," he hollered.

"Are you that ticklish?" she said. She wiggled around until she lay directly on top of him, then poked her fingers into his ribs. He squirmed left and right in an attempt to prevent giving her fingers access.

"Stop it. Or you'll be sorry," he threatened.

"I doubt if anything you could do would make me sorry," she cooed, then she tickled him good.

"No! Stop!"

Sitting astride him, she managed to get in a few more gouges.

"It's too small in here for this!"

"You mean," she said, taking mercy on him and holding off the tickling, "that you can't get away from me." She stretched out full length on him once again.

"Exactly," he replied. "But then I don't really want to get away from you, I just want"—in one swift motion he had her beneath him—"the upper hand."

Wrapping her arms around his neck, she pulled him down to her. "That's all right with me."

"I'm glad you see things my way," he said, and pressed his lips to hers.

She reached for the soft skin of his backside, but he quickly realized her intent and grabbed her hand.

"No pinching," he said.

"I was only joking," she replied.

"Sure you were."

Deciding they'd done enough talking, Katie ran her hand up his chest and around his neck once more.

"Kiss me again," she whispered.

And he gladly complied.

Early the next morning before the sun had fully risen and after Katie and Spence had explored the wonders of each other again, they held each other close and listened to the quiet. With the flaps now raised, the brilliant colors of sunrise flooded the interior of the wagon. They snuggled together, enjoying the view, basking in the moment of togetherness, ignoring the unspoken questions they refused to allow to come to the forefront. Spence knew only that he could never let her go, no matter what the price. And now Katie felt certain she could have it both ways. With each of them figuring they could work out the details later, both of them let their thoughts go where neither of them had ever considered going before.

Spence nuzzled her ear. "I guess this isn't exactly the proper time to ask . . . I mean, I should have done things right and made an honest man out of myself first . . ."

"This is the perfect time to ask," she replied, snuggling against him, kissing his neck.

"Will you marry me, Katie, so we can be together always?"

She raised her face and looked into his eyes, hiding her moment of hesitation. Then promising herself they'd work out the details later, she replied, "Yes."

A great calm settled over Spence. He hadn't been sure

that she would accept, since he knew how important her photography was to her.

"What do you think the chances are that we'll be able to find a preacher out here?" she asked. "We've hardly met a soul."

"Probably none, unless we happen to come across a circuit preacher. But in the first town we come to, we'll find one."

"What do you suppose Tim will say?" she asked.

"Plenty."

"You're right." She paused. "Do you think he'll punch you?"

"If he gets a chance."

"Are you worried?"

He grinned at her. "Do I look worried?"

"No." She smiled. Then settling back, she said, "Hmm. Katie McCord. I like it."

"Mrs. Spence McCord," he said, testing the words slowly. "I more than like it."

"Well, we'd better get going if we're going to find that small town with a preacher."

"All right," he said with regret and let her go.

Katie slipped down to the river to bathe. When she finished, she pulled on the blue muslin dress that Spence had bought for her. Patting it into place and smoothing the creases, she returned to camp. So much time had passed since she'd worn a dress that it felt strange to have the material floating around her naked legs. But when Spence caught sight of her, the appreciative look in his eyes far outweighed the disadvantages of long skirts.

Standing across the fire from him, she pinned up her hair and smiled.

"I wasn't sure if you liked the dress or not," he said, returning her smile.

When she finished with her pins, she spread her skirt

to better view the material. "Somehow I like it better now than before."

"Somehow you look even better in it now than before." In two strides he was standing in front of her, pulling her into his arms and kissing her upturned face.

"Are we going to have breakfast?" she asked, teasing him.

"Maybe not. That dress is giving me other ideas."

"Mr. McCord, whatever shall I do with you?"

"Just leave that up to me," he said as he swung her up into his arms and marched back to the wagon.

Chapter Eighteen

After weeks of traveling across the hot and dusty prairie while continuing to follow the Platte River, Katie and Spence finally rode into a small town. The first thing they did was to get a room in the only hotel available and the second was to get a meal that consisted of anything but beans.

Katie cut up the fried steak on her plate with great anticipation. Whipped potatoes, gravy and an assortment of vegetables accompanied the meat but were less interesting at the moment. She popped the chunk into her mouth and nearly moaned with ecstasy.

"You act as though you've been starved," Spence teased.

She pointed at his plate with her fork. "And what about you?" Fried potatoes, steak, eggs, biscuits and gravy were piled so high it was impossible to tell if there was a plate underneath it all.

"I have been starving," he whispered, leaning across the table toward her.

236

"That's not my fault," she returned.

"Yes, it is."

"And I haven't been sleeping very well," she countered.

"That isn't my fault," he said.

"Yes. It is."

Both chewed on their steak, contemplating the other, watching the mischievous sparkle in each other's eyes.

"We could remedy that," he suggested, "by getting separate rooms. If you want to."

"I wasn't complaining," she said.

"Neither was I."

A commotion at the front desk interrupted their dinner, drawing the attention of everyone in the dinning room to the wide doorway where they had a clear view of what was happening.

A woman wearing a large, flowery hat that far outweighed the rest of her stood ramrod-stiff in front of the clerk. In her hand she clutched a parasol as though it were a weapon.

"What do you mean," said the woman, her voice a sing-song of accusation, "you don't know who or where he is?"

"Mrs. Abernathy, not everyone that comes in here tells me his occupation. Or their problems," the clerk replied, then muttered, "Thank goodness." He picked up his paper and began reading.

With her parasol, Mrs. Abernathy pushed his paper aside. Obviously, she had no intention of being dismissed so easily.

"The livery man told me he came into town late this morning. Could you at least look and see the name of the man who most recently checked in?" she scolded.

"I could," he answered, unruffled and unimpressed with her proper demeanor. "But maybe the person wants to keep his privacy. Did you think of that?"

"Why must you be so difficult? I simply want the

name of the man who owns the photographer's wagon."
A forced smiled pinched her lips as she said, "Please."

"No," he said emphatically.

Katie watched the entire scene unmoving until she heard her wagon mentioned. Tossing aside her napkin, she rose from her seat. Spence stayed where he was, enjoying his meal. He had long since discovered that she could handle herself in any situation that came along.

"Mrs. Abernathy," Katie said, extending her hand. "I'm Katie O'Rourke and the photographer's wagon you're speaking about is mine." She smiled pleasantly, waiting for the woman to shake her hand.

"Oh," Mrs. Abernathy said, finally accepting her offered hand. "You're the photographer." Her sharp glance took in Katie's simple blue dress, scuffed shoes and bright locks of hair.

"Yes. Is there anything I can do for you?"

"Well. I don't know."

"I do," interrupted the clerk. "Her daughter's getting married in the morning and there isn't a picture-taker for more 'n a hundred miles." He smiled. " 'Cept for you."

"A wedding," Katie replied. "That's such a special moment in a young woman's life."

"She's thirty-five," whispered the clerk. "And that's what makes it more special than you know," he added with a wink.

Mrs. Abernathy shot him a warning look. "Mind your manners, Barney. And your *own* business."

He shrugged. "I always try to do just that." Turning his back, he opened his paper again.

Mrs. Abernathy tugged Katie's elbow, pulling her across the small lobby to get a little privacy.

"Caroline's wedding is in the morning," she informed Katie as though the clerk hadn't already mentioned it, "just as soon the preacher arrives in town." She shook her head sadly. "I have regretted her haste in making this match, but"—she lifted one hand, palm up, in a helpless gesture—"there you have it. She's unwilling to listen to me, or to reason. So I want this occasion to be a memorable one for her, since Lord knows the rest of her life probably will not amount to more than toil and trouble." Mrs. Abernathy sighed and gave a single shake of her head.

"I'd be happy to photograph your daughter," Katie said.

"I should ask about your fee, but unless it's outrageous, I'll pay it. This is an important day to Caroline."

"Where would you like the photograph taken?"

"At my home. In front, maybe. Or perhaps in the carriage in front of the house. Yes, that's it." She sighed again. "So many decisions in such a short time. How can I possibly get it all done? Well, I simply must. And that's all there is to it," she said with finality, thumping her parasol tip on the floor. "My house is directly behind the mercantile, which I own. The preacher is expected to arrive in the morning for Sunday services. He comes every other week. Sometimes. But since he missed last week, his appointed time, we can be certain he will be punctual this week. Come early so you can set up your camera and meet Caroline." Mrs. Abernathy nodded and said, "I must be on my way, now. Good day, Miss O'Rourke."

Katie nodded, but the woman was already going out the door.

Returning to her meal, Katie sat across from Spence, who was scraping up the last of the gravy with a biscuit.

"I think your dinner's cold," he said.

"I don't mind. I'm hungry enough that it doesn't matter." She picked up her fork and resumed eating without saying anything more.

"So what was the fuss all about?" he asked.

She shrugged, acting unconcerned. "Oh, the woman's

daughter is getting married and she would like her photograph taken before she embarks on a life of 'toil and trouble.' "

"A wedding, huh? That means there's a preacher in town," he said.

"Not exactly. He's arriving tomorrow," she said before biting into a biscuit.

"What great timing, Miss O'Rourke." He grinned at her. "What about a dress? You need a new one."

"Mrs. Abernathy just happens to own the mercantile."

"We'll go right after you finish your dinner." He pointed to her nearly empty plate with raised brows. "Would you care for some pie?"

Without looking up, she replied, "No, thank you. Maybe later." She drank her coffee, wiped her face with her napkin and said, "I'm ready."

Spence paid for their dinner, then took her elbow. Together they walked down the dusty street since there were no boardwalks to connect the few businesses. The hotel was by far the largest of the buildings with the bank next, then the mercantile, a post office and barber shop/bathhouse and the livery with a blacksmith. A few east-and-west streets ran parallel to the main street where the homes of the townspeople were located. Conspicuously occupying one end of the main street was a small schoolhouse. And just as conspicuously missing was a saloon. The town was quiet, and probably always stayed that way.

The darkened interior of Abernathy's Mercantile took a little getting used to, so Katie stood just inside the door waiting for her eyes to adjust. The rich aromas peculiar to such establishments filled the air along with the earthy fragrance of freshly dug vegetable roots.

Spence stepped around her, making his way to the fabric section of the store. Katie followed as soon as she saw the lovely boutique tucked away in the corner.

Headless dress forms wore gowns that any New York debutante would have loved to own. Kneeling before one of the dresses with a row of pins in her mouth was a pleasantly plump woman who was probably somewhere in her thirties. Katie knew she had to be Caroline.

She lifted one finger in a request for a moment of time, then quickly pinned up the hem she was working on. Taking the last pin from her mouth and pushing it into the fabric, she said, "There! All done." With a little effort she rose to her feet. Her cheeks were a rosy pink, and a happy sparkle shone in her eyes.

"What can I do for you?" she asked.

"You must be Caroline," Katie said.

"And you must be the photographer." If Caroline looked happy before, she looked absolutely vibrant now. Katie thought about herself and concluded, that's how love makes you feel. Mrs. Abernathy was wrong to decide that this match was a mistake.

"I just can't believe my good fortune," Caroline went on. "A wedding photograph! I never would have dreamed it possible."

"I'm glad we're here, too." Katie didn't say so, but she couldn't believe her own and Spence's luck, either. She would have a lovely dress to be married in, and a preacher would be arriving in the morning. "We were hoping to find a preacher in town."

"Oh! You're going to be married, too!"

Katie nodded, smiling happily. Caroline's enthusiasm was more than a little contagious.

"We came in to look for a dress," Spence said.

Caroline turned toward the array of finished dresses. "I have one for almost every occasion, but I seldom sell many here."

"Where do you sell them?" Katie asked, surprised that there might be another town nearby.

"I send them to St. Louis to a dress shop. The lady

who buys them likes my designs and so she sends me the material I need. It's a nice little business."

"Are all of these sold?" Spence asked.

"No. Some are new designs and are not ready to sell. Like that green one. Not that it isn't finished, I just haven't made up my mind if the cut is right. You know, the lay of the material." Caroline smiled. "I'm sorry. I'm sure you didn't want to hear about the details of stitchery."

But Katie wasn't listening anyway. She had her eyes fastened on the lovely emerald green dress with an almost pearlescent sheen. A high, stiff neckline was softened by matching lace at the base of the neck and cascaded down the front while a bustled tier of gathers formed the back of the dress. She guessed she'd been so long on the prairie that even a bustled dress looked good, and this one in particular was beautiful enough to be a wedding dress.

"We want that one," she heard Spence say, indicating the green dress.

Caroline nodded in agreement. "It will be perfect on you."

Katie had the feeling that the dress had been waiting for her to make the trip just to get it, she felt that strongly about wanting it.

Spence excused himself and went off to look at other supplies, leaving Katie to talk with Caroline about dresses, weddings and photographs.

"I'm all butterfingers today," Caroline said to Katie as she tried to tie the string on the package for the third time. "I always hate to fold them and wrap them up. The creases are such a dickens to get out again. But I found that if you stuff the sleeves and the bodice with paper, it isn't nearly so bad. Of course, you'll be wearing it tomorrow," she said with a smile. "So just hang it in your room right away and it should be fine."

"Thank you," Katie replied. "I will."

Then returning to the subject uppermost in both of their minds, Caroline said, "Imagine. Our wedding day will be the same."

"Yes," Katie replied, smiling. "What about your dress? Did you make it, too?"

She nodded. "Would you like to see it?"

"I'd love to."

"It's at the house, which is right out the back door. I need to tell Jeff to keep an eye on the store while we're gone."

Katie found Spence and told him she'd see him later at the hotel, then she waited for Caroline.

"Come with me. We'll put your package back here," Caroline said. They walked through the curtained doorway into a storage room and finally out the back door.

"Mother is taking her afternoon nap, but we won't bother her. She sleeps very soundly." Caroline opened the door of the large two-story house that seemed too big for only two people. There was certainly enough room for a husband to join them, and children, too.

In a downstairs bedroom, Katie stared with admiration at the lovely wedding dress. Caroline had a remarkable talent.

"You made this?" Katie exclaimed.

"And designed it."

"You would do well to have a business in St. Louis or even New York," Katie said honestly. She fingered the lace attached by the tiniest stitches.

"Mother thinks so, too." Caroline lowered her voice, even though she'd told Katie how soundly her mother slept. "She's unhappy about my marriage to Stephen. But she doesn't understand that being a successful woman doesn't compare to being happy. And when I'm with Stephen I'm so happy!" She clasped Katie's hands in her own. "You know what I mean, don't you? Loving someone and being loved is all that I need."

Katie wondered about the "toil and trouble" that Mrs. Abernathy had predicted.

"Will you be living here?"

"No, oh, no! Stephen owns a ranch north of here. I haven't seen it, but he tells me it's beautiful. When he comes to town, which isn't as often as we'd like, we spend all our time together making plans. He's really quite wonderful. And the children are, too."

"Children?"

"Yes, he has two girls and a boy." Caroline blushed to the roots of her dark hair. "And I'm expecting his child."

Katie's eyes widened in surprise. She could just imagine the hair-raising scene when Mrs. Abernathy discovered this news.

"I've been working every spare minute trying to get my dress finished before Brother Jeremiah arrives. He's the circuit preacher. The problem with him is that you never know if he'll show up, but I'm confident that he'll be here tomorrow since he missed last week. He never misses two in a row."

But Katie cared little for the information about Brother Jeremiah; she was still concentrating on the news about an unborn child. Her gaze shifted to Caroline's midsection.

Protectively, Caroline sheltered her stomach with her hands, and smiled. "I'm past three months. Mother doesn't suspect. It wouldn't matter if she did."

"What about Stephen?"

"He's as happy as I am. Maybe even more anxious to get me to the ranch, where he says he can watch me every day."

"Why did you wait this long?"

"Mother's health hasn't been good, or so she's led me to believe. I've since come to the conclusion that she's been hoping for a long time that I would travel east with her and open a dress shop. But I've waited for this day all my life. I have no interest in going east. This is where I belong, with Stephen, with our family. I've waited long enough. Tomorrow I'm going to be married, one way or another."

Katie saw the determination in Caroline's eyes, and decided that her mother was wrong to assume that her daughter would not do well as the wife of a rancher.

"You will be a lovely bride tomorrow," Katie said. "I wish you the best of everything."

"And I wish you the best."

"So, where would you like the picture taken?" Katie asked.

"I believe in front of the house. It's far too stuffy inside to suit Stephen. Actually, we'd like to have the wedding outside, too, but Mother wouldn't hear of it. So I'll compromise." She smiled happily.

"Then I'll set up my camera in front of the house."

"Katie . . ." Caroline paused. "You will be careful not to let Mother know about the baby, won't you? I shouldn't have said anything, but it's been so difficult to keep it to myself for so long, and with our wedding days being the same, I guess it just sort of seemed appropriate to share my happy news with you."

"Of course I'll be careful. You can count on that." And truthfully, she hoped not to be around when Mrs. Abernathy found out.

"Thank you." Caroline touched the wedding dress with one last loving pat, then said, "I suppose I should get back to the store."

The two of them went quietly through the house and across the backyard to the mercantile. Katie retrieved her package and said good-bye. In the short walk to the hotel, she wondered about several things: weddings, babies and marriage, not necessarily in that order. Babies didn't generally come first, but it did happen. Could it happen to her, too?

* * *

Later that evening as Katie and Spence lay in bed together, snuggling and touching, Katie wondered about the things Caroline had said. Her happiness with Stephen meant more to her than the talent she had in designing dresses. How much did Katie's photography mean to her? More than marriage to Spence? She didn't see why she had to choose. Didn't their traveling together prove that she could have both?

"What are you thinking so hard about?" Spence asked.

"Why are you so sure I'm thinking hard?"

"Because you've drawn that same circle on my arm about a hundred times."

She stopped drawing. "I have not."

"You have. So tell me what's on your mind." He took one of her curls and tickled her nose with it. "Tell me."

"Nothing really. I was just thinking about what I was going to do with my pictures." It was as close as she could get to telling him what exactly was on her mind.

"I've wondered that myself. You've never explained what your intentions were."

"Oh," she said, offhandedly brushing at the strand of hair. "I always thought I'd show them in a gallery."

"Hmmm. A gallery. That's where other pictures hang on the wall, too?"

"Yes, but it's not that simple." She didn't want to go into it right then. A sort of sadness had begun to build in her chest. She knew she wasn't like Caroline. Her photography meant too much to her to give it up so easily, if she could at all.

"Nothing ever is," he said, holding her closer. "Nothing ever is."

Katie wore her blue dress the next morning out of respect for Caroline's wedding, even though she knew that the britches would be easier to work in. Her own wedding dress would remain hanging in her room until later. She and Spence would be married in the afternoon.

Spence pulled the wagon in front of the Abernathys' house where a large gathering of people had already begun to assemble. Apparently the church service and wedding would be a combined event.

Katie set up her camera in the most appropriate place and stationed Spence where he could protect it from inquisitive adults and rambunctious children. When all was ready, she went in search of Caroline and her mother.

As Katie stepped in the front door, Caroline stepped out of her bedroom wearing her wedding dress, with her mother close behind protesting vehemently.

Katie thought the bride looked especially radiant. The creamy silk of the dress accented the rosy pink of her cheeks, and the cut of the dress slimmed her plump figure. Although Katie wondered if the plumpness might be because of her condition.

"Caroline! I insist that you remain in your room until the ceremony begins." Mrs. Abernathy strutted behind her daughter, wearing a dark blue silk that could have come from Godey's.

"Mother, it's hotter than blue blazes in there and I simply can't tolerate the heat. Besides, we all know that if Jeremiah was coming he'd have been here long before now. Likely he's drunk in a ditch somewhere. Again."

"Shhh! Don't speak such language. We have guests waiting outside."

"They all know it, too. It's not a secret." Caroline paced the floor, her face concentrated in soft lines of decision making.

At that moment the front door opened and in stepped a man dressed in a plain suit of dark serge.

"Stephen!" cried Mrs. Abernathy, her face suddenly turning white. "You can't come in here yet!" She tried to hide Caroline behind her.

247

"For heaven's sake, Mother," Caroline said, escaping the older woman's clutches.

"Oh," Mrs. Abernathy moaned. "It's bad luck for the bride to be seen before the wedding. And we've already had more bad luck than I can bear."

Caroline stared at her mother with a new resolve.

"Step into the bedroom with me, Mother. I have something to tell you." She turned to Katie. "I may need some help."

Katie nodded and trailed along behind.

Chapter Nineteen

"A baby!" Mrs. Abernathy grasped the bedpost in a near swoon and Katie stepped forward to steady her. "Caroline, oh, Caroline! How could you?" Regaining her wits somewhat, she pierced her daughter with a stare. "*When* did you? I mean, I was always here . . . you were always here. . . ."

"That's after the fact, Mother. I don't want to discuss it."

"But he's just a farmer! A sod farmer!" she moaned.

"He's a rancher. And even if he were a sod farmer, it wouldn't matter to me. I love Stephen."

"I had such plans for you, for us, in St. Louis or New York—"

"I never wanted that, Mother. You did."

Mrs. Abernathy began crying. "You have such talent," she said, sniffling, and Katie handed her a hanky from the dresser. "I just hate to see it wasted out here in the middle of nowhere. And this town is in the middle of nowhere, too. I just hate it. I always have."

"What good is my talent if I have nobody to love or to love me?" Caroline asked softly, tears welling in her own eyes.

"I love you, dear," said her mother.

"I'm sorry, Mother," Caroline replied. "I know you do. I didn't mean to be hurtful. But I want a husband and a child of my own. Making dresses isn't enough. Talent alone will not sustain me. I need love. I need a family of my own."

Katie slipped out of the door, giving them the privacy they should have. With her back to the parlor, she pulled the door shut with a soft click. Caroline sounded so sure of herself and what she wanted from life. Katie thought she knew, but now she was confused because a whole new dimension had been added to her life and she didn't know how to make it all fit together. Unlike Caroline, Katie wasn't willing to give up anything. She wanted it all. But could she realistically have it all? A lump formed in her chest and she knew that she couldn't.

She glanced through the open front door to see Spence in conversation with Stephen. Both men's arms were crossed over their chests as they talked about cattle. A boy around five or six tugged at Stephen's coat. Reaching out a hand, he tousled his son's hair.

Katie dropped into a nearby chair. The rooms swarmed with neighbors, all well-wishers for the bride and groom. But there would be no ceremony, not for Stephen and Caroline, and not for Spence and Katie. The new sadness over her dilemma overshadowed the fact that there would be no wedding, and that only made her more sad.

The bedroom door suddenly swung open.

"Caroline, don't do it!" warned her mother. "Lord in heaven, don't let her do this!"

"Hush, Mother." Caroline crossed the room and stepped onto the porch, motioning to Stephen. He quickly joined her and after a few moments of quiet words, he nodded. Katie saw him squeeze her small hand tight in his large one.

"Everyone!" Caroline called out to the crowd.

Mrs. Abernathy moaned.

"We all know that Brother Jeremiah won't be here after all," Caroline announced. "But the ceremony will go on as planned."

Mrs. Abernathy moaned again.

"Stephen and I would like you to witness our vows to each other, and we're sure the Lord will bless us. When Brother Jeremiah gets around to it, he can do the honors all over again."

Katie stayed where she was, as did everyone else. In quiet reverence the crowd waited and listened while the couple stood on the porch. Mrs. Abernathy, who had apparently collected herself, held her head proudly erect as she listened, too.

"I, Caroline Abernathy, do promise to love and to cherish you as my husband. I will love and protect those who the Lord has given into our care. And I will stand beside you, never wavering but always steadfast in my devotion. I ask only that you love me in return, giving me the whole of your heart."

Stephen held both of her hands in his. His face was ruddy either from the work on the ranch or from having to share his innermost feelings in front of people he hardly knew.

With a deep, earnest voice he said, "You have my promise to love you with the whole of my heart. I will protect you and care for you until my dying day. As the Lord is my witness."

Caroline smiled at him and he broke into a happy grin, pulling her into a hug and kissing her full on the lips beyond the proper length of time.

A hoot and a holler went up and the merriment began.

Katie hurried outside to prepare for the photograph. She climbed onto the step at the back of her wagon, pulling the curtain behind her. The orange calico that she had used in the beginning of her journey had long since gone to tatters and been replaced with one of Spence's cast-off shirts. Her mind flitted between the task at hand and her growing concern over their marriage. In the beginning she had thought of herself as a true pioneer, and she was. How many women had ever done what she had, and in fact was still doing? Very few, if any. And what about the future?

She placed the receptacles on the drop-down shelf in the order she'd gotten so used to that she was sure she could do the entire process in her sleep. Within reach of her right hand was the collodion, a mixture of sulphuric ether, alcohol, salts of bromide and iodide of potassium. The smell no longer made her nose wrinkle; it was part of her living quarters and part of her. In front of her was the developing bath, an iron sulphate solution including acetic acid. Ahead of that was the fixing agent of cyanide potassium.

When everything was where she needed it, she removed the glass plate from the dust-proof box that had served her well, then with a pair of tongs she dipped the plate into the collodion. When it all flowed properly across the plate, she removed it and held it suspended until it attained the proper amount of stickiness. Carefully, she lowered it into the silver nitrate and waited four minutes.

In her mind she heard Caroline say again, "Talent is not enough to sustain me. I need love."

Quickly she slipped the plate into the slide holder and emerged from the tent.

Stephen and Caroline stood facing each other, a picture of happiness before the photograph had actually been taken. Katie inserted the glass plate, exposed it and returned to the wagon.

Almost without thought, she put the plate through the series of developing baths, washing and fixing, then a final washing, drying and varnishing. Next she placed the paper in close contact with the glass negative in a printing frame and emerged once more from the wagon to place it in the sunlight, where it would "take." Then returning to the wagon for the last time, she stabilized the print and added a toner.

The finished photograph of the bride and groom stared back at her. They were, indeed, a very happy pair.

Katie flipped back the flap and stepped down. Caroline waited anxiously not two strides away.

"Here you are," Katie said.

"Oh! Stephen, look." Caroline handed it to Stephen and they bent their heads together over it. "I can't tell you how much this means to me," she said to Katie, giving her a hard squeeze.

Katie nodded and smiled, but suddenly wanted to be away from all the merriment. She needed time alone to think, to decide. She said all the proper things, then excused herself to clean up the wagon.

When she was ready to bring in the camera, Spence was there handing it to her.

"Thank you," she said and slid it into its protected space.

"Would you like to leave now?" he asked.

She nodded.

"I'll take care of the farewells," he said.

She nodded and went around the wagon. In no time he was on the seat beside her, and they drove in silence down the street until they pulled up in front of the hotel.

"I know you're disappointed about the preacher not showing up," he said. "We could wait if you want. He might show up tomorrow."

"No. I'd rather leave today. What about you?"

"There are other towns and other preachers," he said.

He had misunderstood her downheartedness, and she didn't want to dispel that misunderstanding even though it was unfair of her. Maybe by the time an opportunity came up again she'd have things straightened out. She hoped so, because right now her heart just plain hurt.

With every mile they traveled, Spence could feel Montana getting closer, could almost smell it in the air. The dust and wind of the prairies gave way to the dust and wind of the West. Most might not notice the difference, but Spence did. He'd been looking forward to this since they had first pointed Katie's wagon toward the mountains two months ago.

Two months, he thought. He glanced over at her where she sat quietly observing the landscape. She'd gone back to wearing her britches right after the wedding fiasco, but he hadn't minded at all. She was right; they were sensible, and they looked good on her, too. And as long as there wasn't anyone else around to appreciate the view that was meant only for his eyes, he didn't care.

He had planned to follow the north fork of the Platte on up to Fort Laramie but had changed his mind. Instead they had forded the south fork, almost losing a wheel in the process, and headed to Cheyenne. It was the last big town before reaching the Circle M T, if you didn't count Deadwood, which he didn't. Another day and he figured they'd be in Cheyenne, where there was bound to be a preacher. There was no way that he wanted to take Katie back to Tim's without first speaking their vows. He loved her too much to put her through the embarrassment and harassment that Tim was sure to inflict. So one more delay was in order.

Spence pulled the horses to a halt on a small rise where they had a good view of the growing town. The

Union Pacific railroad was the main attraction here, with the cattle business a sure second.

"It is impressive," Katie said, and it was. After all the loneliness of the prairie, coming onto so much civilization seemed almost overwhelming. "Every town has its own flavor, doesn't it? You can practically feel it even from here."

"I know what you mean," he replied. Then with a flick of the reins he urged the horses on but kept a watch out for holes. Limping into town with a broken wheel wasn't exactly what he had in mind. But he was close enough to home that the worry had sort of seeped out of him, and being with Katie just made it better.

He stopped in front of a large hotel, where he unloaded the valises and her wedding dress. Inside, they waited at the desk for a clerk to sign them in.

Katie stared with open curiosity at the plush carpets, brass railings and velvet draperies of rich burgundy. Around them milled women dressed in the finest and men who lightly ushered them. In one corner, a group of men smoked cigars and laughed loudly, clapping each other on the back.

"They've come for a cattlemen's meeting," Spence told her.

"What sort of things do they do when they're all dressed up that way?"

"They're backers or buyers."

"Oh."

They waited for a few more minutes, then Katie offered, "Why don't you go ahead to the livery and I'll get the room. I'll be fine."

He glanced around one last time, but since no clerk could be seen, he agreed to her suggestion, saying he wouldn't be long.

Katie stood facing the pigeonholes behind the desk where envelopes filled some of the numbered spaces. At her feet were the two valises and in her arms was her wedding dress. After another few minutes of waiting, her patience had begun to wear thin. Where was the clerk anyway? From behind her came the sound of laughter again, only this time it belonged to a woman, a familiar woman. Turning around she came face to face with Lorena Kendricks.

"Well, well, who have we here?" Lorena said, a broad smile on her silky soft face. "Molly, isn't it?"

"Katie. Katie O'Rourke."

"Yes. I remember the O'Rourke part," Lorena said. "Tim's little sister." She gave Katie a quick appraisal, then wrinkled her nose. "Just get into town?"

"As a matter of fact, we did."

"We? Is Spence still with you?" she asked, her brows raised in surprise.

Katie decided she wasn't answering any more questions. "If you'll excuse me, I'm looking for someone."

"Of course, dear. Enjoy your stay. You are staying here, aren't you?"

Katie gave her a quick nod, then gathered her valises and headed for an out-of-the-way corner to escape Lorena's probing eyes and questions. She'd wait for Spence to check into their room. As she walked away she heard Lorena call to a clerk passing by, asking for the key to room twenty. Katie hoped to high heaven that their room was on a different floor; better yet, maybe she could talk Spence into a different hotel.

When Lorena went up the stairs, she turned and gave Katie a sharp glance, leaving her feeling as if she'd been visually clawed.

After thirty minutes or so, Spence came through the double front doors. Surprised to see her still waiting, he went to her and picked up her bags.

"No rooms?" he asked.

Tempted to lie in order to be sure he'd agree to try another hotel, she hesitated but said truthfully, "I don't know. I haven't asked."

"Well, let's ask."

"Wait, Spence," she said, grasping his shirt sleeve. "Couldn't we go somewhere else?"

"But this is the nicest one in town, and I want our stay here to be the best in every way."

"I don't need the nicest. Really. Half as nice would be just as good, even better. I'm hardly dressed to compete with the women here."

He kissed the top of her head. "You're not in competition with anyone, but if you were, you'd win hands down. So come on." He headed for the desk, and she had no alternative but to follow.

The clerk handed Spence a key and said, "Room twenty-eight."

Well, Katie thought, at least it wasn't right next to Lorena's. Although being on the same floor was hardly comforting. When they reached the top of the stairs, Katie was thankful that their room was to the left and Lorena's was all the way down to the right.

Spence unlocked their door and pushed it aside, letting Katie go in first.

The room was darkened by heavy draperies at the tall windows, but instead of giving a sense of being closed in, the room felt secluded and private. A large four-poster bed occupied one end of the room, leaving space for a settee and two chairs.

"Do you like it?" he asked.

"Like it! It's beautiful, and such a difference from the back of my wagon."

He set aside the bags he'd carried, and wrapped her in his arms. "But I wonder if it will be half as much fun."

"Somehow I doubt it," she replied.

"Well, we could always go down to the livery."

She laughed. "What do you suppose the livery man would say about that?"

Spence nibbled at her ear. "We'll probably never find out."

Katie let him kiss her, enjoying the warm, delicious sensations that he always aroused in her. During moments like these she could easily put aside her fears and concerns, her confusion and frustration. At a moment like this she could not honestly imagine another day without him by her side. But would he by her side? Would he understand her need to see her photographs in a gallery, to finish what she'd started?

When he held her so securely and tenderly, her emotions insisted there was nothing to decide, but her logical mind reminded her of the life-long goals she would have to give up just when she'd come so close to attaining them.

"Spence?"

"Hmm?"

"I need to talk to you about something."

"I know, we need to find a preacher and make an honest man out of me. I've been suffering with the worst kind of guilt just thinking about facing your brother." He sought her lips and kissed her deeply. "Not that I'm sorry about anything. I love you, Katie, and I want you to be my wife. Have I told you that yet?"

"Yes, you have," she replied breathlessly. With parted lips, she waited for another round of soul-searing kisses. He didn't disappoint her.

At last she drudged up the strength to say, "I need to talk to you about something else."

"Something more important than finding a preacher?"

He nibbled at the edges of her lips, making it difficult to think, let alone talk.

Turning her head slightly, she said, "Not more important, but just as important."

"The only thing that could be more important is if you

know something that I don't about . . . Are you . . . ?"

"What?" she responded, puzzled at first. "No. No, nothing like that." At least she didn't think so. Actually, she hadn't stopped to count the days, or was it weeks, since she'd had a monthly. "I need to ask you some questions. Would that be all right? If we just sat down and talked for a while?"

"I can think of better things to do," he said, "but if you want to talk, we will."

She took him by the hand and led him to the settee.

"This looks serious," he said, smiling at her.

"It is." She tugged at him to sit down facing her. "You know why I wanted to make this trip in the first place."

"To photograph your way across the country." He leaned over and kissed her lightly. "I admit I thought it was silly at first, but it didn't take long to see that you meant business."

"I still do."

A puzzled look crossed his face. "What else is there to do?"

"Taking the pictures is only the first stage. Granted it's the most important, but it's only the beginning."

"The beginning of what?" She sensed his withdrawal in the tenseness of his body.

"I want to try to get some of them into a gallery somewhere, maybe New York, maybe somewhere else. There are some really wonderful photographs, like Granny at the barn raising and Silas with Bossie and . . . you with my wagon on the prairie." She had spoken in a rush when she saw him visibly pull away from her.

"Can't you just send them?"

"No."

"You have to go back? I thought you didn't want to go back!" He was raising his voice.

"I don't! Not to live, anyway."

"I thought you liked the land out here. You seemed to want to try your hand at everything."

259

"I do like it. I love it. I did want to try doing everything. I still want to try more."

"But only in New York, right?" He rose from the settee.

"I knew you wouldn't understand," she said quietly, studying his strong face. All the fear and confusion she'd been feeling was now mirrored there. "I had hoped . . ."

"What? That we could be married and you'd run off to New York, leaving me behind to my solitude?" He ran his fingers through his hair in a helpless gesture, then paced the floor in front of her. He halted in his tracks, stared down at her, then sat beside her. "I love you. Why can't you be happy just staying with me? It's all that I'll ever ask of you."

Tears of sadness filled her eyes and a lump clogged her throat until it hurt. "I don't know," she said softly, her mouth contorting with each painful word. In her mind she heard Caroline's words: "Talent alone will not sustain me. I need love."

Katie needed both.

"Well," Spence said, getting to his feet again. "I guess it's a good thing we got this figured out before it was too late."

Too late? her mind echoed. It was already too late. She loved him with all her heart and soul. Through her tears she watched him cross the room and go out the door. The worst pain she'd ever experienced ripped through her as she flung herself onto the settee and wept. Deep, gut-wrenching sobs that she could not control rolled over her, pulling her under, giving her no release.

Too late. . . .

Chapter Twenty

Spence walked the streets until dark. He avoided all of the usual socializing places like the cattlemen's club and the saloons, and especially the whorehouses. He needed time to think and he needed to be alone. Walking was the only option left.

Before long he found himself at the livery where he had left the horses and wagon. He paid the man in charge an extra coin for the use of the hayloft for the night. He climbed the ladder and chose the loose hay near the open loft doors where he could see the expanse of sky lit by the stars. At least it was quiet here, with nothing more than the familiar sounds of the horses below him. A cool breeze swept through the doors, but he hardly noticed the chill in the air. That, too, was familiar.

How many times had he stared at the sky on nights such as this, he wondered, with only himself for company? So many times he couldn't count them all. So why did it matter if he spent that many and more in the same way?

Because now he loved Katie.

He inhaled deeply of the fragrant hay that nestled beneath his body, warming him. That, too, was a familiar part of his life. All of these things were comforting, but they didn't replace what he'd just lost.

Nothing could replace Katie.

A distant star fell across the sky, and he felt the pain of having nothing to wish for, except perhaps that she would change her mind and come with him to Montana as his wife. But that was a useless wish. She was a complicated woman with needs he didn't understand.

But hell, he thought, all women were complicated, so how could he understand them? If they weren't sneaking and manipulative like Lorena, they were soft and loving with minds of their own like Katie. A man didn't stand a chance of winning in a game like that. He was better off never picking up the cards in the first place. But once he'd picked them up, what was he supposed to do? Pretend he'd never felt anything and go back to living the solitary life?

Without Katie, life would be worse than solitary. But the choice was hers, not his. She'd made up her mind that she didn't want him, just like Lorena had so many years ago, but he'd gotten over that.

He'd get over Katie, too. Or else he'd die trying.

In the meantime, he had a debt that still needed repaying. He'd promised to bring her to Montana to Tim, and that's what he intended to do. Repaying that debt would be just one more thing from the past that he could put to rest right along with the pain of Lorena's rejection.

But this new pain would take some time, maybe forever.

Spence awoke early. The sound of the bellows was enough to bring a drunk man around, and the clang of the hammer on the anvil could bring the dead to life.

He searched through the hay for his hat and swung down the ladder, brushing bits of straw from his clothes when he reached the bottom. He walked toward the sound of the smithy and found the man dousing the hot iron in a bucket of water where it sizzled and steam filled the air.

"What's the chance that you'll have that wheel fixed today?" Spence asked him.

"Not much. Got a couple of orders ahead of you," he said without looking up. Then he banged on the metal with his hammer until Spence's ears rang.

"When do you suppose you'll get to it?" he asked when the noise subsided.

The man shrugged. "Can't tell. Check back later in the day and I'll see how close I am."

Spence nodded but said nothing as the man went back to pounding on the anvil.

Outside, the early morning sun had risen, giving promise of a clear day. The smell of the cattle pens told him he wasn't far from the Union Pacific, and he felt an instant desire to be back on the range. But first he had to set a few things straight with Katie, then get her safely to Tim.

He crossed the lobby, took the steps two at a time and turned to the left. He'd left the key inside their room and so was forced to knock or go back to the desk and ask for another one.

"Katie?" he called through the door as he knocked.

He heard the squeaking of the springs and knew she was awake. He knocked again. "Katie, open the door."

"Go away." Her voice was muffled, and an unbidden picture of her buried in the blankets with her gown hiked past her knees came to mind.

"We have to talk."

"No."

He stood with his head down, contemplating the doorknob, listening to her toss in the bed.

"Do you want everyone in the hotel to hear what I've got to say?"

"It won't matter to me if they hear or not."

He was nearly ready to go down to the desk for a key when he heard the familiar voice of Lorena Kendricks from the other end of the hall.

"Well, if it isn't Spence McCord. I declare, will wonders never cease?" She strolled toward him, stopping within touching distance. "Did you forget your key?"

Her voice was as sweet as sugar, but her eyes speared him with malice.

"Hello, Lorena," he said, but he had more important things on his mind and wanted to get on with them. On the other side of the door the room had suddenly become quiet.

"I said, did you forget your key?"

"Not exactly."

"Oh, the little 'lady' never gave you one, is that it?"

When he didn't answer, she shrugged, rolling one shoulder provocatively in that same practiced manner he remembered.

"What are you doing in Cheyenne?" he asked.

"Why, I'm here as the . . . guest . . . of Mr. Crandall. You remember him, don't you? He's come for some sort of cattle meeting."

Spence grit his teeth at the thought of Lorena spending time with the man who had so recently backed the Circle M T. Her parting threat of "Mark my words, you'll rue the day . . ." echoed in his mind so clearly he thought she'd actually said them again.

"Well, Mr. Crandall is waiting for me." She turned away, then stopped. Looking over her shoulder in another studied pose, she said, "Now, you two lovebirds had better patch up your differences. You know what they say about letting the sun go down with angry words between you." She gave him a cold and calculating smile that hid nothing. "Well, you can never tell what might happen, can you?"

As soon as Lorena had disappeared down the stairway, the door to the room swung wide and Katie stood before him in the same nightgown she'd been wearing for the last two and a half months. The lace collar was frayed and a tear above her left breast showed the soft skin beneath. He remembered the night they'd torn the gown; he wondered if she did.

"What did she want?" Katie practically spit the words at him.

"Never mind her. I want to talk to you," he said, pushing his way past her and closing the door.

"Never mind her? How can you never mind her? She's always there!" Katie flopped her hands against her sides. "St. Louis. Cheyenne. What's she doing here anyway? Following you?"

He'd wondered the same thing, but he wasn't about to discuss Lorena. He had more important things to settle right now. "The wagon won't get fixed today, most likely, so we'll have to figure on leaving tomorrow at the earliest."

She stared at him open-mouthed. "We?"

"Yes, we. I promised Tim I'd deliver you safe and sound to his front door, and that's just what I'm going to do. It's part of a debt I owe him."

A momentary pain crossed her eyes, and he regretted his words. But she quickly masked it with anger.

"A debt? What kind of a debt? You owe him money, as in a wager?" Her voice began to rise. "As in a bet!"

"No. Nothing like that," he said, not at all wanting to discuss any more of his past, wishing it would leave him in peace once and for all.

"Then what!" Her hands at her waist tucked the gown nicely around her hips, so he fastened his gaze on her snapping blue eyes.

"Never mind. Just get dressed so we can go down to breakfast."

"I don't want to never mind. And I don't want to eat breakfast."

"I'm hungry and I know you're hungry, so get dressed before I dress you." He leaned toward her until she backed up a step. "I mean it," he added.

"I'll eat in the room."

"Get dressed," he warned.

She hesitated, trying to stare him down, but he wasn't about to budge.

"Then turn around," she insisted.

"Turn . . ." With an exasperated sigh, he shrugged and turned around.

Within minutes she was dressed in her frayed britches and scuffed shoes. Her hair was quickly pinned up in the same way she'd worn it since he first laid eyes on her.

"All right. I'm ready."

"Good. Let's go."

He held open the door for her and she passed by him with her nose raised. She stepped smartly down the hall five steps ahead of him, and he kept his gaze on her bouncing curls rather than the firm roundness of her bottom.

At the entrance to the dining room she stopped suddenly and he nearly ran into her back. When he looked up, he saw Lorena seated at a table with Crandall. Taking Katie by the arm, he steered her toward the opposite side of the room, through the maze of tables where nearly all eyes turned to stare at her outrageous clothes. At one point she struggled to free herself from his grasp, bumping into a table and nearly upsetting a cup of coffee.

"Stop manhandling me," she said to him without lowering her voice. Then she looked at the well-dressed woman seated at the table, steadying her cup. "There should be a law against abusing women."

"I believe there is," the woman said, eying Spence critically.

He graciously tipped his hat and said, "Excuse my sister. She hasn't been the same since the Indians killed our ma and pa when she was five." He lightly tapped his temple.

The woman gasped and looked sympathetically at both of them. "Poor dear."

Spence took Katie by the elbow once more, keeping a tight grip on her this time until they reached a distant table.

"I can't believe you said that!" She snatched her arm free and sat down.

"You started it."

"I've never said you were crazy!"

"No, you only suggested that I abused you."

"You did! My arm will be purple in the morning." She rolled up her sleeve to inspect the damage, uncaring if anyone around them saw her exposed bare skin.

"Put your sleeve down," he demanded, because he did care if others looked at her bare skin.

"You can't tell me what to do."

She was right; he not only couldn't but he shouldn't. Clenching his jaw, he waited until she finally rolled down her sleeve. A waitress came and took their orders, leaving them to stare at the other diners, the walls or the tablecloth, but not at each other. When their food arrived, Spence busied himself with the steak, biscuits, potatoes and gravy. But Katie only picked at the food on her plate.

"What's the matter?" he asked. "Aren't you hungry?"

She shook her head. "I'm not feeling very well."

"You need to see a doctor or something?"

"No."

She sounded so low in spirits that he didn't press the

issue. His own appetite wasn't the best either, and he found himself eating without tasting.

After another ten minutes of silence, Katie said, "I'd like to go back to the room."

"I'm afraid that will have to wait," he said, glancing up to see Crandall with Lorena in tow heading toward them.

"Hello, McCord. Glad to see you."

Spence rose from his seat and shook hands with the man. Crandall turned to Katie and waited for an introduction.

"This is Katie O'Rourke, Tim's sister," Spence said.

"Nice to meet you, Miss O'Rourke. Is your brother here in Cheyenne?"

"No," Katie responded, unwilling to make polite conversation, especially about Tim.

"Well, perhaps I can go on up to the ranch after the meetings are over," Crandall said. "We can conduct the rest of our business there."

Lorena clutched Crandall's arm to get his attention.

"Excuse me, my dear," he said, smiling at her. "This is Lorena Kendricks. Her husband was a good friend of mine in the banking business back East."

Lorena smiled up at him. "I came all the way to St. Louis because he promised to show me the wild West. And here we are!" She stared at Spence. "Imagine."

"We don't want to bore Mr. McCord with our personal affairs, Lorena."

"But I thought you wanted everyone to know about our engagement?" she whispered loudly, looking hurt.

"Well, not just yet," he replied, getting a bit red in the face.

Katie couldn't bear to listen to any more of Lorena's silky-smooth voice or her talk about engagements and future weddings. She decided that this was as good a time as any to make her escape.

"Excuse me, please," she said, and hurried from the table without looking back.

Upstairs in her room, she leaned against the door after locking it. Tears filled her eyes, spilling over onto her cheeks. All her bravado and sass had been nothing more than a means to cover the hurt, but now that she was alone she had to let it all out. She ran to the bed and fell onto it face down, burying herself in the depth of the covers, but the refuge she sought was not there. Rolling to her back, she stared at the ceiling, wiping her face dry with the back of her hand.

All night long she'd tossed and turned, wondering, hoping that when she saw Spence again he would have changed his mind, that he would understand her needs and be willing to come to a compromise. But the stilted breakfast made it all too clear that he wouldn't. Instead, he expected her to continue on with him to Tim's.

Well, she wouldn't.

He could just buy a horse or get on a stage or walk, for all she cared, all the way to Montana. She didn't need him. She'd learned a lot about traveling, about cooking on campfires, about dangerous critters, about fires, about . . . love.

Her face crumpled into a spasm of crying again. She did need him. She loved him. But she also knew that if she turned her back on her dream she'd grow to resent him. And that would be worse than losing him now. Wouldn't it?

She let the crying take her to exhaustion; then she slept.

Katie awoke to the busy sounds in the streets below her window. She crawled out of bed and crossed the room to stare down at the commotion, feeling more like a bystander in life than ever before. Everyone seemed to have a purpose, somewhere to go, something that needed doing, and probably someone special to do it for.

Well, she had to face up to the fact that it was time she went on her way, alone. This was her dream, her goal, but somehow it had lost a little of its shine. Somehow she'd taken Spence into that dream and made him a part of it, and now it seemed like only half of a dream.

She stripped down to her underclothes and bathed her face and arms in a basin of cool water. The wet cloth soothed the puffiness of her eyes and the redness of her cheeks.

A hard knock at her door brought her to attention. She knew it must be Spence and was glad she'd locked the door again.

"Go away!" she called, laying the wet cloth across her entire face.

But the voice wasn't Spence's.

"I know you don't like me, Katie," Lorena said. "But I think you need to hear what I have to say."

"Go away. You can't say anything I'd want to hear."

"It's about Spence."

For a moment she felt a ripple of panic, then calmed it down. If anything had happened to Spence, it wasn't likely that Lorena would be the first one to tell her.

"Sorry. Not interested."

"This is important, Katie. Just open the door."

She sighed in exasperation. The woman would stand there all day undoubtedly, nagging and whining until she let her in. Well, she'd open the door but she wouldn't let her in.

Katie unlocked the door and opened it just wide enough to talk through. "What do you want, Lorena?"

With a strength that Katie hadn't anticipated, Lorena shouldered the door wide open.

"We have to talk. But not here," she said. Slowly she pulled a small gun from her reticule and pointed it at Katie. "We'll go to my room." Lorena glanced over Katie's lack of dress and smiled. "You're going on a long trip, but don't worry, you're dressed appropriately."

Lorena backed up, pushing the door still wider. Nodding, she indicated that Katie should step into the hall.

"Nobody's coming. Nearly all the men are at a meeting and the women are out shopping. And don't try anything. This little gun is quite handy and I'm an excellent shot, especially at this range. Believe me, I know what I'm talking about."

Katie's heart hammered against her chest. She had no intention of testing Lorena's words, unless she waited until they were in the hall and then called for help.

"If you try anything at all, I'll shoot you. I prefer not to, but the result is all the same. I'll simply say that I saw a man dart into one of the rooms after I heard a gun go off."

A sinking feeling in the pit of her stomach told Katie that Lorena could probably make anyone believe she'd not done it.

"Walk ahead of me and stay close." Lorena slipped the end of her reticule over the gun, keeping it pointed at Katie. "Now start moving."

The walk down the hall was the longest of Katie's life. Every instinct within her said to run, to scream, to turn on Lorena and not let her do this. But every move felt as though she were walking through deep water, unable to react quickly, unable to save herself.

Her thoughts were jerky, moving from slow to panic to slow. As she approached the stairs to the floor below, she wanted to turn her head and catch the eye of someone who happened to be passing by the foot of the steps, but any move might be interpreted as a call for help. If only someone would step out of a room and find her there in only her underwear and a gun in her back.

But no one did.

The number 20 appeared on the door before her and she stopped without being told.

"Well, isn't that interesting. You know where we're going. It almost seems like fate, doesn't it?"

Numbly, Katie thought that she was right.

"Push it open. It isn't locked."

Katie pushed the door wide and stepped inside, then Lorena closed it behind them, locking it.

"Well, it seems only fair that I explain a few things to you. After all, you're doing me quite a favor." Lorena inclined her head and said, "See that trunk?"

Katie momentarily took her eyes off Lorena, spotting the trunk near the foot of the brass bed not two feet behind Katie.

"That's your traveling trunk. I'm going to loan it to you." She paused, looking thoughtful. "Actually, I'm going to give it to you, so don't worry about sending it back. Now, I suppose you're wondering what you need a trunk for since you have no clothes to put in it. You're a very smart woman, Katie." She smiled and shook her head, as though pleased with her own intelligence. "The trunk isn't for your clothes. It's for you. This will be your means of transportation, or should I say the means with which to transport you? Yes, I think that's the correct way to put it. I've even poked a few holes in the side so you can get a little air. I'm not totally heartless."

"Why are you doing this?"

"I told you that I was going to explain a few things, just give me time. Now, where was I?" Lorena pulled up a straight-backed chair and sat down. "This could take a while so excuse me while I make myself comfortable." She kept the small derringer aimed at Katie.

Katie herself had been on that end of a gun, but she hadn't been nearly as comfortable as Lorena appeared, which led to one conclusion only: she meant what she said. If there was any move to be made, it had better be the right one.

"It all started when I married Charles. Poor Charles. He wasn't as smart as you and he underestimated me. I can see that you aren't about to do that." Lorena smiled.

"I don't care about Charles," Katie said. "What about me?"

"Well, believe it or not, there is a connection. Both of you were in the way of my having Spence. You notice I used the word 'were,' because now neither of you are."

"You'll be caught. Spence will figure it out."

"I don't think so. He'll just think you ran off with another man, especially when he reads your note." Lorena frowned prettily. "Now don't distract me. I was starting to tell you about Charles.

"I needed Charles," she went on. "He was a very important part of my life. He had money and position. I had neither. He was quite easy to manipulate, unlike Spence, so it really didn't take long before I had all the money and prestige I wanted. Then, you see, I no longer needed Charles." She shrugged, giving a slight wave of the gun. "So he was robbed and shot, and I became a widow. A very wealthy widow, I might add."

Katie kept her eyes narrowed on Lorena, letting her tell her story, hoping she became so engrossed in its details that Katie might find an avenue of escape. The feeling of treading deep water gradually lessened and her thinking lost that disjointed feel.

"Of course, I did it all for Spence as well as myself. I loved him that much. I still do."

"That isn't love," Katie heard herself say.

"Don't interrupt," Lorena said sharply. She moved the gun from one hand to the other before going on. "Months ago when Crandall came to see me, he asked if I was interested in seeing the West. He was a good friend of Charles's, you know. Anyway, he thought it might do me some good and maybe help me over my grieving. Charles never told his friends about my past or my association with Bailey. Wasn't he a dear to keep my secret?"

When she switched the gun back again, Katie was sure she'd found her avenue of escape. She only needed to wait for the right moment.

Lorena kept her eyes on her prey, yet never wavered from her story. Katie held her gaze, half listening but alert for the opportunity she needed. Her only chance was to make a move when Lorena shifted the gun. During that split second when the trigger was out of reach of both hands, she would rush ahead in an attempt to wrestle the weapon from her opponent.

Fighting down the anxiety rising within her, Katie forced herself not to do anything that would give away her intentions. Her lips were dry, but she dared not wet them. Her hands trembled, but she dared not clench them.

"Can you imagine my surprise," Lorena said, "when Crandall told me that he had business in St. Louis with Spence McCord? And at Bailey's, too. It was as though I'd been dealt the winning hand, and I couldn't let that get away."

She frowned at Katie. "But I hadn't anticipated seeing you. When I boarded the boat near Louisville, it was my mistake to take you for some urchin." Her jaw tensed. "I had no idea you would be the obstacle in my path. I thought it would be Crandall."

"I thought you wanted to marry him."

"You are so smart." She arched an appreciative eyebrow. "Unfortunately, Crandall doesn't know what he's in for when it comes to marriage with me."

"How does Spence come into all this?" Katie was amazed at the workings of the woman's mind. She'd never in her life met anyone so devious.

"Once I've disposed of you, I'll marry Crandall in order to own his share of the Circle M T. After that . . . well, another unfortunate shooting accident in an alley as we're strolling in the evening, and . . . once more I'm a rich widow. A very rich widow."

"And you think Spence will want you then."

"Of course. He wanted to marry me once, but I wasn't satisfied with who I was. I needed to prove that I was as good as anyone." She smiled smugly at Katie. "Now I'm satisfied."

"You're wrong, Lorena. You've lost your chance for real happiness," Katie said, and a dart stabbed her own heart at the words she'd just spoken.

Lorena braced her back, anger burning in her eyes. "He wanted me once, he'll want me again. I have more to offer him now. He won't be able to refuse my share of the ranch and me with it."

"Love doesn't require an offering. Love means giving freely." And her heart was pierced once more.

"You can take your platitudes with you. You might need them where you're going," Lorena said.

She shifted the gun.

Katie's heart jumped and she lunged forward with all her strength. Lorena gasped and fumbled the derringer as she attempted to get to her feet to throw off her assailant, but the gun slid through her fingers, down the front of her dress, and lay on the floor. Katie fought hard to hold Lorena prisoner in the chair while she kicked at the weapon, striving to get a good grip on the woman's arm, her dress or even her hair. For long seconds they grappled until Lorena finally managed to free herself enough to scramble away, taking Katie with her to the floor.

With her life depending on it, Katie clawed and scratched at Lorena in her effort to reach the gun first. Twice the gun was knocked out of reach, and each time both women rolled first one way, then the other. Katie's breath rasped in her chest and the blood pounded in her temples. She fought against the weight of Lorena holding her to the floor. She gritted her teeth and with one huge lunge toppled Lorena, then got to her feet, stretching toward the gun two feet away. But Lorena grasped Katie by the legs and gave her a hard jerk until her feet came out from under her and she was falling backward . . . backward . . . until her head struck something hard and everything went black.

Chapter Twenty-one

Spence climbed the stairs to Katie's room with the news that the wagon was fixed and they would leave right away. There was no reason to delay as far as he was concerned, and he was sure she would agree. He needed to wrap up this debt and be finished with it. There was a ranch to run, and he desperately wanted to get his mind back on his work. But when he reached Katie's room he found the door wide open.

"Katie?" he called, but it was plain to see that she was nowhere around.

Inside, he found her britches and shirt draped over a chair. The basin had clear water in it with the cloth lying in the bottom of the bowl.

"Katie!"

He searched under the bed and in the chifforobe, knowing that it was foolish to do so. When he found her scuffed shoes under the settee, a feeling of panic gripped him like none he'd ever known. Even the prairie fire had been something he'd been able to combat and protect her from, but this was something he couldn't explain. Where would she go without her clothes or shoes?

Nowhere. Not unless she'd been forced.

He ran from the room, took the stairs two at a time and strode to the front desk.

"Have you seen Miss O'Rourke?"

"No, sir," replied the clerk.

"How long have you been here at the desk?" His fear turned to angry agitation with the clerk, who looked barely old enough to shave.

"All morning, sir. The manager won't hardly let me go to the privy unless I get someone to sit for me."

"It's afternoon," Spence reminded him.

"Believe me, sir, I know that."

"Has anyone asked to see her?"

"No, sir."

"This is the only stairway coming down to the lobby, isn't it?" he said, pointing at the stairs to the second floor.

"Yes, sir, it is."

Spence looked around, wondering what explanation there could be for her disappearance. She couldn't be out on the streets without clothes, unless she'd gone out and bought some, which was highly unlikely. So she still had to be in the hotel somewhere. But where? And who would want to harm Katie? She knew nobody in town except him, and nobody knew her. Except Lorena.

"Has Miss Kendricks been out today?"

"Not out."

"But you have seen her."

"Yes, sir. A while ago she sent a trunk to be shipped to Denver on the next train. Said she had a sister there, in one of those, you know . . . one of those houses. Mighty kind of her to think of her sister like that, I'd say, wouldn't you?"

Lorena had no sister that Spence knew of, unless she

was speaking in a broad sense about the bordellos in Denver. A new panic rose in his chest.

"How long ago exactly did she send the trunk? And which train is it due to leave on?"

"Well, now, I can't rightly say how long because I'm not much on watching the clock. It doesn't help when you need to use the privy."

"Which train?" Spence asked, wanting to throttle the youth.

"I think it was supposed to go on the first train that was leaving. She said it didn't matter, since there was only clothes in it. You could go to the station and find out, I suppose, or just ask Miss Kendricks. She's in twenty."

Spence wasn't sure which plan would save the most time, or if Lorena would tell him the truth if he spoke to her. But searching for a trunk at the station in Cheyenne could be hopeless, and what if it had already been shipped? If he was right, and he knew he had to be, Katie was in that trunk. And if she was on a train bound for Denver, he'd run it down if he had to.

"Thanks," he said to the clerk before hurrying across the lobby again and up the stairs. Within moments he pounded on Lorena's door.

"Lorena!" he shouted. "Open the door. Now!"

"Good Lord," she said, opening the door. "What's gotten into you?"

Her hair was down, hanging loose around her shoulders, and she wore a wrapper belted snugly at the waist. She appeared to have been napping, but he wasn't buying that.

"Where's Katie?" he said as he pushed past her.

"Katie? Whatever makes you think she'd come here?"

"She wouldn't. Not willingly. Now tell me where she is."

"I haven't the vaguest idea. I'm not exactly her keeper. Are you?"

"Yes, I am." He wanted to shake her and force her to tell him what she'd done, but he kept his hands to himself. "Where did you send that trunk, and which train is it supposed to leave on?"

Her lips thinned into a straight line and she glared at him. "I don't know what you're talking about."

But he knew now for sure that she did.

He grabbed her by the shoulders, squeezing until her feet nearly left the floor. "If anything happens to her, I promise you'll rot in hell and me alongside of you if necessary. You understand that?"

"Let go of me!" She struggled against his grip.

"I mean it, Lorena. With every ounce of breath I have left in me, I'll see to it that you pay."

"I don't know where she is! Take your hands off me!"

He let her go, and she stood unsteadily on her feet, rubbing her arms.

"Get out of here before I send for the sheriff!"

"You do that. I want to see him myself as soon as I find Katie."

"You don't scare me, Spence McCord. I'm ahead of you ten steps." She gave him a smug smile. "Go find your precious Katie. If you can."

Another threat came to mind, but he decided to save it. He'd wasted enough time, too much, and she wasn't about to tell him anything. He turned and hurried from the room.

Outside on the boardwalk, the sun beat down as a dry wind swirled through the streets, and he wondered how long a person could survive in a trunk. And why hadn't Katie cried out to alert someone? Was she hurt? Was she dead?

He ran through the alleys in whatever shortcut offered itself until at last he stood on the platform of the depot. With his breath coming hard, he could barely speak to the ticket master.

"Train to Denver . . ." was all he could get out.

"Sure thing, mister. But you didn't have to be in such a all-fired hurry. Got about twenty minutes or so."

"Any other trains—"

"Nope. The last one left an hour ago but it wasn't bound for Denver, directly. Just making a stop before it heads west."

Spence passed his hand across his face. Had he missed it? How would he ever catch up to a train that left an hour ago? He prayed to God she wasn't on that train.

"Where are the trunks that will be loaded on the one that leaves soon?" he asked, his breath coming easier now.

"What you want with a trunk that's due to be shipped out? Is it yours?" The man eyed him skeptically. "We can't have anybody taking what isn't theirs, you know."

"It's mine. Believe me, it's mine."

"And you want to reclaim it?"

"I do." More than anything he wanted to reclaim her. They could work out something, anything. He was willing to do whatever he had to in order to convince her to stay with him.

"Well, then, tell me your name and I can maybe point you in the right direction," said the man.

"The tag says Kendricks."

The man peered at him over his spectacles. "Kendricks, huh?"

Spence nodded. He wanted to hurry the man but didn't want to raise so much suspicion that he ended up being delayed. The trunk had to be hot, suffocating, he thought, and if she was hurt . . .

"Well." The man paused. "Try over yonder." He pointed to a warehouse with a loading dock. "If you don't recognize it, come on back."

Without a word, Spence took off at a dead run, dodging people, baggage and children. He had to find her!

Melody Morgan

She had to be on this train and not the one that had left an hour ago. She had to be on this train.

Katie awakened slowly and gagged against the rag stuffed in her mouth, wondering what was making her so ill. And why did her head hurt with such fierce pounding? The motion beneath her was not like any she'd felt before, not a buggy, not a train, not even a wagon. She was in a small box with her arms cramped behind her and her knees shoved nearly to her chest. The motion stopped and the box dropped with a thud, making her grunt with pain.

Voices! She heard voices.

Struggling against her bonds, she rolled back and forth, trying to call out, trying to scream, but the sound was trapped in her mouth by the rag. Her elbows felt raw from banging against the back and bottom of the trunk.

She knew she was in a trunk. Lorena's trunk. She remembered the threat, the gun, the whole ugly story told by a vindictive woman. A woman who was bent on the destruction of everyone who crossed her.

The voices were receding!

"Help!" But she knew the word was so muffled it couldn't be heard by anyone but herself. The word echoed in her brain, drowning out all reason. Frantic to be free, she tried kicking the end of the small cubicle, but her efforts were futile. She kicked and she screamed and she rocked but succeeded only in bruising herself. The darkness bore in on her, taking her breath, taking her life.

Calm, she told herself; *stay calm and breathe slowly. Don't let Lorena win. Don't let Lorena take away everything you ever wanted.*

Spence.

A tear trickled across her face, followed by another and another. She would never see him again, never be able to tell him how much she loved him, would always love him. If he could only find her . . .

When Spence reached the warehouse, he was thankful that it was a little cooler inside out of the sun, but that would be of little benefit inside a trunk.

He grabbed the first man he saw. "I'm looking for my trunk. The tag says Kendricks."

The man shrugged. "Don't recall the name. But I seldom read the tags."

"It's headed for Denver."

"Oh. Most of those are already loaded. Through that door." He pointed to the other side of the warehouse where a wide door opened onto another loading dock and the Denver train waited beyond that.

She had to be there! She had to be in that car! Without asking, he made his way across the warehouse, then checked the tags on all the trunks sitting on the dock. He read each quickly, glancing more than reading, but none of them said Kendricks.

He jumped into the luggage car and began reading tags again but had to slow down in order to see the names in the dim light. He'd nearly given up hope when he found one that said "Bailey." Of course, she wouldn't have used her real name. How could he have thought she would?

"Katie!" he called. "Answer me!" He looked around for something to use as a pry bar. "Katie!" His heart thundered in his chest when he got no answer.

There was nothing strong enough to break the lock. He rushed from the car and searched along the inside wall of the warehouse, grabbing the first thing made of metal. Dodging through the maze of trunks, he hurried back to the car, losing his balance once and banging his shins.

"Katie!" he called again, standing before the trunk in which he knew she was trapped.

Without waiting for an answer he feared would not come, he wedged the pry bar under the lock, using his foot and his weight for leverage. It wouldn't give. He slipped the bar through the hasp, barely able to make it fit, twisting it with all the pressure his body could apply. The lock weakened but didn't break. He twisted it back the other way, metal straining against metal, muscles bunched in desperation, in fear. At last the lock let loose and he fell to the floor with it. Scrambling to his knees, he pushed up the heavy lid.

Inside was Katie, lying as still as the hot air that surrounded her. She wore only her chemise and undergarment; her hands were bound behind her back and her mouth was gagged. She squinted up at him, her blue eyes filled with tears.

"Katie," he said, softly, reaching inside to untie her.

He took the cloth from her mouth, and she began to cry. "Oh, Spence. I thought I'd never see you again."

"Shhh. I'm here. Hold still while I get this undone."

She continued crying so softly he barely heard her, but the tears on her face were like daggers in his heart. When her hands were free she raised them toward him, wrapping them around his neck as he stood and lifted her out. He held her tight, vowing never to let her out of his sight again. Weak with relief, he sank to the floor with her in his arms and his back against another trunk. With his free hand, he followed the contours of her body from her ankle to her neck just to make sure she was all right, then he spread his fingers in her hair and pressed her head into his shoulder.

"Spence." She nestled against him in the perfect fit he remembered so well as he cradled her in his lap. "I thought I'd never see you again," she repeated. Her tears wet his shirt and the skin beneath.

"I love you, Katie," he said hoarsely. "I don't ever want to lose you." He brushed kisses over her hair, mur-

muring words that he'd never used before, words that felt so right.

He smoothed back the tendrils of damp hair that stuck to her face, wiping her tears with his thumb. Her clothing was damp with sweat from the heat that had been trapped inside the trunk. He stroked her bare leg where it curled against his side, then grasped her toes and tucked them protectively inside his palm.

"All I ask is that you let me keep you safe," he said. "Safe beside me. Always."

Sniffling, she whispered, "I don't want to be anywhere else. Hold me tight." She pressed against him, clinging.

"We'll be together. It doesn't matter where or how." He took her face in his hands. Then he kissed her with an intensity born of relief and need, a nearly desperate need to keep her close. Her response echoed his in its yearning as the soft suppleness of her body flattened against his, and he moaned quietly.

When at last the kiss ended, there was a mutual touching of lips in reassurance that what they'd almost lost would be forever theirs. He kissed her brow, her closed lids, her cheeks; she kissed his chin, his neck, his searching mouth.

He tangled his fingers in her hair once more. "I know that I can't ask you to forget your dream," he said.

"I'll give it up," she said.

"No," he said, running his thumb along her cheek. "We'll work it out."

She sighed and turned her face toward his neck, still clutching him tightly as though her very life depended on it.

"I love you, Spence."

He drew her up against him, burying his nose in the sweet fragrance of her hair, wishing he could pull her inside of himself where he could keep her safe always, where they could become one.

A shudder ran the length of the train in preparation for moving down the track to pick up the passengers who waited at the depot.

"We're headed for Denver if we stay on board," Spence said into her hair. "And I don't have a ticket."

"I didn't want to go anyway. Let's get off."

He pulled back, looking at her. "I hate taking you back to the hotel dressed like that," he said.

"Don't worry about me. I'm so glad to go that it wouldn't matter if I had nothing on."

"Here," he said, setting her away from him long enough to take off his shirt. "Put this on. I don't want anyone staring at my soon-to-be wife but me."

She smiled at him for the first time since he found her and said, "Now I'll have to worry about all the women staring at my future husband."

He slipped the shirt over her arms, pulling it closed in front. "You don't have to worry about anything at all." He kissed her lightly on the lips. "Ever."

"That's a wonderful promise," she said. "I think I'll hold you to it."

The train jerked, then moved a few inches and stopped.

"We'd better go now," he said, getting to his feet and helping her up. He jumped down from the car and walked alongside as it slowly moved away. Raising his arms, he lifted her down until she stood before him, then he picked her up, catching her behind the knees.

Spence walked across the tracks, avoiding the crowds that waited to depart the station, while a plan formed in his mind about Lorena. She wouldn't get away with this, not if he had to tie her to a chair while he went to the sheriff. Katie could have died in that trunk, and would have if he hadn't found her, and Lorena knew it. He never would have thought she was that devious or cruel; he never would have thought she was capable of murder.

Katie's exposure to the curious stares was more than Spence could bear. His anger at Lorena grew with each long stride. When the hotel came into view at last, he told Katie they were almost there. She hid her face deeper against his neck. Inside the building, he walked past the clerk at the front desk and straight up to the room. Surprisingly, the door was still open, and he kicked it shut after he entered. Laying her on the bed, he took the cloth from the basin and wiped her face.

"I'm all right, Spence. Really," she said, taking his hand and smiling at him. "Just being with you and knowing that you love me—"

He kissed her again, interrupting her words, and her arms circled his neck.

"We seem to be making a regular habit out of doing that," she said.

"It's a habit I plan never to break."

"I didn't say it was a bad habit," she replied softly.

"Far from bad," he said, planting short kisses on her lips, her brow, her cheek. He sat on the side of the bed, holding her hands in his.

"I have to go talk to the sheriff," he said. "You'll be okay, won't you?"

She nodded, and her eyes searched his. "Spence?"

"Hmmm?"

"Lorena is a frightening woman. I mean, you can't imagine what horrible things she's done and is planning to do."

"I know what she did to you, and nothing could have scared me more."

"Spence. She said she murdered her husband."

"Charles?" Why that surprised him he didn't know. It was still unbelievable that he knew so little about Lorena after all. How could he ever have thought he loved her?

Katie nodded. "It's true. And she's planning on marrying Mr. Crandall. And murdering him, too, just so she

287

can get his share of the ranch when he dies. I don't suppose now is the time to ask, but what ranch is she talking about?"

"The Circle M T," he replied. A shiver of apprehension went up his spine. Her plan was solid enough to actually work, if Crandall fell for her wiles, and that wasn't unlikely. "I have to warn Crandall on my way to see the sheriff. Don't leave this room for any reason."

"I won't."

"I could get another one so she won't know that you're here," he said.

"No. I'll be fine." When he still looked unsure, she repeated, "I'll be fine."

He kissed the curls on the top of her head, and she followed him to the door.

"Lock it," he said.

"I will."

He waited in the hall until he heard the key turn in the lock. At the top of the stairs he hesitated only a moment before heading toward Lorena's room. He meant to keep that promise he'd made to himself by tying her to a chair if necessary while he went for the sheriff.

"Lorena," he called through the door. "Open up."

He waited, rattling the doorknob in his impatience. "Open the door, Lorena. Now."

Still nothing.

He pounded on it twice with his fist. "Lorena!"

He turned and strode down the hall, cursing under his breath that she had outsmarted him and gotten away. How far could she have gotten in the time it took to find Katie? God knew it seemed like hours since he'd last seen Lorena and his terrifying search had begun. Could she have been on that very same train?

Downstairs at the desk he found the young clerk, who stared at him wide-eyed. "Where's Miss Kendricks?" Spence nearly shouted.

"Gone, sir."

"I said, where?" Spence narrowed his gaze on the quirming boy.

"Don't know, sir." Then thinking better of his answer, he added, "I mean, she didn't tell me."

"When did she leave?"

"Right after you did. The first time. When you were asking about—"

"Was she alone?"

"Yes, I think so." The boy's gaze wandered to the other side of the room, and Spence looked up to find Crandall walking toward them.

"If you're looking for Lorena," Crandall said, "she seems to be gone. I've been looking for her, too."

The boy handed Spence an envelope. "She left this for you." Without delay, Spence tore it open.

"I'm not finished with you yet," was the terse message.

Folding the paper, he stuffed it into his shirt. How could he have made such a foolhardy mistake not to drag her to the sheriff before he left the hotel? But then Katie would have surely died in that trunk long before the train ever reached Denver. He'd made the right choice. Keeping Katie safe was worth letting Lorena go.

"Could we talk in private?" Crandall said to Spence, bringing him out of his thoughts. "In your room, perhaps? The lobby isn't a good place for what I have to say."

Spence nodded and led the way back upstairs, where he knocked on Katie's door. "Open up, Katie, it's me. And Crandall."

In a moment the door swung wide, revealing Katie in her britches. Both men entered and she closed the door.

"Could I see that paper?" Crandall asked, holding out his hand. "I'm with the Pinkerton Agency. I've been awaiting Miss Kendricks for quite some time now."

Spence handed over the letter, staring at Cranda[ll]
with near disbelief.

" 'I'm not finished with you yet,' " Crandall rea[d]
aloud. "And I'm not finished with you either, Miss Ke[n]
dricks. Not by a long shot."

Spence and Katie sat side by side, holding hands an[d]
answering all of Crandall's questions. Then they aske[d]
him a few of their own.

He told them that a relative of Charles Kendricks su[s]
pected foul play when Charles had been killed and s[o]
he'd hired the agency to look into the rich widow's pas[t.]
That was how Crandall made the connection betwee[n]
Spence and Lorena, luring her into a meeting at Bai[l]
ey's. Crandall said that Bailey was always willing t[o]
help the agency whenever possible, although h[e]
shouldn't repeat that information and begged them t[o]
keep their secret.

"Lorena is a clever woman," Crandall said. "And [it]
may seem as though she's slipped through our finger[s]
but we're holding the aces since she doesn't know we'[re]
on to her. I'll wire ahead to Denver and have her a[r]
rested. She'll be quite disappointed, I'm sure."

"She was certainly looking forward to becoming [a]
widow," Katie said. " 'A very wealthy widow,' were h[er]
exact words."

Crandall smiled. "She'd have been sorely disa[p]
pointed again, I'm afraid. The only money she woul[d]
have inherited from me wouldn't have paid her trai[n]
fare out of town."

Spence, instantly alert, leaned forward. "What abo[ut]
the backing for the Circle M T that we agreed on?"

Crandall smiled broadly. "I bartered with someon[e]
else's money. Bailey's. She's you're partner, not me."

Spence frowned at him, speechless.

"Bailey?" Katie asked. Then she, too, smiled. "Baile[y?]
Isn't that nice?"

Spence wasn't so sure, especially since he'd have to tell Tim. And there was already plenty to tell Tim.

"Isn't it, Spence?" Katie said, poking him gently in the ribs. "I mean, it just seems sort of right, don't you think? After all, the three of you started out together."

Maybe she was right, he thought. They had all three had such dreams, and now after so many years, maybe things would fall together for each of them.

"What do you think Tim will say?" she asked. The mischievous twinkle that he loved so dearly was back in her blue eyes.

"I imagine Tim will have plenty to say about a lot of things, starting with us."

"I can hardly wait," Katie said.

Chapter Twenty-two

Katie let Spence help her on with the emerald green dress they'd bought from Caroline. Neither of them had any fear of bad luck on their wedding day. They'd already been through all of that and were determined there would be nothing but good luck for them from now on.

"You're beautiful."

"You're rather dashing yourself in that new suit," she replied, staring at his reflection in the mirror. She pinned up her hair, hampered by the soft kisses he dropped on the back of her neck. "We won't be able to get on with this wedding if you continue doing that." She closed her eyes and leaned against him, enjoying the warm sensations rolling over her.

"Well, we've waited this long, a little longer won't hurt," he said, nibbling on her nape.

"Oh, yes," she answer breathlessly. "I mean, no. We aren't waiting for another day." She sidestepped away from him, keeping out of reach. "Besides, isn't the preacher supposed to be here soon?"

"Actually, he's late." Spence took a step toward her, but she backed up again.

"You don't suppose we'll have to do what Caroline and Stephen did, do you?" she asked, putting a chair between them.

He walked around the chair, but she stayed on the far side of the circle he was making.

"We'll have a preacher if we have to knock on every church door," he said as he lunged across the chair.

She squealed and made a dash for the settee, keeping it between them. "Spence," she warned, drawing out his name.

"Katie," he mimicked, circling the settee.

"It'll never do to appear at our own wedding . . . you know, mussed."

"I plan to do more than muss," he said with a leer.

Laughing, she replied, "Listen to the things you say. For shame." With one hand on the carved wood edge of the settee, she kept circling. When she reached the front, he lunged across and caught her wrist. She squealed again, but laughed too much to put up a proper struggle.

"Ah, ha!" he said, stepping over the settee. He pulled her down onto it with him, stretching out full length as much as the furniture would allow. "I've got you where I want you now."

"I'm so disappointed," she said, breathless from their tussle. "I thought you had something more daring in mind."

"I do. But you're not supposed to get ahead of me."

She laughed. "Then I'll be patient."

He touched his lips to hers with gentle kisses that had an underlying urgency while his hand sought the firm softness kept from him by the silk of her bodice. She arched against him, clasping him tightly to her.

A knock at the door brought them up short of breath.

"I think we have company," she said, nibbling on his ear.

"Shhh. Maybe they'll go away."

"It's probably the preacher."

"Tell him to come back later."

"All right," she said, trying to raise up on one elbow.

"No, wait. No more delays." Spence sat up. "I'd better let him in."

"If you're sure," she said with a smile.

He let his gaze follow the length of her clear to the top of her curls. "You look like you've been mussed."

"And you promised me more than that. I'm so disappointed." She raised an eyebrow wickedly.

He pulled her to her feet. "This won't take long," he said, brushing at the wrinkles in her dress while she pinned up the strands of hair that had fallen free.

"It won't matter if it does," she replied softly. "We have the rest of our lives together."

Spence let the preacher and his wife into the room, then they exchanged greetings before the preacher explained the procedure.

Katie stood close to Spence's side, her hand in his, feeling as if they were already married and this was merely a formal ceremony to seal their union. As the preacher spoke the familiar words, Katie listened as though she'd never heard them before. And when he was ready to pronounce them man and wife, Katie interrupted him, remembering the vows that Caroline and Stephen had given each other.

"I'd like to add something," she said. She turned to face Spence and, clasping his hand in both of hers, pressed it firmly against her heart. "No matter what lies ahead and no matter what lies in the past, I promise to always love you with the same steadfastness as the beat of my heart."

Spence held her gaze until she felt he'd searched the depth of her soul. "I love you, Katie O'Rourke," he whis-

ered. Then he took her in his arms and kissed her
deeply.

Seeing that things were getting ahead of schedule,
the preacher quickly pronounced in a loud clear voice,
"I now pronounce you man and wife. You may kiss the
bride."

When Spence and Katie finally stepped apart, smiling broadly at one another, the preacher intruded upon
them by shaking hands. The preacher's wife sniffled
and dabbed her eyes with a handkerchief, saying, "Such
a lovely couple. I wish you the best, Mrs. McCord."

Then at last they were alone.

"Mrs. McCord," Katie said, testing the word. "It
sounds very nice."

"It looks pretty nice, too," Spence said. He grinned at
her and tugged her into his arms.

"Oh! Wait. How could I forget? We need to take our
wedding picture!"

"Couldn't we do it later?"

"No, we have to do it now." She fussed momentarily
in the mirror. "Come on. We have to go get the wagon
and find someone to expose the plate."

"Katie—"

"We can't wait," she insisted. "There won't be much
daylight left if we don't hurry."

"Maybe we should eat supper, too," he said drily.

"Are you hungry?" she asked. "So am I. As a matter
of fact, I'm starving, but it will have to wait."

They walked to the livery where the wagon stood unhitched behind the barn. She convinced the smithy to
expose the plate and in return promised to photograph
him in front of his shop.

"This is taking too long," Spence said to her under
his breath while she looked around for a suitable site.

"But it just doesn't feel right," she said. "It seems so
planned, so posed. I've spent a whole journey trying to

capture life and people as they really are, and this jus
doesn't fit."

"How about the wagon?" he suggested, hoping t
hurry her along.

"No. That doesn't feel right, either." She glanced u
and down the street until her gaze fastened on an empt
building across the way. "That's what I've been lookin
for," she said.

"An empty building?"

"It's empty now but it won't be for long." She hurrie
across the busy street and bracketed her hands agains
the dirty window to peer inside. "It's perfect."

"Perfect for what?" he asked, staring at her.

"A gallery." She looked up at him. "Don't you thin
so? I could sell the house and studio in New York an
buy this! I'm sure it will take some time to establish
gallery this far away from the usual places, but I knov
it will work. I just know it will!"

Spence studied the intense longing on her face an
knew there would be no stopping her. He had only
moment to be grateful that at least it was close to th
ranch, closer than New York or St. Louis anyway, be
fore she threw herself into his arms. He accepted th
kisses she plastered all over his face and looked forwar
to a lifetime of these unexpected pleasures.

"You're making quite a spectacle of yourself, Mrs
McCord. And right in front of your new gallery at that
What will everyone say?"

"I don't care what they say. I only care what you say.

"I say, okay."

She kissed him again, leaving him longing for more
then hurried back across the street to the livery.

"Hurry," she called over her shoulder, and he didn'
have to be told twice.

The wagon was hitched in record time as the su
slowly sank toward the horizon. When the wagon wa
finally sitting in front of the empty building, Katie se

to work pulling out her basins and chemicals, mindful of her wedding dress so as not to spoil it. Meanwhile Spence set up the camera in the middle of the street where she instructed him.

When everything was ready, the smithy came to take Spence's place. By now a large crowd had accumulated, watching the proceedings with great interest, and creating a semicircle around the newly married couple and their photographer's wagon.

Katie and Spence stood hand in hand beside the wagon, she in her silk, fashioned gown and he in his new suit and hat. The lowering sun made her uncovered hair a spectacle of bronzed curls as she turned her head at the last moment to look up into her husband's face. The moment was right, the place was right, and the photograph was a success.

With the shadows beginning to deepen, Katie hurried to take the smithy's picture, and the crowd waited and watched again.

Afterwards, she was approached by several women and a few men who were interested in having their photographs taken. Katie happily told them she would soon be setting up a gallery and studio, just as soon as she could complete the plans they were making.

"Are we finished yet?" Spence whispered in her ear when a prospective customer departed. "This is our wedding day, you know."

"I know," she said, smiling at him. "And you have a promise to fulfill, I believe."

He grasped her elbow and steered her toward the hotel. Inside, she halted when they passed the dining room.

"Oh, what about supper? I'm absolutely starved, aren't you?"

"No," he said, "not at all." And he nearly pulled her along after him up the stairs.

Inside their room, he closed the door and locked it.

Then he pulled off his jacket, tossed his hat onto a chair and walked toward her, his intent obvious.

"Spence," she warned, a wicked sparkle in her eyes as she backed away, keeping a good distance between them. "I don't want my dress wrinkled or ruined."

"We'll take it off."

She dodged behind the settee again.

"We aren't going to play games, Katie."

"Why not? I rather liked it the first time," she said, circling the settee as she had before the preacher arrived.

Spence sat down on a chair and watched her while he removed first one boot, then the other. Setting them aside, he advanced on the settee, stepping onto the seat and over the back.

Katie gave a small shriek and, laughing, escaped to the other end of the room, where she kept the bed between them.

Spence bypassed the bed, his strides long and purposeful until he had her within reach. But Katie jumped onto the soft ticking and rolled across its width in an attempt to thwart his progress. Before she could climb off the other side he had her in his clutches, towering over her, capturing her beneath him.

"Now look what you've done," she said, merriment shining in her eyes. "My dress is forever wrinkled."

"I don't care," he said. With infinite tenderness he pressed his mouth to hers, barely able to contain his need. He deepened the kiss, and she accommodated him.

"I don't care either," she agreed, weak and breathless, when at last he allowed her to speak.

"Maybe we should take it off now," he said. He slid away from her and pulled her to a sitting position. He unbuttoned the front and slipped the silky material from her arms, exposing the bare skin. Pulling her to her feet, he removed her chemise over her head. Her

face was flushed and the glitter of mischievousness was gone, replaced by an intense seriousness. With both hands on her cheeks, he kissed her softly, feeling her breath against his lips when he parted from her.

Katie slipped her hand to unbutton his shirt, one button at a time. Then she found the waistband of his trousers, hesitating only a moment before helping him shed them.

In even less time, her dress pooled at their feet, cooling her skin as it brushed down her bare legs.

"I'm still wearing my shoes," she said.

He glanced down to see that she was right, then lifted her onto the bed and removed the tedious buttoned shoes.

"We'll get you some boots tomorrow," he said sincerely as he stretched out beside her. "No more delays like this."

"No more," she repeated, and she circled his neck with her arms, pulling him to her.

Time became unimportant as they touched, and talked, and soared to heights they'd never attained before. Whispered words of endearment and cherished glances were given, then stored away in their hearts to be savored during those times that they knew they would be apart. Promises were spoken and sealed with burning kisses, igniting fires that they thought had cooled.

Katie lay in Spence's arms, warm and sated, full of love for the man who was now her husband and would be forevermore.

"Can I ask you something?" she whispered, drawing circles on his chest.

He grasped her hand and held it still. "Ask me anything."

"I was just wondering about the debt and a few other things."

He settled deeper into the blankets, tucking her closer to his side, enjoying the fit.

"It doesn't matter anymore," he said. "But I'll explain it if you like."

She nodded, her curls brushing against his cheek.

He took a deep breath, then let out a sigh. So many things had happened since he'd first met Tim that he hardly knew where to begin.

"It was during the war that Tim and I met. I fought for the gray and he fought for the blue, as you already know. Actually, the war had ended but none of us knew it at the time. And we were scared. Both of us were just boys, really, fighting for causes we didn't understand, watching new friends being blown to bits or maimed in the worst kind of way.

"Tim's regiment advanced on ours, giving us the worst of it. I took a hit in the leg and went down face first, and I just lay there expecting to get it in the back. Another unknown fatality for the Confederacy. But the next thing I knew, someone had rolled me over and pulled my hat off. He took my gun, my shirt, my knapsack, leaving me nothing but my frayed britches and worn-out shoes."

Spence rubbed the soft skin of Katie's arm, bringing his mind to the present and keeping the story where it belonged: in the past.

"Tim grabbed a shirt and hat from a dead Yankee and stuffed me into them, saying things like, 'These won't do him any good, and I've had enough of this damn war.' And so had I.

"When the call came to fall back, he helped me limp along with him. I thought for sure I was headed for an execution, but instead he said, 'You owe me, pal. Name's Tim O'Rourke. When this war's over you can find me in St. Louis, if we live that long.'

"I told him my name and he said I should just keep

my Johnny-Reb mouth shut and let him do all the talking So I did."

"That sounds like Tim all right," Katie said. "But for once I'm glad he was so bossy."

"He told everyone that I was from another company and that I must have somehow wandered into theirs during battle, which was the truth. He saw to it that I got patched up without losing any important limbs, and the next thing we heard, the war was over. And what was more, it had been over for a week."

Katie pressed closer to him. "It was over and those men and boys died so needlessly."

"I know."

They lay in the darkened room, each thinking somber thoughts and being grateful for the chance to spend their lives together.

"What happened then? Did you look for Tim in St. Louis?"

"No. We went there together and that's when we found Bailey," he said, then added, "And Lorena."

"I know about that part."

He turned to stare at her in the dark. "How could you know about that? Did Lorena tell you?"

"No. Bailey did."

He rubbed his thumb along her arm. "That's a part of my life I'd like to forget."

"Consider it forgotten," she said. "It doesn't matter to me. The only thing that matters now is us." After a pause, she went on. "And now you have Bailey for a partner. Just exactly what kind of partner is she? I mean, I thought in the beginning that you worked for Tim."

He tweaked her nose. "You misunderstood. Tim and I became partners in St. Louis and headed west to Colorado, where we started a ranching outfit. It was small, but we didn't mind since we only had ourselves to worry about."

"Now that's all changed, isn't it?"

"You bet. Now I have plenty to worry about. A ranch, a wife and a photography business that's only a few hundred miles from home."

"Are we that far away?" she said, pulling back from him.

"Yes."

"Maybe I should rethink this idea and get one closer to home."

"Where the buffalo and Indians roam or the bandits hang out in Deadwood? I don't think so. Cheyenne will do just fine. You won't have to be here all the time, will you?"

"Of course not. I'll just start the gallery and find some wonderful photographer who enjoys taking propped and posed pictures more than I do." She paused. "I still might like to keep the wagon, though, and travel again. Did you say there were Indians and buffalo and bandits? Now, those are some things I haven't had the occasion to photograph."

"Oh no you don't," he said, rolling her onto her back. "I'll have none of that."

"I wouldn't go alone. I'd want you with me." She kissed him, lingering at the edge of his lips. "Always."

"We'll discuss it later," he replied. "When I can think better."

Katie wiggled beneath him. "I can wait."

Chapter Twenty-three

Katie had been in awe since they crossed the Belle Fourche River, but nothing they'd come through thus far had prepared her for the beautiful sight before her now. Ahead of them beyond the Powder River sat a small house with barns behind it and cattle surrounding it. Everywhere there were cattle.

"Is that Tim's house?" she asked, excitement and pride welling within her.

"That's it."

A plume of smoke rose from the chimney, telling them that Rachel must be in the midst of cooking supper. There was no resemblance whatsoever to the soddies they'd visited, and she was glad. Instead, the house was made of logs and was low and rambling, just the sort of house in which to raise a large family.

"It's been a long time," she said.

"You mean getting here?"

"No. It's been a long time since I've seen Tim. And I've never seen any of his family." She wondered how it would be to live nearby.

"You'll like Rachel. Everyone does."

"And the children?" Involuntarily, she pressed a hand to her stomach.

"Nothing like their father," Spence said, teasing her.

"That's too bad," she returned. "He deserves a dose of his own medicine."

Spence chuckled and agreed with her.

"Where's your cabin?"

"Ours," he corrected. "It's a few miles to the west where it's even more beautiful. But don't expect too much of the cabin. It's nothing like Tim's, because I've been gone fetching me a wife."

She snuggled up close. "And I'm so glad you did."

Soon they arrived at the front door, where a welcoming party lined up to greet them. Tim stood with his hands on the heads of two little boys, both redheaded and one a little taller than the other. Beside Tim stood Rachel, a bundle in her arms. Coming around the sides of the house were a few of the hired hands. Everyone rushed forward, shaking hands and hugging, laughing and just staring at one another.

"Katie girl, how are you?" Tim asked, taking her into a bear hug that nearly squeezed the breath from her lungs.

"I'm fine." He'd grown a little older, a lot bigger, and surprisingly, she found she'd missed him terribly. She hugged him back.

"You look pretty healthy." He held her hands and stepped back to look her over carefully. "And what's this?" he said, taking note of her worn britches and shirt. "My sister dressing like a boy?" He frowned and glanced at Spence.

"She seems to have a mind of her own," Spence said with a shrug and a smile. He looked at Katie and winked.

Immediately Tim took in the whole situation, the

wink, the clothes, the familiar way the two laughed with each other, and he stepped in front of Spence.

"Just how much of a mind of her own, I'm wanting to know," he said in a heavy Irish brogue. "And how much of a mind of your own!"

"Tim, there's something I should tell—"

"You're damn right there is!" Tim hauled off and punched Spence, catching him unaware and making him reel.

"Wait—" But Spence never had a chance to finish his sentence. Tim came at him, wrestling him to the ground, where they grappled while Spence tried to defend himself.

"Stop it!" Katie screamed as she tried to pull Tim off her husband. "Tim, you jackass! Leave him alone!"

They rolled across the ground, grunting, nearly dragging Katie into the fracas with them. Rachel, who had joined Katie, was doing her best to stop them, too.

"I said, stop it!" Katie grabbed Tim's hair and yanked. "Will you stop it, please!"

The men rolled away from each other, Spence eying her brother warily and looking guilty as all get-out.

"What's the matter with you!" Katie said, mad enough to give Tim a good kick in the shins. "I'm a grown woman, so stop treating me like a child. For once in my life!"

Spence and Tim got to their feet.

"You'll be marryin' my sister before the end of this week!" he shouted at Spence. "That you will."

"We're already married," Katie said. "That's what he was trying to tell you, if you'd let him talk instead of knocking the stuffing out of him." She gave him one last glaring look before tending to the cut on Spence's lip.

"Lord have mercy! Just what's been going on here?"

Katie turned around to find Mrs. O'Shea standing in the doorway, wiping her hands on her apron, a look of concern on her face. Katie flew into the arms of the sweet woman she'd missed so much.

"Ah, Katie dear," she crooned, patting her back. "My girl's married now, you say?"

Katie squeezed the soft body tight. "Mrs. O'Shea!" she exclaimed with delight. "You *did* come out West, just like you said in your letter!"

"Let me look at you now." She held her at arm's length and peered into her eyes. She smiled knowingly and whispered so nobody but Katie could hear, "And married just in time too, I'd say."

Katie laughed and hugged her again.

"Well," Tim said, his jovial self once more, "I guess a little celebration is in order, then." He hugged his wife to his side and said in a low voice, "You see how well it all worked out? Just as I intended."

Inside the big kitchen, Katie tried to help with the meal, but Rachel handed the baby to her and pointed her in the direction of the rocking chair. The little bundle in her arms felt so fragile and looked so beautiful, and fit so well.

The oldest of Tim's boys came to stand beside her as she gently rocked to and fro.

"You're Michael, aren't you?" she asked.

"Yes. And that's Rebecca," he replied, touching the baby with his finger. "She cries a lot. Mother says that all babies do that. Even me. When I was a baby, I mean." He smiled, showing her a grin that was missing a tooth. "David doesn't like it when Rebecca cries. He always goes and hides. Usually in the outhouse."

Katie laughed. "Where is he now?"

"Hiding under the table. Over there." He pointed toward the table where the men sat drinking coffee. Spence caught her gaze and winked. A flush of happiness enveloped her, warming her clear to her heart as she bsmiled back at him.

* * *

During supper, it was brought up that Erin, James and the boys were planning to come west because they had no intention of being left behind without any family. Mrs. O'Shea was certain that the news of Katie and Spence's marriage would be all it would take to set them packing. Katie hoped so; she missed Erin something terrible.

Rachel apologized for not cooking a dinner that was fitting for a celebration, but Katie assured her that being together meant more than having a feast. As it was, there was more than enough food to go around, with plenty of coffee and even cake for dessert. When it came to cleaning up, Katie insisted on helping, and Mrs. O'Shea raised her eyebrows in quiet approval.

Spence had disappeared out the door with the other men before the cleaning up began and hadn't come back even by the time the boys were in bed. Katie knew he'd missed the ranch and had a lot of catching up to do. He also had a lot of explaining to do about Lorena and about their new partner, Bailey. Katie hoped this new development didn't cause a problem for Rachel, who was so easy to like, and Katie found she liked her even more as the evening went by.

A clock somewhere in the house sounded nine. This was the longest that she and Spence had been apart for weeks, except for the night she'd spent alone in the hotel. She kept glancing at the door waiting for his return, feeling peculiarly lonely. She hardly heard the conversation between Rachel and Mrs. O'Shea, and could barely give a proper answer when called upon. Another thirty minutes passed before the door opened and Tim and Spence finally returned. Katie rose to greet Spence, unabashedly kissing his cheek and pulling him to sit beside her at the table.

Mrs. O'Shea yawned and made her excuses for the night, leaving only Tim and Rachel, Katie and Spence sitting across from each other. Before long, Rachel took

Tim's arm, insisting that he needed his rest, and everyone said good night. A pile of blankets had somehow appeared on a chair by the back door that until now Katie hadn't noticed.

With a single lamp burning in the center of the large table, the shadows lay around the edge of the room in a comforting fashion, encouraging a yawn.

"You're not tired, are you?" Spence asked.

"Hmm. A little."

"Well, I guess we'll hit the hay, then." He rose from his chair and collected the blankets. "Ready?"

"Where are we going?" she asked, looking surprised that he had his hand on the doorknob. "To the wagon?"

"No. The hayloft."

Blowing out the lamp first, she crossed the room and took his hand. "I've never slept in a hayloft before."

"I'm certainly glad to hear that," he responded.

"Have you?"

"A time or two." He opened the door and waited for her.

"Is that something I need to be concerned about?" she asked.

He leaned down and kissed the top of her head. "There's nothing for you to be concerned about. Ever."

He'd told her that once before but she liked hearing it again. "Just thought I'd ask."

Inside the barn he pointed out the ladder, and she climbed up to the loft and flopped onto the soft hay.

"This feels almost as good as a feather bed," she said.

He spread the blankets beside her and she rolled onto them, snuggling into their depths. Kicking off the new boots he'd bought for her in Cheyenne, she wiggled her toes inside her stockings.

He dropped down beside her, kicked off his own boots, then lay back, resting his head on his crossed arms. Katie rolled against him, easing the curves of her body into the lines of his.

"Whose idea was this?" she asked, drawing circles on his shirt.

"Mine."

"Any special reason?"

"No."

"You just like to be outside under the stars."

"Something like that."

"But not alone."

"Something like that."

She circled one button until it came undone.

"We're not exactly under the stars," she said.

"Pretty close."

She circled another button until it, too, came undone.

"What did Tim say when you said you wanted to sleep with your wife in the barn?"

"Not much."

She raised up on one elbow and stared down into his face. "Can't you say more than two-word sentences?"

"Anyone ever tell you that you talk too much?" he asked as he pushed her down and covered her with his body. "I brought you up here to get you alone, but talking wasn't what I had in mind."

"Pray tell—" she began, but his lips on hers cut off her words. "Mmm," she moaned throatily as she clasped her arms around his neck.

The strong, sweet scent of hay rose up to greet them with every move they made, planting the idea forever in Katie's mind that love and earthy scents went hand in hand. She waited with anticipation as he tugged at her shirt and then her camisole until his hand finally lay on the bare skin of her stomach, inching toward the firm mound of her breast. But before they could go on, she had to know how he would react to the news she'd been saving. Pulling away, she ended the kiss.

"Spence?"

He took a lock of her hair and wound it around his finger. "Hmm?"

"I have something to tell you."

"You like being here," he guessed.

"Yes, I do. But that's not what's on my mind."

"You want to move to our cabin tomorrow. Well, I'm afraid that it won't be ready for a long time."

"That's all right. I can wait. For a while, anyway."

He tickled her nose with the curl he held. "That's good." He nibbled on her ear, making her squirm.

"How would you feel about us having a baby so soon?" she asked, almost holding her breath while she waited for his answer.

"A what?" He moved back in an attempt to see her in the dark.

"Like Rebecca. But probably with dark hair like yours and curls like mine. Of course, it might not be curly but then again it just might be, you can never tell—"

He put his hand gently over her mouth. "Katie?"

"What?" she mumbled through his fingers.

"Did you say a baby?"

She nodded.

"Like Rebecca," he said, still not believing what she was telling him.

She uncovered her mouth, holding his hand tightly in hers. "Well, it might be a boy."

"A boy." He lay back on the blanket beside her, unmoving.

Katie couldn't be sure what he was thinking. She wanted to ask him what he thought, she needed desperately to know how he felt, but then again she was afraid to ask. She wanted him to tell her without her having to ask. Then again what if he—

Spence reached his hand in search of hers and, finding it beside him, squeezed it. Smiling into the dark, Katie squeezed it back.

"I hope she has red-gold hair like yours," he said, staring at the underside of the barn roof.

"I hope he grows as tall as you." She rolled her head toward him, trying to see his expression.

The night sounds crept into their awareness as they listened to the nicker of horses and the distant howl of an animal. The smell of woodsmoke carried to them on a breeze, and somewhere in the bunkhouse one of the men coughed.

"A baby," he said again. He turned toward her, lying on his side, bracing his head on his palm so he could look at her. A full moon overhead spread its light through the cracks in the walls of the barn.

"When I think of how my life was before I met you, Katie O'Rourke McCord, I wonder how long I would have survived in such loneliness."

"I thought you liked your solitude."

"I thought I did, too."

He leaned over and kissed her cheek. "Now I know better."

She smiled. "You don't think you'll miss the quiet after the baby arrives?"

"Not for a moment."

She took his free hand and laid it on her stomach. Not nearly enough time had passed yet for any sign of movement, but it was comforting to have him touch her there.

"The cabin is going to have to be bigger," he said.

"But we can still move in, can't we? I don't want to live with Tim and Rachel after the baby comes; that would be too much of an imposition."

"We'll make it livable and move in as soon as possible, then start an addition."

She cupped her hands over his.

"How long before she gets here?" he asked.

"I'm not sure when he'll get here, probably late winter or early spring."

"Come here," he said, carefully folding her close and stroking her back, shoulders and hair.

"I'm not going to break, you know."

"I can't be sure of that now."

"Well, I can." She wrapped her arms around his neck. "Are you going to kiss me or not?"

When he hesitated, she brushed her lips across his, then gradually deepened the kiss as he'd taught her to do. Like a spark in the wind, he responded until a full-fledged fire grew, enveloping both of them.

Spence allowed a breath of space between them and answered, "You're right. We do have some unfinished business that needs tending. After all, isn't that the reason we came up here?"

"Sometimes you talk too much," she replied, pulling his head down to hers.

Neither of them heard the rustling of the hay beneath their blankets, or the nicker of the horses in the stalls below. Neither of them saw the falling star that arced across the sky or knew they'd lost the opportunity to make a wish.

But then, neither of them had a need for that. Their wishes were being fulfilled in each other.

JAUNCEY

Melody Morgan

"A lovely romance."   *—Romantic Times*

After inheriting property in Laramie, Wyoming, Jauncey Taylor makes big plans for the future—until she discovers her inheritance is a bordello. Then she chases off former customer Matt Dawson, even as she wonders what ecstasy she could taste in his kiss. But Jauncey won't find out until she makes an honest man of the rugged cowpoke—and turns the bawdy house into a house of love.

_51992-5 $4.99 US/$5.99 CAN

ABIDING LOVE

MELODY MORGAN

Bestselling Author Of *Jauncey*

No one in the sleepy town of Grand Rapids, Ohio, would have ever expected to see shy Irene Barrett tearing up the local barroom. But after joining a women's temperance group, the spinster schoolteacher finds herself face-to-face with the handsome owner of the Broken Keg Saloon—and gazing into a pair of gray-blue eyes as intoxicating as the sweetest wine.

A drifter made good, Ross Hollister has no business courting a well-bred lady. Yet the banked fires of passion smoldering beneath Irene's straight-laced demeanor compel him to make her his own. But first Ross will have to show Irene that nothing—not the townsfolk's censure or his own sullied past—can prevent two hearts from sharing an abiding love.

_3825-0 $4.99 US/$6.99 CAN

"Doreen Malek's storytelling gifts keep us deliciously entertained!"
— *Romantic Times*

When an innocent excursion to Constantinople takes an unexpected twist, Sarah Woolcott finds herself a prisoner of young and virile Kalid Shah. Headstrong and courageous, Sarah is determined to resist the handsome foreigner whose arrogance outrages her—even as his tantalizing touch promises exotic nights of fiery sensuality.

Never has Kalid Shah encountered a woman who enflames his desire like the blonde Westerner with the independent spirit. Although she spurns his passionate overtures, Kalid vows to tempt her with his masterful skills until she becomes a willing companion on their journey of exquisite ecstasy.

_3569-3 $4.99 US/$5.99 CAN

Captive Legacy

Theresa Scott

"Theresa Scott's captivating writing brings you to a wonderous time and shows you that love inself is timeless."
—*Affaire de Coeur*

Heading west to the Oregon Territory and an arranged marriage, Dorie Primfield never dreams that a virile stranger will kidnap her and claim her as his wife. Part Indian, part white, Dorie's abductor is everything she's ever desired in a man, yet she isn't about to submit to his white-hot passion without a fight. Then by a twist of fate, she has her captor naked and at gunpoint, and she finds herself torn between escaping into the wilderness—and turning a captive legacy into endless love.

_3880-3 $5.99 US/$7.99 CAN

THERESA SCOTT

"More than an Indian romance, more than a Viking tale, *Bride Of Desire* is a unique combination of both. Enjoyable and satisfying!"

—Romantic Times

To beautiful, ebony-haired Winsome, the tall blond stranger who has taken her captive seems an entirely different breed of male from the men of her tribe. Though Brand treats her gently, his ways are nothing like the customs of her people. She has been taught that a man and a maiden may not join together until elaborate courting rituals are performed, but when Brand crushes her against his hard-muscled body, it is only too clear that he has no intention of waiting for anything. Weak with wanting, Winsome longs to surrender, but she will insist on a wedding ceremony first. When Brand finally claims her innocence, she will be the bride of his heart, as well as a bride of desire.

_3610-X $4.99 US/$5.99 CAN

Dorchester Publishing Co., Inc.
65 Commerce Road
Stamford, CT 06902

Please add $1.75 for shipping and handling for the first book and $.50 for each book thereafter. NY, NYC, PA and CT residents, please add appropriate sales tax. No cash, stamps, or C.O.D.s. All orders shipped within 6 weeks via postal service book rate. Canadian orders require $2.00 extra postage and must be paid in U.S. dollars through a U.S. banking facility.

Name _____

Address _____

City _____ State _____ Zip _____

I have enclosed $_____ in payment for the checked book(s).

Payment <u>must</u> accompany all orders. ☐ Please send a free catalog.

Forever Gold

CATHERINE HART

**"Catherine Hart writes thrilling adventure...
beautiful and memorable romance!"**
—Romantic Times

From the moment Blake Montgomery holds up the
westward-bound stagecoach carrying lovely Megan Coulston
to her adoring fiance, she hates everything about the virile
outlaw. How dare he drag her off to an isolated mountain
cabin and hold her ransom? How dare he steal her innocence
with his practiced caresses? How dare he kidnap her heart
when all he can offer is forbidden moments of burning,
trembling esctasy?

__3895-1 $5.99 US/$7.99 CAN

WEST WIND

Linda Winstead

Annabelle St. Clair has the voice of an angel and the devil at her heels. On the run for a murder she didn't commit, the world-renowned opera diva is reduced to singing in saloons until she finds a handsome gunslinger willing to take her to safety in San Francisco.

A restless bounty hunter, Shelley is more at home on the range than in Annabelle's polite society. Yet on the rugged trail, he can't resist sharing with her a passion as vast and limitless as the Western sky.

But despite the ecstasy they find, Annabelle can trust no one, especially not a man with dangerous secrets—secrets that threaten to ruin their lives and destroy their love.

_3796-3 $4.99 US/$5.99 CAN

Dorchester Publishing Co., Inc.
65 Commerce Road
Stamford, CT 06902

Please add $1.75 for shipping and handling for the first book and $.50 for each book thereafter. NY, NYC, PA and CT residents, please add appropriate sales tax. No cash, stamps, or C.O.D.s. All orders shipped within 6 weeks via postal service book rate. Canadian orders require $2.00 extra postage and must be paid in U.S. dollars through a U.S. banking facility.

Name _____

Address _____

City _____ State _____ Zip _____

I have enclosed $_____ in payment for the checked book(s).

Payment <u>must</u> accompany all orders.☐ Please send a free catalog.